# INTRODUCTION

ERNEST HENHAM's early psychological horror story, *Tenebrae: A Novel* (1898), appeared toward the end of an exceptionally fertile resurgence of Gothic fiction: *Dr Jekyll and Mr Hyde* (1886), *The Picture of Dorian Gray* (1890-91), *The Island of Doctor Moreau* (1896), and *Dracula* (1897). Oddly, Henham's publisher, Skeffington & Son, specialized in theology, children's picture books, and (perhaps not the father's side of the business) novels of lurid sins and melodramatic suicides. Were it not for its psychological ambiguity, *Tenebrae* might be thought to be either homage to E. A. Poe's works aimed at mass-market tastes—indeed, one does suspect it grew into a full blown novel from a lengthy story in situation and imagery much like "The Fall of the House of Usher" (1839-40)—or, for the sake of satirical humor, a deliberate parody of Poe's Gothic effects and insane narrators. In either such case one might then adapt the wry opening sentence of Arthur Symons's review of Francis Thompson's first volume: "If Crashaw, Shelley, Donne, Marvell, Patmore and some other poets had not existed, Francis Thompson would be a poet of remarkable novelty." But the likeliest possibility is neither homage nor parody; rather, we have covert self-expression touching personal and cultural anxieties so unmentionable that the cloak of Gothic fiction was the safest means by which they might be explored. In Victorian society (and, one might add, almost any other culture) who can express what, and when, and where was a closely controlled matter of precept and proscription. It has been observed, for example, that after the French Revolution (1789) an expressed wish for the death of any authority-figure, particularly the father, was socially taboo because it renewed anxieties about disruption and chaos. Our contemporary society is so much more open that often only legalities prompt distancing techniques, such as euphemisms in polite society ("That just tears the rag right off the bush!") or the not infrequently hypocritical asseveration that "any resemblance to actual events or persons, living or dead, is entirely coincidental."

Henham's dark romanticism explores the violence and aberrant sexuality of the narrator, an individual perversely self-destructive, a social outcast racked with personal fears, and one for whom the supernatural is hellishly hallucinatory. His dawning realization—to give a nod to Giovanni Palestrina's *Peccantem me*—is the somewhat less-than-cheerful realization that "there is no redemption in hell." In the handling of these somber Gothic themes Henham is by turns serious and comic, very much in the tradition of Walpole's *The Castle of Otranto* (1764) or *The Mysterious Mother* (1791) with their exaggerated intensity of warped desire turned violent. But his story, apart from Poe's influence, especially recalls the unapologetic supernatural staginess of M. G. Lewis's *The Monk* (1796), described by Francis Jeffrey as a "mixture of extravagance and jocularity which has impressed most of his writings with the character of a sort of farcical horror."[1] Henham's horror, then, is part of the Gothic genre's prototypical mix of styles and discourses, both literary and non-literary, lifted from popular theatrical entertainments, evangelical pulpit oratory, exaggerations of exotic fauna and flora in Britain's far-flung empire, myths, legends, and even travel guides like that of the *Western Morning News* for Dartmoor, with enough picturesque or sublimely gloomy rocks, trees, and tarns to flesh out a shelf of novels.

Henham's novel is also heir to the later impressionistic techniques of Oscar Wilde's *Dorian Gray* and the decadence of Charles Baudelaire, author of the Symbolist *Les fleurs du mal* (1857) and translator of Poe, whose art evokes ecstasy and eroticism, ideal love and betrayal, a beauty hidden by darkness and a darkness staining the light. The narrator's insane uncle, rejoicing in his Baudelairean life of alcohol and concoctions of drugs, is equally a sort of comic Dr. Jekyll—he even teaches his nephew to sweeten coffee with arsenic, something Martha Stewart has never suggested. He is the narrator's familiar spirit, responsible for demonic possessions since he styles himself "king of the insects," which is to say, Beelzebub, the king or lord (*Beel*) of the flies (*zebub*, a generic term for insects, including flies), another name for Satan. This may be a lampooning of Henham's clerical uncle with whom the young boy

---

1  *Edinburgh Review,* 20 (November 1812): 445.

# Tenebrae

# Also Available from Valancourt Books

By the Same Author
All Edited by Prof. Gerald C. Monsman

*A Pixy in Petticoats*
*Furze the Cruel*
*Sleeping Waters*


More Victorian Gothic & Horror

*The Beetle*
by Richard Marsh
Edited by Minna Vuohelainen

*The Sign of the Spider*
by Bertram Mitford
Edited by Gerald C. Monsman

*The Blood of the Vampire*
by Florence Marryat
Introduction by Brenda Hammack

*Carmilla*
by J. Sheridan Le Fanu
Edited by Jamieson Ridenhour

*Ziska: The Problem of a Wicked Soul*
by Marie Corelli
Introduction by Curt Herr


HTTP://WWW.VALANCOURTBOOKS.COM

VALANCOURT CLASSICS

# TENEBRAE

## A Novel

BY

## ERNEST G. HENHAM

Edited by Gerald C. Monsman

Kansas City:

VALANCOURT BOOKS

2013

*Tenebrae: A Novel* by Ernest George Henham
First published London: Skeffington & Son, 1898
First Valancourt Books edition 2013

This edition © 2013 by Valancourt Books
Introduction and notes © 2013 by Gerald C. Monsman

ISBN 978-1-934555-29-3

Design and typography by James D. Jenkins
Published by Valancourt Books
Kansas City, Missouri
http://www.valancourtbooks.com

# CONTENTS

lived—all the vices the righteous vicar abhorred are chalked up to this toadying uncle. For Henham, such psychic opposites as puritanical righteousness and unlicensed depravity both are blights to the soul. Taking his cue from those innovators who regenerated a decades-dominant Romanticism, Henham composes a horrifying scenario—the schizoid contestation between the conscious and the subconscious mind of its first person narrator. Henham might or might not have been aware of his multiple subtexts; but *Tenebrae* overtly deals with the narrator's self-justifications and self-deceptions. What he repressively cannot admit to be the truth defines his madness as his self splits off from its moral environment. *Tenebrae*, then, becomes something more than mere literary sensationalism of only historical interest.

Although in reality *Tenebrae* is the offspring of earlier Gothic and Symbolist traditions, Henham disguises a late Victorian cultural uncertainty and irresolution behind his diverse mix of sources. Thus the novel's overlaying appeal to popular taste and intended commercial success is not in conflict with its artistic design because both are outcomes of the same anxieties. The emotions in his scenes are classically paranoid-schizoid, allowing his readers to experience with cathartic intensity the traumas of real life crises and fears through a fictionalized or surrogate reality. But if the "turbid lineaments" of Henham's own struggles with an inhibited personality are autobiographically disguised in Gothic images and conventions, which life events produced which passages? His morbidity and "bewildering mysticism," especially in several of his earlier novels, might suggest a psychological distress stemming from his orphaning, his troubled relationship with his clerical uncle, his struggle with his health, and possibly a sexual angst produced by a childhood of severe religious repression. *Tenebrae*'s narrator "lusting . . . to kill" suggests a dangerously repressed sexuality—not Henham's actual impulse here but his fittingly artistic sublimation of those inhibitions by a description of the narrator's acting out.

Part I ("The Foreshadowing") describes the protagonist's alienation from his once loved younger brother who has taken his girlfriend away from him—as he says, "seduced her affections." Hints by his old nurse and the mad uncle are inescapably confirmed when he voyeuristically spies upon the lovers. He even interrogates his visual evidence by comparison to a literary anecdote of misunderstood motives, only to reflect that he had overheard their love-making also. Whereas the elder brother's world grows dark, mad, and filled with hate, the younger's appears sane and contented. A key parallel in this novel's structure is the theme of contrasting fraternal brothers in the biblical tale of Cain and Abel, especially the extra-biblical interpretation from the Midrash that identifies the real motive for murder as jealousy over a desirable woman. The narrator's palm-print lifeline is a foreshadowing of the mark of Cain that afterwards appears as blood upon his forehead. Another echo in *Tenebrae* comes from Shakespeare's *The Winter's Tale* (1611) in which King Leontes becomes possessed with jealousy, convinced that his childhood friend, King Polixenes, has seduced Hermione, his wife: "I have drunk, and seen the spider" (2.1.45). Polixenes had recalled the age of innocence when he and Leontes were boys, pure even from original sin. Suddenly, the spider in the cup, sexual jealousy, corrupts that deep affection. Henham, it is true, gives his narrator's jealousy a genuine foundation—"My brother had been guilty of vile treachery, and therefore I hated him. The woman abused me, while sharing in my brother's deceit"—but in both works obsessive suspicion over which reason has no sway becomes a poisoning of the soul.

In Henham's tale, the traditional polarities of good and evil or darkness and light overlap in the context of sexual rivalry. The elder brother is wealthy, introverted, nervous, and violently envious of his handsome but poor younger brother, who is too weak to confess honestly to his older sibling his sexual conquest. The woman's excuse, that her new lover didn't want to give his brother "pain," rings hollow. Both brothers, after all, are flawed—insecure and uncertain of their identities, sharing a dark symbiosis of love now turned to deceit and hate: "We shared, as it were, the same heart, the same mind, equal portions of the same soul. Only the law of Nature compelled us to pass through life beneath the identity of separate bodies." For that reason, he explains: "Had I not loved you so greatly in the past, the hatred of the present had been less." With an allusion from William Blake's "The Sick Rose," the older brother gives the girl roses from which his phobia—a spider—creeps forth. The "dark secret love" (Blake) of a guilty romance has penetrated and sickened what should have been an open and trusting affection, destroying innocence, beauty, life. Not long before the fratricide the narrator destroys in the fireplace a picture-frame with his and his brother's photographs: "I had burnt my own portraiture with his; in figuratively destroying him, I had inflicted a like injury upon myself." The narrator thereafter mutilates and throws his younger brother from a cliff onto the sea rocks: "Physically and mentally my brother was far weaker than myself. . . . With my small knife I stabbed the eyes which had looked into hers, the lips which had been pressed upon hers, the hand which had fondled her, even the heart which had throbbed for her." He then scrambles down to weight his body with stones. In a last ghoulishly convulsive gesture the victim thrashes out at the narrator—seemingly anticipating such later famous cinematic moments as that in Henri-Georges Clouzot's movie *Diabolique* where Simone Signoret pops out of the bath, "quoted" subsequently in numerous other film endings, such as Adrian Lyne's *Fatal Attraction.*

In Part II, "The Under-shadow," Henham creates a neologism formed by analogy with "overshadow," implying not the penumbra created from the sun's light above but a deeper "darkness visible" (Milton) from hell. The title of Henham's novel is the Latin noun, singular or plural, meaning "shadows" or "darkness"—and also "gloom," "blindness," "night," "death." He adapts his phrase, *"Ave, Tenebrae! Ego moriturus vos saluto"* from Suetonius's *Lives of the Caesars* (A.D. 121) in which combatants fated to die once addressed the emperor Claudius: "Hail, Emperor, those who are about to die salute you." Henham's version is in the first person: "Hail, Darkness! I who am about to die salute you." He was doubtless aware of its ironic pagan contrast to the invocation of darkness in the Catholic and Anglican services during Holy Week at which the crucifixion is commemorated by a gradual extinguishing of candles: "Hail, darkness, as I walk towards you . . . ." After the darkness of betrayal, suffering, and death, Christ brings redemption connoted by the light of Easter morning. In Henham's novel, darkness becomes an anthropomorphic horror: a spider in an all-but-haunted house mirrors a fantasy love that, unrequited, exacerbates the vengeance of a dangerously egocentric madman. The ordinary spider in the garden is described by the mad uncle as "the largest I have seen for a long time. His great body is covered thickly with long hairs. Then there is the cross. You cannot help seeing it. It is a white cross, and very distinct." Henham here is thinking of the common garden "diadem" or "cross spider" (*Araneus diadematus*) with five or more large white dots in the shape of a cross. But by the end of the narrative it has become an infernal apotheosis the size of a bear with a human face, the dark double of the narrator and also a *diabolous ex machina*, Lucifer himself as the anti-Christ.[1]

The narrator believes in an ethereal "Presence" flowing around him, out of which his growing guilt slowly takes its material incarnation, an idea found in Old Norse skaldic and Eddaic poetry. Following in the first part the foreshadowing of vengeance in the form of an everyday spider, the ghostly "under-shadow" of Part II begins as a black "scar" on the wall that feeds fat on crime and guilt to become the embodied vampiric spider, the "living substance of a crime." The narrator exclaims hysterically: "'There—huge and horrible in the centre of the wall. Its body is like ebony, except for the silver cross . . . . Why does it bear that mark? Such a sign they erect over graves.'" He then recalls the Lord stigmatized Cain: "'It was the mark of the white cross upon the black soul. That was the mark set upon the forehead of Cain.'" From a sexual point of view spiders symbolize the core fantasies and conflicts from various developmental levels; they emblematize feelings of repulsion and anxiety, of being "caught in the web" of desires, emotions, and personal feelings of dependence and need. When an intensely ambivalent person battles against a break with reality, the spider often emerges as a symbol of the feared and deeply repressed aspects both of the self's potentially psychotic core and of the vampire woman who debilitates and drains her prey. Here the narrator's *soi-disant* fiancée, suspecting he has murdered his brother,

---

1 The predecessor to Henham's vampiristic spider is found in Bertram Mitford's classic *The Sign of the Spider* (1896) that may have provided Henham with the idea of a spider the size of a bear with a human face. Both Mitford and Henham's human-faced spiders incorporate features of the death's head spider (*Eriophora ravilla*), the crab spider (*Misumenoides formosipes*), the skull spider (*Pholcus phalangioides*), and the jumping spider (*Phidippus audax*).

pretends to love him and only marries him to revenge herself on him: "I had resolved to hang over you, like the vampire, the fury, until you should . . . sink to your damnation by the frenzied act of the suicide." His marriage is grotesquely consummated in his hallucination of the spider that drops from the ceiling onto his face like a massy *vagina dentata*.

As the protagonist visualizes the spider inexorably advancing to destroy him, his wife enters pursued by the crazy uncle. By now the spider has become a deeply metaphorical image that combines the storm of the older brother's anger, his younger brother's deceit, and the wife's revenge—murder, deceit, revenge are the spiders he sees in the cup. The uncle's arsenic, laudanum, opium, nicotine, and alcohol are their literal complements. Despite foreshadowing and such analogues as his burned photograph or his uncle's report of two spiders fighting, "the smaller one wanted to get away . . . but the larger one—he was cowardly, nephew—ran up behind, and attacked him," the narrator fails to see what has been adumbrated from the beginning. All along he had seen the spider as the Other—as the revenge of his brother, or of the woman, or of his sin itself in ghostly bestial shape: "Each was a child of that Shadow which Crime had made." But what about himself, not the sin but the *sinner*? The true spider appeared when he looked at himself in the mirror: "A more hideous face surely had never passed into life from Nature's mould, for the features were pinched and diabolic, the lips a twisted blue line, the mad eyes were filled with blood. But presently I understood that I was gazing upon myself." He reluctantly admits: "The Lord had set a mark upon Cain—the mark of the Shadow, the mark of the eternally damned. And I was Cain." The venomous wife provides a knife to entice her husband into suicide to avoid further agony. After the uncle leaps to his death possessed by the evil spirits of his "new mixture," the narrator is discovered—with an echo here from *The Picture of Dorian Gray* (1890-91)—dead with his wife's knife in his heart, fulfilling Friedrich Nietzsche's psychological dictum that decadent souls express themselves most creatively in their own self-destruction.

GERALD MONSMAN
Tucson

*August 29, 2012*

## NOTE ON THE TEXT

*Tenebrae: A Novel* was published by Skeffington & Son of London in early 1898. The British Library copy bears a receipt stamp dated March 21, 1898. The first edition was published in crown octavo format, bound in green decorative cloth, and sold for six shillings. The front cover of this edition reproduces the front cover of the original edition. The present edition was set from the copy of the first edition in the collections of the University of Pennsylvania Libraries and was compared to the copy in the British Library. No differences were noted between these two copies. This edition reprints the original edition verbatim in all respects, with the exception of a couple minor printer's errors, including one missing period and one comma which should have been a period; these errors have been silently corrected.

The publisher wishes to acknowledge the kind assistance of Mr Robert Brown of Winchester Antiquarian Books, who shared a reproduction of the cover of his copy for use in this edition.

# TENEBRAE

# CONTENTS

## PART I

## The Foreshadowing

## PART II

## The Under-Shadow

# PART I

## The Foreshadowing

# TENEBRAE

## CHAPTER I

### PEACE

The meek-eyed Peace;
With turtle wing the amorous clouds dividing.

MILTON.

Thursday morning, 10th April.

SONG birds rejoiced in every tree, as each sought a mate; upon the odorous earth, scented blossoms were glorious, while the bushes were lined with the fresh green of spring. Beyond rolled small pink clouds, tender as the red lips of early love, marking the eastern spot where the sun had arisen.

Peace! The perfect serenity of a heart unmarked by guilt. What gifts may the world offer in comparison with such? Peace!

Peace! The word rings with the fantastic sound of some soft evening bell over smiling waters—yet dies away in a lingering echo that suggests the death knell.

I leant from my window, inhaling the breath of morning. I noted the slow formation of tiny leaflets upon the grey strands of the creepers, and felt the balm-laden waves of air rolling and rippling upon my features. Suddenly there arose shuffling movements from the garden beneath, while a weird voice cried, in shrill accents of strange anger,—

'What! What! You won't take the fly? You won't eat the breakfast that I have provided for you? I can see you. Yes, there are your black legs showing under the rose leaves. I'm going to kill you. Do you hear that? You're going to die.'

7

This was merely my uncle, an old man, who suffered from the fearful malady he had brought upon himself by continual abuse of his body. Formerly he had been a nameless adventurer and wanderer over many lands. Then he had drifted back to me, a human derelict, that contained only a single germ of life. He had destroyed his powers in the gloomy west by internal use of arsenic and laudanum, by external application of morphia; in the bright east he had slept the long opium dream, and had revelled in the mad fever of alcoholism. Now he clung feebly to life, with the old lust still within him, beneath a constant horror that was induced by his insanity.

He was engaged in an occupation which came more as a duty to him than a pastime. He called himself the king of insects, so upon each fine day he might have been seen in the gardens, either capturing flies, or hurrying to some bush in search of a particular subject of his strange kingdom. With a fly between finger and thumb, he would pause before the web of one of those most detestable objects of created life—the spider. Deliberately he would insert his capture between the meshes of the sticky web, and wait for the grim insect to pounce down upon its hapless prey. Then he would stand upon the gravel path, laughing fearfully, and knotting his strange fingers together, while the fly buzzed in its last agony, and the horrid spider glutted its lust upon the victim's life.

Sometimes he would release the fly at that last moment; at other times he would introduce one spider into the home of another, and watch them fighting to the death. Should one endeavour to run away, he killed it for its cowardice.

On this occasion I knew that the spider refused to stir from its lair, and thus had aroused the anger of its would-be benefactor. He cursed at it, then knocked it from its nest with his stick.

He watched it as it lay curled up at his feet, then squeezed its pulpy body maliciously with the toe of his boot.

'You will try to deceive me, will you? You have disobeyed me, and now you would feign death. Ah, ah, we shall see. I will punish you. I'm going to torture you; then I shall kill you.'

The insect moved away, but he followed and squashed it slowly beneath his foot. Then I heard other footsteps, and presently my old nurse appeared in sight.

'Eh, sir, and what are you after now? Plaguing those poor flies and spiders as usual, I'll be bound.'

The old man looked up with a weird chuckle. 'I have killed him. See the dead body lying near that stone. It was a disobedient subject, so I have punished him. It is not murder. No, no. This is justice. It will be a warning to the others.'

'Come away in, sir. Your breakfast is waiting. Leave the poor things alone.'

But he went along, and hung over a rhododendron bush. 'I have not finished yet. I must go round and see my subjects.'

She followed and pulled at his arm. 'Now come along with me. There's your nice breakfast spoiling, and all for nothing.'

He replied only by a cry of fear. 'Look where you're treading! He's my enemy, for he kills and eats my insects. Come away from the horrid creature.'

She started. 'What is it? One of your nasty creatures crawling over me?'

'No, no. The big toad. Look at his red eyes and great speckled mouth. Take care! You will tread upon him.'

Then she understood, and did not step aside. 'Don't be afraid, sir. It's gone away now.'

There was something of interest he had discovered within the rhododendron bush, which was covered thickly with light green buds.

'Look! look!' he cried, thrusting his spare body forward. 'See! Here is a wonderful subject.'

Then he glanced up and saw me at the window. 'Ah, nephew! Come down here. He is worth looking at.'

'What is it, uncle?' I called.

'He is all in silver and brown,' cried the old man, bending over more closely. 'He lies right in the centre of the web, without moving—ah, no, I can see his black jaws stirring, and his eyes—he has fine eyes, nephew.'

Though the morning was warm, I shuddered.

'Don't touch it, uncle.' The words fell from my lips involuntarily.

'He would not hurt me. He wouldn't bite me.'

'Come away inside, sir,' repeated the old woman, more impatiently.

'Nephew! This is a good Christian. This is a pious spider. There is a silver cross upon his body. Come down and see.'

Again my fear swept over me. I had noticed this often, for nobody in the world knew more about these insects than I. Always had I wondered and trembled at the dread significance of that sign. Why should this foul and hellish insect be invested for its brief life with the symbol of man's redemption? What was the meaning in it? What the object?

'Ah, ah. I will bring you down to see this wonder presently, nephew. He is the largest I have seen for a long time. His great body is covered thickly with long hairs. Then there is the cross. You cannot help seeing it. It is a white cross, and very distinct.'

He began to grow excited. Presently I saw him led away, muttering incoherent remarks to invisible occupants in every bush he passed. The morning seemed brighter when he had gone, but my peace of mind had been terribly disturbed. I went to my breakfast, and afterwards walked out in company with my reflections.

I passed along the wide extent of garden, until I came to a rustic seat, around which blossomed pale yellow aconites, with many another of the season's flowers. Here I seated myself.

I was a young man—standing only upon the threshold of the thirtieth year. When a man of that age seeks isolation in the heart of Nature, finds rapture in the murmuring of the trees and soft song of the birds, it is generally because he finds himself overwhelmed by the subtle passion of love.

I was happy on that spring morning, I say. Happy! The trivial word has no weight in diagnosing the rapture at my heart. Joy formed a glorious environment, which bathed my body in its pure golden waves of feeling. For I loved, and knew myself to be loved. When a man may make such a pure confession to the confidence of his soul, he has lived and known the pleasure of life. Then lies nothing beyond in the years to come, but the mere shadow of that bliss.

Yet what a fury is that inexplicable power! How it thrills its fiery course through the veins! How the heart burns, how the brain throbs with the delight of life! Yet, withal, what a grim monster of jealousy is there!

Such is an old story, time-worn as the grey earth itself, yet ever young in the minds of all. I loved, and what did it matter that thousands were placed even as I? That millions of dead witnessed to the fleeting nature of this transitory passion? That eternity hovered behind, with its selfish message of salvation? I loved. That sufficed for me. Others might go their way, and sway this mighty world with their discoveries of Nature's hidden secrets. But such had no affinity with me. All I sought for was peace—and the realisation of my heart's desire.

And she, whom I had endowed with the poor gift of myself, she who was photographed in both my eyes, was indeed fair. Only the painter may inadequately delineate beauty with his dim eloquence of silence; the art is withheld from him who guides the pen. Description of a graceful curve, a wondrous colouring, is impossible. Imagination flies from the lifeless touch of words. Only the lover may describe the perfections of his particular mistress, and then only to his own heart. So let it suffice to say that she was a woman, and I loved her.

From selfish consideration, I turned to thoughts of others. There were three, who had enwrapped themselves round my life, three strangely dissimilar in every way, apart from a single common characteristic—their affection for me, the master of the house.

Surely, in the matter of love, Fortune had blessed me with singular favour. Above all stood my brother, who was in age but a year my junior. Here was one who possessed for me all that wealth of devotion which Jonathan of old showered upon David.[1] Here was a man who loved his brother as he did himself, who had, moreover, no thought apart from that brother's happiness. He was a man with a great heart, and he loved—my God! what has come over my eyes? The ink turns red upon the paper. The pen is dripping blood. Blood, I say. God! My brain is in flames. There it is again. The horror surges up before my eyes. Ah! leave me—leave me.

Peace. I was forgetting. I am calm again now. I am curiously liable to such fits when I think of my brother. For he is dead now. Ages have rolled away since we buried him. His was a strange, a mysterious sinking into death. Many wondered why he departed so suddenly, and abandoned the brother he loved. But the world is

---

1 See Chapter II epigraph.

full of greater mysteries. Of what account is the life or death of one unknown man from the myriads that walk upon the earth? Nothing—nothing at all.

Then there came the memory of my old nurse, a faithful woman who had been for years in the family of which I was now the head. She had led up my brother and myself from infancy, with that loving attention which is so often wanting in the mother. Now she was the general guardian of all my domestic affairs. And lastly, I thought of my uncle, whom I pitied.

These, then, were the three of the home circle with whom my life was bound up—the loving brother, the faithful housekeeper, the drivelling uncle. A curious family, perhaps, yet peaceful and happy. My God! how peaceful and happy!

I remained upon the rustic seat, in peace with my own mind, until I became suddenly disturbed. Over my head was rough woodwork, where ivy twisted and fell in graceful festoons of shining green. The sun rays pierced the tree branches and struck full upon my face, causing me to move slightly to one side. But as I did so, without warning, without the least sound, a horrible creature dropped from the tangled mesh above, swung upon a glistening silver strand, with hideous legs working through the air, then dropped in grim silence upon the seat. It would have fallen upon my hand, had I not withdrawn it with a shock of sickening terror.

The creature was a black spider, bloated and ungainly.

For some seconds repugnance at this grim visitant impaired each sense. My eyes were fixed upon the hairy body, which swayed slowly from side to side. There was no cross there, but I noticed other markings upon that dark skin, yellow lines and tracings, which seemed to me—I may have been in error, for my imagination was fevered—to represent the ghastly form of a human skull, that symbol of all things solemn, and of death.

Then the creature drew itself round upon the seat, faced me, and deliberately commenced to move in my direction. Every line of its horrid body rippled with the fiendish action that lay beneath.

With a fearful shudder I took a long stick and swept the creature from the seat. It dropped from the woodwork, swinging upon a single strand. This I broke, and it fell to the ground. I placed an end of the stick above that spot where the creature was feigning death. I closed my eyes, and dug the point well into the soil.

Then, without glancing at the result of my work, I hurried away, with an unaccountable feeling of nausea.

## CHAPTER II

### AFFECTION

Thy love to me was wonderful, passing the love of women.
2 Samuel i. 26.

4 o'clock p.m.

Many might have imagined that my house was set in the midst of extremely dreary surroundings. They might even have applied to it such terms as gloomy and desolate.

Before the grounds stretched a grass-grown road, little frequented and always silent. This might have borne a dreary aspect in the rainy autumn, when the long sedges and solemn bushes stood dripping with moisture, and mud lay piled on either side. Also, there were many decayed trees dotted along the ragged hedgerows, and these often showed ghastly on moonlight nights.

In a south-westerly direction ran the jagged line of the cliff, beneath which the sea moaned and sobbed, in the sorrow of calm or the anger of storm. Running back from the sheer edge spread a wood of pines, terminating at the grass road before mentioned. This was a part of my large property, as was also the desolate moor, which ran for a great distance almost direct north on the opposite side. It was a pathless reach of broken ground, with occasional blasted oaks that uplifted gaunt, crooked arms to the sky, and a melancholy patch of ink-black water lying stagnant near the centre.

The house itself, erected in the days when romance and imagination happily controlled the genius of the architect, was unmistakably stern in its gradual decay. There were many creepers clinging to the aged brickwork, which showed frequently in discoloured patches, but most of these shared in the antiquity of the materials to which they adhered. In many places the woodwork had rotted considerably, and was almost entirely overspread by a minute yellow fungus, which at a short distance bore an unnatural appearance of grotesque colouring.

Each window bore a certain vacant and *searching* appearance, an unconscious freak on the part of the long dead architect, yet one which pleased me greatly. These windows—I would allow no white curtains to detract from their grimness—seemed to follow any frequenter of the grounds with the questioning gaze that lurks in the eyes of a well-painted portrait. Some there were which forgotten ancestors had deemed it advisable, or necessary, to close up, and which now peered blankly through the clinging ivy, striking into the spectator's mind a latent suggestion of guarded horrors lying concealed behind, of rooms possessing no door, nor any means of entry from within. All this, however, was pleasing to my naturally morbid imagination.

With all speed I hurried from the house towards the road beyond, for I had an appointment to keep. I stepped from the path, where a few half-dead poplars shook mournful heads, and left behind me the gates of rusted iron. The next moment I found myself face to face with my brother.

(Before I write further, I must strive to quiet the wild revulsion at my heart. The agonising affliction presses upon me, an awful passion is consuming me. The time is short now. The horror of the end is inevitable. But peace—peace as at present. For the time I am free.)

Perhaps we were strange brothers, with our extraordinary affection for each other. As children we lay in the same bed; we played through boyhood's happy days without a quarrel; together we were influenced and corrected.

So we had reached man's estate, joined together by the great unspoken love which controlled our every action. We shared, as it were, the same heart, the same mind, equal portions of the same soul. Only the law of Nature compelled us to pass through life beneath the identity of separate bodies.

We formed the last representatives of an ancient family, proud of its history and its name. Upon the early death of father and mother, the large estate fell to me, the eldest by a year. In comparison with me, my brother was poor, but that mattered little, for the understanding between us was complete. My property was his. We shared in all things alike. All understood our positions. They knew me to be the rich owner, my brother the poor dependant.

So we met together on that spring afternoon, at the iron gates which led to the lonely road. He was breathing hard, as though heated with running. Yet he was the first to speak.

'I am glad it is you. I was afraid I should miss you.'

His manner seemed to me strange. It was as though he feared his tongue might convict him of wrong-doing. His glance had something of suspicion, while the eyes shifted aside when they met mine. I had come upon him unexpectedly, when he was unprepared to meet me.

'Why?' I asked merely.

'I think I know where you are going. To the road at the back of the wood—'

'Of course,' I cried. 'And I must not stop here any longer. I am due there already.'

I was about to step away over the fresh grass, when he put out his arm and stopped me. 'Wait a moment. I hurried on to tell you,' he said.

'What?' I cried in fear. 'Nothing has happened to her?'

'I met her by an accident, as I came up from the shore, and walked with her. She had a sudden faintness, and was compelled to return home. I hurried on to catch you in time.'

I was alarmed at his information. 'It is nothing serious? You are sure of it?'

'Quite,' he replied, with conviction. Then he added, 'She would not even allow me to accompany her home.'

This placed the matter beyond question. 'Did she not send me a message?' I cried.

He bit his lips, and I almost thought it was in anger. Then I saw he was thinking. 'Yes,' he said slowly; 'to-morrow afternoon—'

'At the same place?' I interrupted.

'At the same place,' he repeated, with the same slow emphasis.

'The same time?'

He seemed actually afraid to trust his voice. He merely nodded, then made as though he would have passed me.

I placed my hand upon his arm. 'You are not going to leave me,' I said. 'Let us take a walk together.'

He came with me, though I had the thought that he obeyed unwillingly, and we paced along the grass-grown road in silence for a time. This was nothing unusual. We understood each other so well that speech was often unnecessary. So we passed together from the grass-grown road, and commenced to wind a devious track among the rugged stones which lay everywhere scattered over the surface of the moor. Though the prospect ahead was clearly lighted by afternoon sunshine, save for a white line of fog which hung heavily across the eastern horizon, at the first glimpse of this lonely moor an unaccountable feeling of depression, a distinct sense of gloom permeated my mind. Why, I cannot imagine, for at the time I was entirely happy. That strange superstition for the unseen, which had ever exerted a powerful influence over my career, rose in a strong impetus of feeling, and sent a shudder through my entire frame, when I glanced upon the worn, windswept rocks, the blasted trees of grotesque and melancholy shapes, and the occasional patches of long grey grass whispering drearily beneath a rising breeze.

A coldness crept into my body, an unmistakable sense of loss tormented my mind. There *was* no pleasure in life. There was nothing between maturity and dissolution, but a mad striving after the unattainable. Should any dim delight present itself, enjoyment was banished by physical affliction, or the unhealthy fancy of imagination; should success arrive, appreciation became at once overshadowed blackly by the gaunt apparition of death. There was nothing in life, beyond this appalling fear of death; there was nothing in that recession to the unknown which was not entirely horrible.

Such in brief were some of my thoughts, as I stepped out with my brother upon the lonely moor. I brushed aside the sedges with careless tread, until we stood upon a sodden grass patch, and looked down upon the black waters of the small lake which blotted the centre of this melancholy land.

Presently I spoke. The attractions of that spot had a morbid tendency.

'It is said that there exists a race of uncivilised people who fear stagnant water. They believe that the spirit of evil inhabits its dark depths.'

My brother turned to me. 'They may well think so. Anything might lie beneath such a surface as this, and remain invisible.'

'Its shape would necessarily be strange,' I continued. 'It may stretch itself along the slimy bottom, waiting to seize upon any who enter its domains. The traveller, passing by night, might slip and fall. He would be drawn down into these dark waters, choked in the monster's vile embrace, and meet a fearful end. There is a mystery in water.'

He made no reply, and I continued, 'How many of the world's secrets lie concealed beneath the dark water! There is nothing like it for hiding away the damning evidence of guilt—the body of a murdered victim, shall we say?'

He gave an exclamation of horror. A great bubble mounted upward from unknown depths, and burst upon the sluggish surface at our feet. The greasy water became animated with small ripples, while a sickly odour of marsh gas beat upon our nostrils.

'That was like the breath of created life,' I muttered.

'It is nothing,' he said. 'Only mud, rotting vegetation, with perhaps the carcase of some animal.'

'Or human being,' I added, my eyes gloating upon the ink-like surface.

He shuddered. Physically and mentally my brother was far weaker than myself. 'This is not a human grave,' he said.

I laughed. 'These dark pools preserve their sombre secrets. What can you or I know of the passions that may have raged over this very spot? Perhaps some gloomy life chapter has found its conclusion here. This grass may once have been spotted with blood. Two, who had loved once, may here have shrieked a last farewell, one to return to the world, the other—' I pointed to the sullen pit below.

'It is possible,' he said slowly.

'There would have been one great cry, then a splash, and after that—silence. The world would go on laughing and sinning as before, while another creature would walk the earth beneath the curse of Cain. How terrible it must be to know yourself, no longer as a man, but as—a murderer!'

He looked at me, and I saw that his hands were trembling. 'Why do you speak on such things?'

'The thoughts are not our own. There are those of good and

those of evil; there are thoughts happy and others morbid. These
suit themselves to the environment of the body.'

I waved my hand towards the bleak expanse of water, with
the inverted images of decayed tree trunks and scraggy bush. 'In
such a spot, the thoughts turn into a morbid groove. This place is
suggestive of a burying ground, its features might well stand for
memorial tablets of the dead. We are induced to consider such
things by the knowledge of our common end.'

'Yet it is not for us to reflect upon unwholesome fancies. You
were never cast in the murderer's mould. You know that the criminal is born for the gallows, not led up to it by a series of life's
mischances.'

I groaned to myself and violently clenched my left hand. The
palm was throbbing as he spoke, while two lines of liquid fire
played across the flesh. I jealously concealed from all eyes that fatal
commingling of the two vital lines of head and life on that hand.
The ominous cutting of these fantastic markings is commonly
known as the Scaffold Sign.[1]

Deliberately he continued, 'The murderer is usually a man of
limited education, who has not the power to cloak feeling, and
who acts always under the quick impulse of the moment. He is
thus unable to grasp the entire significance of his act. Neither can
he appreciate the full torturing horror of the interval between sentence and extreme penalty.'

It was my turn to shiver at his words.

'Such a punishment would be inconceivable to either of us,' I
said. 'A man so sensitive as myself, for instance, would succumb
long before the fatal day.'

He drew me away from the dismal blot of water.

'Let us go back,' he said. 'We have been in this dreary place long
enough.'

The dreadful thought still burned within me. 'A murderer,'
I muttered. 'Think of the days of madness, and long nights of
horror. Every man is an enemy, you are yourself an outcast from

---

1  "He has the Scaffold Sign—a violent and abrupt cutting off of the 'line of the
head' (the one running across the palm) by the line running toward the fingers
from the wrist." "The Murderer's Hand," *Christian Work: Illustrated Family News-
paper*, 29 August 1895: 359.

earth and heaven. Tormented by the frightful image of your victim, racked with the anguish of the death cell and the scaffold. It is all horrible! It is unspeakable!'

'But does not concern us,' he said; and then, 'Nor can it.'

We walked over the broken waste towards the garden entrance at the south side. Our talking was done for the time.

We were strangely affectionate brothers. I have said so before, but I must state it plainly again. Usually we walked with arm linked in arm; sometimes I had a hand upon his shoulder; there were occasions when we still walked hand clasped in hand like children.

As we were about to pass through the gate, I said, more to my own heart than for his ear, 'To-morrow afternoon, at the same time and place. May the hours speed till then.'

I felt my brother start, as though smitten with remembrance. His arm fell away from my body, a dark flush—it might have been either of shame or fear—overspread his features.

## CHAPTER III

## LOVE

Then must you speak
Of one that lov'd, not wisely but too well;
Of one not easily jealous, but, being wrought,
Perplex'd in the extreme; of one whose hand,
Like the base Judean, threw a pearl away,
Richer than all his tribe.
Set you down this.

*Othello*, Act V. sc. 2.

Friday afternoon, 11th April.

MY brother was in the library, but when I looked in upon his
privacy, he was sitting with head bowed upon his arms. I would not
disturb his meditation—it could have been nothing else—so went
on to a room in the south wing, where I spent much of my time.

This blue room was another of my fancies. Here the furniture, the hangings upon the walls, even the depicted decoration of
the ceiling were of the same sombre hue of black. Upon all these
things rested a livid lustre, a weird light, which flickered up and
down the curtains, which played across the ceiling and quivered
along each separate article of furniture. This effect was simply
caused. All the window glass had been stained a vivid blue; the
lamp shades were of the same tint; even the rays of the firelight
were projected through a vitreous screen of blue mica.

I had discovered that this effect of colouring was conducive to
careful thought, while it was, also, restful to the mind. The blue
rays falling across black objects caused a certain dimness throughout the room, even on the brightest days in summer. Everything at
a slight distance bore the appearance of objects viewed indistinctly
through the deceptive covering of a fog. The remote corners of
this chamber were always invisible, and lent to the solitary occupant a feeling of mystery and enchantment.

I entered, and closed the door silently. As I seated myself in a chair of black velvet, sounds reached my ears. Looking round, I perceived, bent over a black-wood table, near one of the blue windows, my uncle, busy upon some unnatural occupation.

He turned towards me his wizened face, which was ghastly in that light. His appearance was that of a corpse, galvanised into temporary animation.

'What are you doing, uncle?' I called.

'Ha! ha!' came his answer, with many chuckles. 'Come here and see. I'm making a fine mixture. You shall have some of it presently.'

I noticed many articles scattered beneath his hands. I came over into the blue glare of the window.

'I have been at it since morning. It is ready now, and we will enjoy it together.'

He waved before me a small flask that was half full of a black liquid. Then he wrapped a skinny hand round the neck of a brandy bottle hard by.

'One gets tired of the old things, nephew. We must make new pleasures for ourselves.'

He half filled a tumbler with the fiery spirit, then with shaking hand mixed a portion of the black fluid. Every drop sank slowly, lengthening into a dark line, that was suggestive of a small serpent.

He shook the glass, while the livid rays of light shot through its contents. He shouted in a wild mirth, 'Taste it, nephew. This is a glorious drink.'

I shrank away from him. He raised the glass and madly gulped down the compound. His face became purple in that light; he staggered back and fell into a chair, his head shaking furiously.

I smelt at the contents of the pungent bottle. 'This is nicotine,' I cried.

He repeated the word feebly. 'It mixes well with brandy. Taste it, nephew.'

I merely summoned a servant, and ordered the articles to be removed. He almost wept when he saw the bottles taken. He went down upon his knees on the black carpet, and begged that they might be restored to him. At length I pacified him, and drew my chair near his, wondering if my father—whom I had never looked upon—had in any way resembled his brother.

'I cannot stay with you long, uncle,' I said. 'I have an engagement presently.'

He regarded me with his watery eyes. One may never know how far to trust a madman. This old man could be singularly acute at times.

He gave a long chuckle of delight, and rubbed his skinny hands together. 'I know—I know. It is good to be young—to enjoy life. Ha! ha! Where the shingle shines with the wet, where the waves tumble. That is one place. Up in the pine wood, where there are strange odours. That is another. Ha! ha!'

I had not seen him so jovial for long.

'Boys and love—they are all the same. I know you two. Ha! ha! Love and folly. Always the same.'

There was hidden meaning in these words. I touched my uncle on the knee. 'What have you seen, uncle?' I said.

'Ha! ha! You are different in face, but the same at heart. I walk about to set my kingdom in order, and I see much, I am not blind yet. Ha! ha! Not blind—not yet.'

His mirth angered me. 'Uncle,' I cried, 'whom have you seen me with? Tell me.'

'She is young and dark. She has a proud face and a fine figure. They'll not last, nephew. No, no. Age comes and beauty flies—'

I put a cunning question. 'That was yesterday afternoon? A little later than this. You saw me then?'

I knew that his memory could not travel back more than a few days.

'I was by the shore. I saw her coming—but you were not there. I walked along, talking to the waters, but I didn't see you.'

'My brother was there.'

'I was up among the pines, and I saw him, but not you. He was there for a long time. Then he was running along the grass road. Ha! ha! I see many things in my walks. He ran hard, while she walked away.'

It was time for me to go. My uncle was rambling, yet—he said that my brother had been running. This was true.

I put one last question. 'She was not well, uncle. You saw her when she walked away?'

He twisted himself up with unnatural laughter. 'Ha! ha! Faint with love. She came near me as I lay among the pines. I see many things in my walks. Her cheeks were red and her eyes were bright. Ha! ha! Faint with love.'

His cracked laughter rose again, while I sprang up, with a strange fever burning within.

The old man cried after me pitifully, 'Give me back my bottles—I must have my bottles, nephew.'

But I only shouted back an incoherent reply, as I hastened from the blue chamber and came out to the white light of day.

My brain throbbed wildly as I sped through the deserted hall out into the grounds—the oppression of the atmosphere stifled me—on, until the iron gates uprose before me in the loneliness, and the gaunt poplars shook their dead heads at me solemnly. I could not think; I hastened, until the pine wood rose in sight. Here all was black and solemn. But there was—yes, my eyes could not deceive me, there certainly was an ornament to the landscape, one single bright spot of colour and beauty.

She was awaiting me at the place appointed. There had been, after all, more of madness than truth in my uncle's words. She was faithful to the man who loved her.

She came forward from the dark shadowed fringe of the wood. We met together on the path, and my last fears vanished when I looked into her eyes, when I saw the happy smile which heightened the perfection of her face.

'You are almost five minutes late,' she said reproachfully.

'I confess it,' I said. 'You must pardon me. I was detained by my uncle.'

'You generally bring me flowers,' she continued. 'You have forgotten me to-day.'

They had been lying in the hall, but I had forgotten them in my excitement. I could send them on later, I reflected.

I inquired after her health. She flushed, and in a low voice told me she was well again. The day before had been unusually warm for the time of year; this had caused a sudden faintness, all effects of which had now passed away.

I linked my arm through hers, and we walked together. It was a wonderfully fine evening. Even the hanging mists seemed to me more full of radiance than the brightest sunset.

I bent over her, and spoke. 'You certainly have many things to forgive. I kept you waiting, and I forgot to bring your flowers. I have been unsettled to-day, for even I have cares, you must know. My poor uncle is more of an anxiety than you can imagine.'

'It is good of you to give him a home,' she said. 'Such men have scarcely a right to dwell with civilised people.'

'But he is my uncle,' I said quietly. 'He has the greater claim upon my protection because he is afflicted.'

'But he brought it on himself.'

The remark struck me as heartless. But women spare no sympathy for men who are conquered by the appetite for liquor or drug. His condition would appear horrible in its degradation to one of her pure nature. Nevertheless, I said,—

'That reflection has no weight with me. The fact remains that he has none to look to beside myself.'

'Your brother—does he approve of it?'

I smiled upon her. 'You know us both by this time. His wish is mine. He loves, hates, acts as I do.'

At this I fancied she trembled slightly. But there was now a fresh breeze springing up from the sea.

'So he kept you this afternoon—from me?' she said lightly.

'And he would have detained me longer. For once his conversation was interesting—he was speaking about you.'

'Me!' She laughed nervously.

'You know he has often seen you with me. Also, he has seen my brother—'

She interrupted me. 'What! Your brother? Where?'

'You have no cause to fear our uncle, even though he may spy upon your actions,' I said reassuringly. 'He is harmless, and always weak, even in his anger.'

'Yes, of course,' she said hurriedly. 'It was foolish of me. Still—still, one naturally shrinks from madness.'

'I will tell him not to come near you,' I said tenderly. 'He will obey me.'

'Thank you,' she said, still breathing strangely. 'It is a silly idea of mine, I know; but it is not pleasant in this lonely place to think that he may be watching me.'

We were in the pine wood by this time, pressing the brown

needles against the peat. Here it was sheltered and pleasant. The wind murmured in the dark masses overhead; the soft air was fragrant with a resinous odour.

Presently we fell into a livelier vein. Idly we laughed and chatted, until a mystic greyness proclaimed the approach of evening. Then she brought back my morbid fear by a light-hearted remark.

'Come! I will tell your fortune. Show me your hand.'

I hesitated, then obeyed, and stretched forth my right hand.

'No. I will see that presently. The other, please.'

I stammered forth an excuse, but she persisted.

'Take off your glove—you scarcely ever uncover your left hand. Have you lost a finger? No matter. I must see it.'

Again I protested, but she laughed away my words. Finding it impossible to disobey, I withdrew my glove, and offered that damning palm for her inspection.

She bent her beautiful head, until the flowers that nodded in her hat caressed my forehead. She brought my open hand closer up to her eyes, as the shadows of evening enwrapped us with chilly loneliness. There followed an interval of silence. No sweet voice of prophecy made the air musical. I saw her lips part, then a quick change came over the face, and she dropped my hand, as though it were a thing that might convey infection. Then she looked me in the eyes, and spoke solemnly, 'I did not think you had *that.*'

I knew well what she meant, but still I asked, 'What is it?'

She took my hand again, and pointed out with a delicate finger the fatal junction of two lines which crawled across my palm in deep furrows as red as blood.

'Do you know what name scientists have given to that?' she whispered.

'The Scaffold Sign,' I muttered, as lightly as I might. 'Well, what of it? Hundreds of better men than I are doubtless so marked. It is foolish to imagine that a man's fate is set forth on his hand.'

She smiled faintly. 'I am willing to admit that you are the exception,' she said; 'but I have my own opinions, though I am only a woman. Those who have examined the hands of criminals will tell you of certain characteristics identical on each. That sign is the most prominent.'

'According to your belief, the man who bears it is born to live as a criminal?'

She nodded, with a frightened expression on her face.

'It is a terrible predestination.'

'It is,' she said; 'but don't let us talk about it.'

I drew on the glove, with a dreadful sinking at my heart.

'You have shaken my belief,' she said cheerfully.

The dusk was drawing round, so we set forth for her home, which lay at the distance of half a mile from the outskirts of my property. At the gate I left her, then returned with slow step and anxious thought. Strive as I might, I could not banish recollection of my uncle's wild words, 'You are different in face, but the same at heart.'

Oh! my God! The torture I have suffered since! The agony I am undergoing now!

## CHAPTER IV

## ALTERATION

But hail, thou Goddess, sage and holy,
Hail, divinest Melancholy!—MILTON.

Monday evening, 21st April.

THE manuscript book that I was reading by the failing daylight was of exceeding rarity; indeed I had reason to believe that the work in my possession was the original, from which no duplicate had ever been taken.

This remarkable book, which had come from some long forgotten source into my family, was the life-work of some ancient Norse philosopher. I had made myself thoroughly acquainted with the language, for the sole purpose of being able to appreciate the learning scattered within.

It was entitled simply, 'The Hidden Man,' and formed a wonderful analysis of the secret power which actuates each movement of the mind. Modern writers would certainly have scoffed at the indefinite theories contained therein.

Considering the great question of Man and Vitality, the saga started indeed with slight data. Merely a lump of clay, resting upon a lofty spot in the hypothetical centre of chaos, exposed to a whirling vapour and continual current of winds.

In process of time this earth assumed a definite shape, owing to the influence of its atmospheric surroundings. Particles, formed by similar process elsewhere, were drifted into these currents, to be assimilated by the omnivorous mass of pervadable earth. Gradually it absorbed within its core the external air, which it held a prisoner. The resultant effect was life and power of motion in the form of primitive man.

The vapour thus imprisoned formed a separate being, which, being of a higher nature than the gross material of its environment, soon came to dominate the baser creature's every motion and action. To such an extent indeed, that the clay, or flesh as it then was called, became nothing more than the mere vehicle of this hidden being.

A desire of the objective to protect itself from the tyranny of the subjective formed, after lapse of ages, numerous bonds and ropes, in the shape of bones and muscles, which erected a barrier, with the object of restricting the mightier power. But the breath responded by withdrawing itself from the resisting tabernacle, leaving it to return to that original state in which it had been discovered. So came death.

That portion of the work which possessed for me the stronger fascination was the second part. Here the philosopher endeavoured to point out how entirely dual was Man, both from an animal and mental standpoint. He was, in fact, a multitude in himself.

*Exempli gratiâ*, there might be a righteous man linked to a scoffing nature, by some wild revelry of overruling fate. The former would be external and obvious; the latter, internal and indiscernible. There might also be some work of creation, vile and worthless to all outward appearance, yet inwardly joined to one all virtue and purity. The following paragraph is an excerpt from the original,—

'Which of the two natures of man we are conversing with, none may tell. Perchance it is the friend, who has our interests at heart; perchance it is the enemy, who will readily shatter our reputation. It may be the generous disposition, who will perform the office we are seeking, with a real desire to assist; again, it may be the selfish nature, who will make a smiling promise to our face, then depart, to encompass a plan for our ruin.'

I was pondering on these words, when the daylight disappeared. I returned the roll of manuscript to its place, then sought the room where I was wont to sit with my brother of an evening.

As I came slowly along and entered, I could hear the wind moaning outside, with heavy gusts of rain beating upon the window glass. It was a cold evening of storm, and of sorrow, doubtless, for many. But the grief of others could not touch my heart.

This room was large, and the loftiest in the house. The ceiling was composed of dark oak, stained by time; the windows were at a great height above the floor, and were of the narrow pointed style usually adapted to churches; the furniture was antique, while an air of gloom pervaded the whole. This was caused possibly by the heavy black draperies which depended from the walls.

My brother rose from a deep chair, and greeted me slowly. It seemed as though the effort of speech was constrained. I looked at him, and endeavoured in vain to detect the particular lines of his countenance which had altered in general appearance of late. His face was not the same, yet I could not discover where the change had taken place. The alteration seemed to be due to a different *arrangement*, if I may so use the word, of those face lines.

Let me endeavour to explain my meaning. Someone, in my absence, might alter the arrangement of the furniture in my own particular room, without making any addition to, or subtraction from, the same. On my return, I should enter this room, with the expectation of finding all as I had left it. For a time I should fancy myself in a strange place, although surrounded by my most familiar possessions. Such an operation cannot be called change, in the full sense of the word. It is rather alteration, by a different mode of arrangement.

My brother moved forward uneasily. 'I expected you earlier. It is rather lonely here to-night.'

'I was in the library,' I said; 'as usual, among my books.'

He smiled faintly. 'You are happy in your love for literature. A compulsory digestion of another's wisdom annoys me. The author cannot destroy his personality. The triumphant and obtrusive "I am" is stamped across each page.'

'That is the affliction of being born a critic,' I said lightly. 'You read only to discover faults; I read for the enlargement of my mind.'

'The philosophy of your Norse saga, the Chaldæan witchcraft, the wild ritual of heathen mythologists. Is that satisfying food?'

He had quoted my favourite works. 'Each follows his taste,' I said. 'Some prefer the unsubstantial food afforded by romance, tales of milk-and-watery love, flavoured with intermittent clash of steel; others revel in the delight of theology, and strive to unravel twisted skeins of monkish doctrine; yet others, who prefer to glide along the smooth metre of poetry. But I prefer Nature in her strange and wild moods. I would plunge deeply into the mysteries of her hidden secrets. For there lies the true knowledge.'

'It is a thankless study.'

'But absorbing. We mortals are wonderful pieces of mechanism. We rise from nothing; we raise a feeble cry in the world, then we sink back to nothing. What is that essence we call life? Why, having it, should we not discover the power of preserving it indefinitely? These are questions which millions have tried to answer, millions who have now neither name nor place in the world. But the questions remain as new and perplexing. They all failed.'

'As you must fail,' he muttered.

'True. But some man must approach nearer the truth than his compeers. I am a man. Why should not I be that one?'

He sank back wearily into the chair. I fronted him, as the lamplight streamed down fully upon his face. Again I sought to discover where lay the change, and again I looked in vain.

The complexion of his face was cadaverous—the artificial light may have caused this; his eyes were large and of unusual luminosity. All the curves, notably those of the lips and chin, were of a refined beauty, although inclined to be statuesque. But there was much character in that countenance, also—as it struck me then for the first time—a singular lack of moral energy.

We sat together, silent in the quiet room, until my brother made a casual remark upon the similitude between the words 'immorality' and 'immortality.'

'So alike that, when spoken hurriedly, one might almost be confounded with the other, yet expressing meanings so entirely contrary.'

'The evil power is certainly immortal, as we understand time—a thing which may be set within the bounds of human reckoning,' I answered. 'Before the problem of eternity—a spherical, therefore endless, continuation—the brain fails. Evil, upon this world, is a more potent factor than good; immorality is the inner essence of all life; such a power may well be expressed in the syllables of unending time.'

'Is there such a thing as a moral passion?' he asked.

'Moral? The word is far-reaching. The thought of the mind, the tendency of the spirit, the inclination of the heart, are all included within the province of morals. A man may be in a state of religious ecstasy—'

'That is not a passion.'

'No, fanaticism—madness, rather. Then we have that extraordinary devotion, which caused hundreds to suffer in the early ages for the cause of Christianity. I think this is as near as we can get to the moral passion.'

'The true passion must have a visible and tangible object,' he muttered. 'The resolution of the Christians arose from a power of belief, added to a selfish desire of assuring salvation. Passion is a flame which darts up, then expires, to reappear later. Their devotion amounted to a vocation.'

'And then we come to human love. That is the passion paramount.'

'Which is immoral in all its ramifications,' he said quickly.

He spoke sharply, as though he expected contradiction.

'Love is not a passion,' I said. 'It is rather that sense of emotional helplessness in which we approach the Deity. The attraction of opposite sex is a passion.'

'Which cannot be moral,' he said slowly. 'Love is like the snow, coldness and purity; passion resembles the fire, with its heat and fury.'

I closed my eyes, and saw a raging torrent of red waves, passing and recrossing in endless revelry. This was with me generally the result of deep thought.

My brother looked at me from the recess of his chair. 'You know how this power touches the body,' he said deliberately.

Then I spoke wildly. 'A complete dedication of self to another; an entire transference of heart, brain and thought; an inextinguishable desire; a lack of energy to act singly. If that is love, I am indeed a victim to its power. But it is a terribly weak word.'

He seemed to shiver as I spoke. 'Why should you ask?' I continued.

He hesitated before replying. 'I was wondering to what extent that influence had grown upon you. How deeply would the withdrawal of that passion touch you?'

His words excited me. 'Have you any suspicion?' I cried loudly.

'You would hold nothing from me. Tell me. Is there anything that
I should know?'

'You have no cause for fear,' he said quietly. 'Only the possible
in life must be guarded against.'

I was for the time silent, then everything became perfectly
plain. Blind fool that I had been! I had marvelled at the change in
my brother; I had sought to find where that alteration lay. As he
spoke, the veil dropped from my eyes, and I saw clearly.

My brother was jealous of the claims another had upon me! He
had been my associate, my sole companion, my more than friend.
We had lived for one another exclusively. It was necessary that this
state of things should exist no longer.

I came nearer, until I stood at the side of his chair. Then I placed
my hand upon his shoulder, and inclined my head towards his. My
perception was *very* keen. It was strange that the truth should have
been concealed from me for so long.

I spoke, in a voice which bore the heart with it. 'I know the
cause of your melancholy. But there can be no change in our affection. My house is yours—you know it—as it has always been. All
shall be in the future as it has been in the past.'

His tongue gave me back no word. 'There will be a change,
I grant. You have always had a brother; now you shall possess a
sister, one who will make our home a place of delights. Alteration
there must certainly be. But what of it, when it comes in the shape
of increased happiness?'

Yet his head remained still bent. I looked down into his face,
but, as I did so, I could feel that his huddled body shuddered
beneath my hand.

CHAPTER V

MISGIVING

Say man's a worm, and power belongs to God.

COWPER.

Friday morning, 25th April.

IT was late in the day when I arose. My head was racked with pain, while I was most unaccountably nervous. I was unhappy, and afflicted by a morbid depression, such as that I had suffered from on a former evening, when standing by the black patch of water upon the moor. I was suspicious of woe impending, yet I had no explicit cause for such fear.

I came into the blue room, where light glared with long livid rays through the tinted glass. I seated myself despondently, and hardly had I done so when my nurse entered, with some slight delicacies she hoped might tempt my appetite. This old woman kept a careful eye upon my every movement about the house. She knew when I had risen, by listening in her simple manner outside my door, then she would hurry away to prepare some breakfast. She stood by me, chatting idly in the garrulous fashion of her sex, with hope of distracting me from my thoughts. I was too weak to oppose myself to the flow of her words, or indeed to heed their meaning. But presently she aroused me by exclaiming, with the carelessness of the old woman accustomed to regard masters whom she had reared to maturity with familiarity, 'The young master is ahead of you this morning. He has been up for a long time.'

Her words vibrated upon a certain current of feeling, and finally touched a chord which corresponded with the indefinite fear that had troubled me of late.

'Where is he?' I said. 'I have not seen him to-day.'

She looked at me with anxiety. 'Why, he has gone out. He took his breakfast all by himself, and then hurried out to the garden. He was in a big hurry about something or other—'

'Which way did he go?' I interrupted.

'Well, I couldn't be quite certain, because the lilacs hide the turn of the path. I suppose he must have gone through the gate, and out along by the cliff. That was more than two hours ago.'

'Why should he hurry away?' I muttered.

She laughed. 'It's not for me to say, is it? I don't look after you two now, as I used when you were both babies, and would toddle along holding to my skirt.'

'Why did he hurry?' I repeated.

'He'll be in presently, then you can ask him yourself. The young master will tell you everything quickly enough, though—'

'Go on,' I cried, more fiercely than I had ever addressed her.

'There—there. Eat your breakfast. Nothing at all, but my old tongue runs away with me at times.'

Then she cried in fear, because I sprang to my feet and caught her by the arm.

'Tell me! I will know. What have you to say?'

'Why,' she exclaimed, in a flurried manner, 'how you do frighten me! You're not at all well this morning. Now I brought in something with me, which will do your poor head a power of good. My dear grandmother gave me the receipt just before she died, and—'

'I want none of your medicines,' I cried angrily. 'I order you to finish your sentence.'

She laughed in a tremulous fashion. 'Well, well. It's nothing, after all, but an old woman's fancy. You mustn't worry yourself over such little things—but you are not well this morning.'

'Tell me.'

'Why, the young master has seemed to change during the past week or so. You see I have brought you both up from childhood. I can see what nobody else can.'

'I have seen it, too,' I muttered.

Then the old nurse warmed to her subject, as a woman will when she has once spoken.

'Only a little time ago, and if I'd told him you weren't well, he'd have been up by your bedside almost as soon as I'd done speaking. I don't understand why he hasn't been near you to-day.'

I shivered, with head between my hands. 'Yes, why?'

'It is a change,' she said solemnly, shaking her white head at me.
'We must all change,' I cried fiercely.

She looked at me wonderingly. Then she began—as she thought—to understand.

She placed her wrinkled hand upon my shoulder. 'There's nothing gone wrong between you and—someone else, has there?' she asked, with anxious affection.

Again that sudden touch of dread. 'Why should there be anything?' I cried. 'Has my brother spoken upon—?'

I swallowed a cup of coffee, which she had poured out for me. It was flavoured with arsenic—a habit my uncle had taught me. This exciting draught aroused me and refreshed each sense with a temporary excess of life. Then I continued slowly,—

'You may as well know the truth. I have watched him carefully. My brother is jealous of me.'

There followed a short interval of silence, while the livid rays of sunlight flickered across the black hangings. In that weird light the old woman's face was unspeakably ghastly. She was agitated, though I could not then understand why. Several times she essayed to speak, but the effort was beyond her. At length I caught the meaning of faintly spoken words.

'Have you spoken to him? Have words passed between you?'

'What!' I cried strongly. 'Words of anger between my brother and myself? That is impossible.'

'You have always been so affectionate, you two,' she murmured. 'Is it all going to end now?'

At such foolishness on her part I positively laughed. 'You know, as well as I, that nothing can come between us. Nothing—but death.'

'You say he is jealous!'

Again I laughed. 'He fears—and naturally—that I may become so engrossed with her as to neglect him. The thought wounds him.'

She had half turned from me, while now I noticed that her bosom was rising and falling in a manner suggestive of excitement.

'What is the matter?' I called, as she seemed anxious to move away. Then my suspicious nature again awoke. 'There is something you are keeping from me,' I cried. 'What is it?'

She looked at me, and I beheld a new expression in her eyes. There was, lurking there, beyond all question, the shivering glance of pity.

I was touched by the love she had for both of us. 'You need not fear,' I said. 'What is mine shall still be his, even when I am married.'

She gasped and placed a hand at her bosom. 'When you are married!' she said in strange fashion.

Her foolish manner angered me. 'Are you jealous also, because there will be a mistress in the house?'

But she only moved away from me, and made to the door with feeble motions.

'God help us,' I heard her muttering. 'God save us. There will be great trouble.'

'You are foolish, nurse,' I cried. 'You seem to fear that your position in my house is not assured.'

She merely stood upon the threshold, her white head shaking drearily. For a time she paused, with the white light of the passage behind her, and the blue rays crossing between us. She made as though she would speak, but no sounds came from her lips. Then the door closed with a sudden hollow resonance, and she was gone.

This conversation gave me much to think upon, so I remained in my loneliness and mused for long. That my brother should be jealous of my newfound love was conceivable, that the old nurse should be so was preposterous. In such a case one naturally searches for the motive, but here one was lacking. When reflection brought no satisfaction, I made my way to the garden, where I settled myself upon the shaded root of a tree that bent up, moss-covered, in a grotesque shape from the fresh green turf. Here, with a favourite work on some abstruse science, I whiled away the hours.

I will now briefly mention the particular shadow of fear which had been destined to fall across my life, a shadow which came in the afflicting form of a weakness, strange, yet not unique.

Since the earliest days of infancy, I had suffered from a peculiar horror of those insects which crawl upon many legs. The sight of so frightful a creature as a centipede would drive a cold shiver through my bones. Its bodily contact with my skin would certainly have frightened me into fever. But the acme of all horrors lay in that most hideous of all created things, the spider. It is no idle exaggeration to state, that I would have rather faced a tiger, although armed with no better weapon than my mere hands, than to allow the huge black spider, that *Ultima Thule* of my fear, to trail its noisome body upon any portion of my unprotected flesh.

The old nurse—my parents having died in my extreme childhood—was accustomed to laugh at this weakness, and often declared that it would pass away when I came to manhood, but she was wrong. As maturity approached, the sentiment grew, if possible, stronger. There was a single dream which alone had the power of destroying my nightly rest. The structure of this visionary fabric was composed somewhat as follows:—

After a long period of total darkness and wanderings throughout an unknown land, I was ushered by some irresistible might into a lonely cave. Here I was abandoned, while the black clouds gradually lifted, and left me encircled by a harsh, dim light, raw and biting, like the fog air of an early November morning. As this increased in strength, I perceived that all the rocky crags were thickly veiled with inky festoons of cobweb, which drooped and waved along the sides, and which depended in lace-like masses from the invisible roof almost to my head.

Each terrifying moment I expected some portion of this sticky web to fall. Goaded into action by a natural sense of fear, I turned to escape from this purgatory of insects. Then it was that I made the most terrible discovery. Another web, with strands like tarred rope, spread between me and the only means of exit. Nor was this all. Gloating in the centre appeared a malignant spider, with body as black as coal and eyes of hot fire, motionless and unspeakable.

Suddenly, from a black mass at the side, writhed an enormous creature, more fearful a monster than has ever been conceived by the fierce madness of the drunkard's mind, and, as this worked its course upward, the cave became alive, seething, with fiendish creatures, less in size, but as repulsive in shape. They came wriggling out of every mesh, fighting from each corner, a black, writhing mass of loathsomeness. Finally, as though with preconcerted movement, they advanced upon me, with feet curling, jaws moving, and eyes burning.

I could not move. There was no passing that grim gaoler behind, but I shrieked aloud in madness of fright until the cave trembled. I shrieked forth wild prayers for release, incoherent supplications which faded away into the vapourings of the madman.

Gradually the monster crept up, swinging in awful fashion from net to net, sure of his human prey. He reached the roof, swung himself along with deliberate movements, until he was above my head, then hesitated for seconds which might have been years, hovering upon a long, single strand, while I laughed aloud in my dreadful insanity. Then he fell, dropping upon my upturned face. My entire body shrivelled up with the anguish. The life burnt out at the indescribable touch. I sank, a blasted corpse, to the ground.

Such was my vision, laughable, perhaps, to those who may listen to a description portrayed in the cold imagery of words, yet to me so terrible as to make sleep, and the night accompanying, things of the deepest dread to my mind.

I glanced idly at the open book upon my knee. It was a lengthy work upon the mystery of death. I read aloud the following lines:—

'It were idle to imagine that the act of dissolution concludes physical suffering. Matter, being in its essence indestructible, is consequently subject to pain as much after the severance from soul as before. So the body cremated endures all the anguish of a torturing death by burning. The body interred within the dark recess of some earth tomb is compelled to undergo the fearful pangs of a gradual stifling, followed by a still tardier process of decomposition. For proof of this, let us take the man who has undergone amputation of a limb. Often he is afflicted with violent pains in the foot, or the hand, of the limb he has lost. This suffering is assuredly very real, yet it cannot arise directly from the body, which is living. Undoubtedly it does exist in the limb which is dying. The sense of pain vibrates from the severed member, back through an indefinite distance to the body, which had originally given it nurture.

'Life is made up of suffering; must we not suppose, being creatures of affliction, that beyond the dark barrier of death lie other woes, not only spiritual but physical?'

The page closed, but I had not then an inclination to continue the dismal analysis. I allowed the musty volume to slip from my hand; then I lay back against the rough tree trunk and dreamily watched small clouds chasing each other over a sky of soft blue, that resembled nothing so strongly as a mystical, but unapproachable sea of rest and imagination.

For one hour of that joyous calm now. For a few moments of that peace of mind, that undisturbed brain! What would I not give to be able again to breathe the fragrant air of the past? What are riches—what is health—what is life, when there is blood on everything I see and touch?

CHAPTER VI

DISCOVERY

Heaven has no rage like love to hatred turned.—CONGREVE.

Thursday, 1st May.

I STEPPED out into the avenue of lilacs, where odorous white blossoms fell like snow-flakes; for I desired to drink in the soft draught of the breeze, that was freshened with brine from the sea. I was strangely happy. My step was free and joyous; a song fell from my lips; even my morbid tastes had for the time deserted me. The blood coursed hotly through my veins; the rich stain of health ebbed along my features.

There appeared now no rift along the clear sky of my future prospect. She, whom I loved, was mine. I was sure of my prize; one last parting word had flushed me with the triumph of the victor. That afternoon all was to be definitely arranged between us. I should meet her—be with her alone in that glorious solitude which lovers sigh for. At length I should feel the bliss of hearing my question answered.

I walked lightly through the gardens, and came through the small gate out upon the breezy cliff path. Here the fresh spray beat against my brow, and healthy brine invigorated each sense. I went along the grass walk, shouting to the circling sea gulls in my joy, crying to the waves that rolled and broke beneath. On either side small whins glared in vesture of green and gold, while heather swept my exultant feet. Finally, into the pine wood beyond, where the air was dark tinted and loaded with resinous fragrance. The inclination of the man in love tends towards isolation. He desires to be alone, that he may muse the better, that he may relieve the flowing ecstasy of his mind by such slight fancies as carving the initials of his adored in rude characters upon some tree trunk, or scratching some trivial message in the sand at his feet.

Presently I returned, having met with none on my lonely walk, which was yet crowded with happy forecasts. I found that my brother was awaiting me, and we sat together at luncheon, while at the further end of the table our uncle chatted busily over his knife and fork.

My brother appeared uneasy and somewhat abstracted. During the whole of that meal he gave me an impression that he was thinking of some absent person.

'Where have you been?' he asked me at length, yet without raising his eyes.

'I went for a walk along the cliff,' I answered. 'It was a glorious morning. I did not see you, or we might have gone together.'

My uncle glanced up cunningly, with his accustomed chuckle. 'Ah, ah, I know. You are always along in the pine wood, one or other of you. I see many things in my walks.'

This old man was the skeleton at our feast. He scarcely ever sat in complete silence, and usually managed to absorb most of the conversation which flowed around him.

'So you did not venture into the wood, uncle?'

A weird light crept into his feeble eyes. 'I dared not, nephew. There were dreadful creatures at every step. Perhaps they will have gone, when I return this afternoon. I must go and look for the doctor's body. They will have killed him, and he will be lying cold along the pines.'

My brother grew yet more uneasy. He turned upon me almost sharply. 'Your time is filled up this afternoon?'

My good humour flowed high. 'Yes,' I said, smiling upon him.

'Then I must go for a ride by myself. I had hoped you would accompany me.'

I turned upon him a look that was charged with affection. 'I am sorry. I would gladly have ridden with you. But there are some duties which are pleasures, you know.'

He joined in my laughter, yet half-heartedly, while I noticed the dark shadow which crept suddenly across his eyes.

My joy was crossed momentarily with sorrow. While I was selfishly happy, the brother, who loved me, was miserable with the thought of approaching loneliness. I should have to devise some plan, which might convince him that, in spite of an ulterior attraction, he was still uppermost in my affections. That evening, when I should return with joyful intelligence upon my lips, I must speak to him plainly; I must show him that his jealousy was ill-founded and unnecessary.

On this subject I was reflecting later that same afternoon, when I reached the edge of the pine wood, and gratefully came within the influence of the balmy shade. Here there was a rustic seat, erected by my instruction for the convenience of myself and others. I laughed at the pleasing fancy thus suggested, then seated myself. I glanced at the time; I was ten minutes early.

It was indeed an afternoon which the poet might have depicted for the ideal scene of love. Though I was waiting under expectancy, the minutes passed quickly, for there was much to look at, and much to admire. The scented blossoms clustering upon the bushes; the insect-filled rays of tinted light, which streamed down through the tree tops; the busy birds bustling to their nests; the squirrels leaping airily from bough to bough; the marvellous shading of the predominant hue, from darkest to extremely light tint of green. Yes, there was much to enjoy in that last hour of my life's happiness.

Suddenly a cold blast of wind shuddered between the tree trunks—the sea lay immediately behind. I shivered slightly, and glanced at my watch. It was five minutes past the appointed time. Then I smiled to myself when I saw how I was being punished. On a former occasion I had kept her waiting a similar time. Now she was enjoying her revenge.

Still, the air was not so warm as it had been. I determined to go along a short distance and meet her on the path.

So I came out again to the road. There was nobody in sight between the wood and a sharp bend, about fifty yards ahead. What matter? I would walk slowly in that direction, when we might meet at any moment. Then there would be a pretended start, a cry of glad surprise, and then—and then—a loving welcome.

I stood at the bend, and gazed down the green vista of the road. The bushes at my side shivered and whispered drearily. The loud and persistent hum of the bees along the air irritated me. Strange that I should have thought it was so warm a day. It was certainly becoming quite chilly.

There was nobody in sight, and the road was straight for a long distance. There was no other way by which she could come. A couple of crows flapped their sombre wings and croaked, then disappeared with heavy flight in the direction of the moor. I had my watch lying in the palm of my hand. A quarter of an hour of my new existence had passed.

I returned to the seat, then paced again to the bend, and afterwards back to the solemn seat again. Half an hour had passed away, and still I had no companion. My brain sickened, as that vague fear swept once more over my body, not as a mere passing wave, but as an overwhelming tide of perpetual suffering. I ran—sped as my brother had once done along the same course—back to the iron gates, while three fearful questions formed themselves into gruesome shapes, to hover along the red atmosphere, which leapt before and around me.

'What is the actual meaning in your brother's change? What truth lies beneath your uncle's words? Why does your old nurse look at you with pity?'

I tried to persuade myself that such fears were groundless. She was unwell, or had perhaps been detained against her wish. I should receive that same day an explanation. There were numerous causes to hinder her from keeping an appointment.

Find your brother!

This was a cry which refused to be stifled into silence. Why should I find him? How could he assist me? Besides, he was then probably miles distant across the moor.

Still, when I reached the grounds, my steps turned towards the stables. The discovery I made there was surely unimportant. It was merely this—the horse my brother rode invariably had not been used that day.

Out again to the garden. Then I came upon my old nurse, with a suddenness that startled us both. She was gathering early roses, but dropped the basket when she saw me.

'Where is my brother?' I said.

She uttered a faint scream and clapped her hands to her face. I repeated the question furiously, and she answered me at length,—

'I don't know. I have not seen him this afternoon.'

I loved this old woman, who had been almost a mother to me, but so great was my fury I could then have killed her.

As suddenly I left, then sped across the lawns, until the shadow of the lilac avenue closed above my head. And here, cramped upon the rustic seat, with an empty bottle clutched in his skinny hand, I discovered my uncle. The gate leading out to the cliff stood open beyond. Evidently he had passed through there but recently.

The rapid beat of my feet aroused him. He shouted forth wildly, then staggered up and lurched to me across the path. 'Ha! ha! Come on with me, nephew. Come with me.'

I saw that his wrecked brain was again over-mastered by liquor. I pushed aside his weak old hands, and would have made for the gate—though I had no definite plan—but he turned back and hung to me.

'Stay with me,' he screamed. Then his manner became suddenly cunning. He drew his body nearer and raised his face to mine. 'Come back to the house, nephew. Give me the keys of the cellar. You can trust me—your poor old uncle. We can lock ourselves quietly in the blue room, and I will show you how to make fine mixtures. Eh? Eh?'

'Let me go, uncle,' I cried. 'I must go. I am looking for my brother.'

'I have seen him. I know where he is. Come with me, and I will tell you presently.'

I ceased my struggles to escape, while the heat of my fury cooled. 'Where is he, uncle?'

'You must stay with me,' he howled, beating at imaginary foes with the empty bottle. 'I have been running away from them for this last hour, but they follow me. There were two great ones, squatting under the lilacs, as you came up. They were watching me, but when they saw you they were frightened and ran away.'

'What? Where is my brother?'

'They had men's faces, but great jaws. They had no arms, but claws like spiders. Look! there is one crawling from that bush now!'

I shuddered frightfully and looked, but saw only the crooked shadow cast by the tree branches. 'Where have you seen my brother? Tell me, and I will come back to you soon.'

He chuckled again. 'Then you will let me have the keys? You will let me go down to the cellar?'

'You shall do as you wish. But tell me.'

'Come away first. I don't like that great toad near your feet. He is opening his mouth at me.'

I led him away from a moss-coated flint, and again pressed him to speak.

'I have been in the pine wood. I was searching for the doctor's dead body.'

'What did you see?'

I felt his shrunken form quiver. 'There were dreadful creatures—'

'I don't want to hear of them. Tell me who you saw.'

He bit his shaking fingers. 'There were men and women. Young people in the foolery of love. I saw two sitting under a tree, and they had their arms wound like snakes round each other's necks. I stood before them and laughed, and told them they would have to die some day.'

'Who—who were they?' I gasped at him.

'Ha! ha! They didn't heed an old man's warning. One of them said I was mad. The other spoke to me and said, 'Go away, uncle. Leave us, uncle.'

The sunbeams became hot tongues of fire that smote me across the eyes.

'My God!' I shrieked, interrupting his ravings. 'When was this? Who was he with?'

'Ha! ha!' he shouted more wildly than ever. 'Come along, nephew. You are mad now. So am I. We will go along together, you and I. Ha! ha! Mad, both of us. Ho! ho!'

I cast him back. He tottered, his feeble hands scratching the air, then stumbled and fell upon the gravel path. He shouted out, and, for the first time, I heard him curse me loudly.

I rushed forward blindly, through the gate, out from the garden, along the winding path by the edge of the cliff, where I had walked so peacefully that very morning. I had no fixed plan of action; I had not even any definite suspicion; I felt only that a fatal blow was about to fall.

I came within the shadow of the wood, and here I paused,

amazed at the aimless speed with which I had hurried. Sweat streamed from my face; the clothes adhered to my body; I could feel the furious pulsations of my heart.

I could not be calm. I plunged into the wood, my erratic tread pressing softly upon the brown pine needles.

I cannot fairly judge how long I had been among the pines when I heard the pressure of footsteps, followed by a soft laugh. In my then mood I thought little of it, though I withdrew a few steps from the narrow pathway to convenience their passing. A couple of lovers enjoying the early days of their love. I entered a waving patch of lofty bracken, behind the slender columns of the trees. Impelled by a certain curiosity, I glanced back once over my shoulder. One hurried glance only, yet a flash of lightning hissed before my eyes, and I staggered forward like a drunken man.

For I had found my brother.

Yes, it was, it could be none other. She was with him, and he was bending over her; he was walking close to her side; he was dropping soft words into her ear. O God! They were pressing body against body! That look upon her face! The smile on his! Above all, that wonderful light in his eyes.

I became calm again, dreadfully calm. Some men would have cried out; others might have leapt forward with thoughts of violence. But I was cool.

So engrossed were they in the delights of each other's presence that I was not regarded. It was already growing dusk. There was a whitethorn bush near. This I placed between myself and them, and crouched upon the peaty soil, with the sullen murmur of the sea in my ears.

In spite of my coolness, my fingers were digging madly into the dry soil. I had mistaken the position entirely. She had been prevented from coming to meet me, but later had ventured out. She had met my brother on the way, and he had informed her that I was away from the house—he had good reason to suppose so. As darkness was rapidly approaching, he had insisted upon escorting her home. True, he spoke to her in the soft tone of affection, but that was right. Was she not loved by the brother, who was as a part of himself?

Presently they stepped forward from the rising gloom, and

stood within my vision on the opposite side of the white-robed bush. Then I saw everything plainly; beheld, as though the search-light of Heaven's discerning eye beat upon these two. And I heard.

He held her to him closely, with an arm wound round her waist; one of her hands rested upon his shoulder; her eyes looked full up to his; his tongue spoke honeyed words. And, I tell you, I heard.

'You should have gone this afternoon, my darling.'

'I couldn't.'

'If only for a few minutes.'

'I could have never got away.'

'Poor fellow. He likes you, and has been kind to you. What a pity it is. If I could only find courage to let him know the truth!'

They passed on slowly, while the hideous echo of their words died away.

I lay in the growing darkness, gnawing my tongue, and writh-ing like a wounded snake. Yet I would not disclose myself, not then. I would wait patiently; the time must inevitably arrive—the hour of my vengeance; the triumph, not now of love, but of hate.

Again I looked after the indistinct forms, as the moon shiv-ered upward from the sea. Then I could almost have wept in my hopeless misery. He was my brother, and he was in my place. His hands, his tongue, his eyes, were performing my offices; his heart was doing the work of mine. Is it that my passion has inflamed his brain? I thought wildly. Can my heated words have aroused his heart to seek for love? We have ever had the same wishes and inclinations. Has he been compelled, against his wish, to adore her whom also I love?

But when I thought on the deceit, the lying affection, the black treachery, I grovelled upon the soil, a prey to the fury consuming heart and brain.

In one swift moment the end came. I hated my brother as fiercely and intensely as I had formerly loved him.

CHAPTER VII

MADNESS?

To be wroth with one we love,
Doth work like madness in the brain.—COLERIDGE.

Friday, 2nd May.

I HAD no plan; I made no resolve. Only, as I dragged my stiffened body from the damp ground and staggered drunkenly along the homeward path, I could see before me the smiling face of the man I had formerly loved, while my ears ached with that soft music he had listened to in my stead.

I passed through the gateway in the yew hedge, and began with weary steps to ascend towards the house—my house, as I then realised with a flush of bitter triumph—with its sleeping inmates, one of whom was a traitor. The early summer night was still and beautiful. A pitying moon formed a white circle in the sky, casting a sheen upon maturing flowers; dead twigs rattled from the trees overhead as I passed beneath; red leaves, curled and dry, relics of winter, brushed drearily along the paths; an owl hooted mockingly into my ears. There were scented blossoms around me; bunches of green foliage, with glistening dewdrops upon the leaves; yet for such things I had no eyes. I could look with satisfaction only upon the unlovely, the dead; for that which was beautiful reminded me of the dream which had departed, and the hope which had decayed. How easily may the man be converted into a brute!

I sought my room. When I slept finally, goaded into unconsciousness by the use of morphia, my terrible dream recurred with a force and vividness it had never possessed before. I awoke, shuddering in a bath of perspiration, when the sun was streaming in through the window curtains. My brain was fevered, but I could readily recall the past, for every incident was limned upon my brain. My fear was great, because the dream had presented itself in a fresh guise.

As the awful spider, evil genius, life-fear personified, whatever you may call it, crept up the side of the cave, the light grew stronger, until it seemed to me that the monster bore the features of one I knew well. The eyes were those of a human being, the grim smile I could recognise. As it crawled up stealthily overhead, I understood that I was looking upon my brother, transformed into this vile creature, whose mission it was to destroy me. Suddenly a new strength and resolution swept over me. As it fell, I sprang aside, among the unknown horrors of the cave, while the creature, disappointed of its prey, lay upon the ground at my side. I leapt upon it in a fury unspeakable; I trampled it madly under foot, until its vitals gushed out upon me; I tore it to fragments with my hands, and at length could realise that my enemy lay dead. But my triumph was short-lived. For, as I fell back, the grim gaoler by the door seized me in his awful claws and sucked away my life.

All the way down the wide stairway I laughed to myself in bitter mockery. Only the day before, I possessed everything—so I thought. Now there was nothing I might call my own; nothing, except an empty reality of riches, the heavy monotony of wealth.

I paused, for I could distinguish voices in the hall. It was my uncle conversing with the man who was now my greatest enemy in the world. I was unable to see them, but I could hear portions of what they said.

'I cannot come with you, uncle. I have an appointment. My brother will accompany you when he comes down.'

'Ha! ha! I was forgetting him. He is my companion now, nephew. Yesterday evening he went mad. We were together in the garden when it happened.'

'Uncle! What are you talking about?'

'We shall always be together now. We are mad, both of us. That is what people will say.'

'What happened yesterday evening?' His voice changed, as though he were afraid.

'You would like to know, eh? Eh? We don't tell everything. He went mad when he saw the big toads. I haven't seen him since.'

My brother's satisfied laughter uprose, and I knew that he was reassured.

'That is all, is it? Well, I must go, uncle.'

'Yes, you are a young man. It is a fine morning, and you will go on your walks. Perhaps you will meet someone. Ha! ha! I know you young men.'

'Be quiet, you old fool.' The words were muttered sharply, but I caught them as I dug the nails into my palm.

'Ha! ha! Old fools are wiser than young fools. They see more, nephew. Perhaps you will go mad, too. Then you will have more sense. Ho! ho!'

The reply was inaudible, but I knew by the following silence that my uncle was alone again.

Biting my nails in a cold nervousness, I made my way back to the room I had recently quitted. That clear voice, the burst of hearty laughter, had again aroused my fury. It was, as my uncle had said, a glorious morning. The sun would be flashing down, with a thousand silver smiles, upon the wrinkled sea; the sands would be glowing with heat and teeming with ever-moving insect life; the grass would be dry and fresh; a warm and fragrant odour would emanate from the pines; all nature would be rejoicing. And he—where would he be?

I stood there in my loneliness, a solitary being in the world, a floating atom along some mystic ray of a mighty universe, a mere man. Yet a single man had, before that day, upturned the world with the force of a great will, had broken into the minds of all by some great deed of daring or vengeance. Might not I be such a man?

There was a timid knock upon the door. I realised the almost forgotten fact that there was such a thing as time, and shouted a reply. My old nurse came slowly into the room with that nourishment the body is supposed to require.

'Good morning,' I shouted to her. 'It is a fine morning, is it not?'

She seemed encouraged by my cheerfulness. 'Well, it is about afternoon. You must have slept a long time, and I thought you would be wanting something to eat.'

I walked up and down the room, with long easy tread. 'I heard voices below just now. Was it my uncle?'

'The old gentleman has just gone out. If you look from the window, I expect you will see him upon the terrace. He seems better this morning.'

'And my brother? I thought I heard him, too.'

She evaded my glance. 'He is out. He asked me when you were coming down, and, as I couldn't tell him, he has gone round to the stables. He is going for a ride.'

I knew she was lying to me. This honest old creature was unable to prevaricate.

I laughed with such apparent mirth, that she was set at ease. 'Why, nurse,' I called, 'do you think you know more about my brother than I do? He would not keep anything from me. I know everything. He has told me himself.'

Then her face broke up at once. It was a simple matter to deceive her.

'You know everything? As much—as much—as I do?'

'More—what do you know? We understand one another well. There has been a secret between us, but it is cleared away now.'

'Ah! I am glad; I'm so glad,' she said impulsively. 'It was a great sorrow to think that you and the young master were set one against the other. And it is all over now, you say?'

'We settled everything last night. I suffered a little, you understand, but then I love him. There is no man like my brother. Now you know why I have kept in my room this morning.'

She came towards me with outstretched hands. 'Ah! That is noble, it is very noble of you. What a good brother you are to him, to be sure! But I never thought you could give up so much as that.'

'Yes,' I muttered. 'It is a great sacrifice. Not every brother would be worth it.'

The old woman was happy again. I had set her doubting mind at ease, and in doing so had averted suspicion from myself. I was growing cunning. My brother was teaching me.

'Now you know everything, nurse. But you must speak to nobody.'

'No, no. But I'm so very glad you've told me. I saw so much that was different, and I was afraid—very much afraid.'

'What have you seen?' I asked sharply. This old woman might be serviceable to me.

'Why! I told you before that the young master had changed, didn't I? I have slept little lately, what with thinking of him and you. Then you are a hard sleeper; you did not hear what I heard during the nights.'

'What? What?' I called at her quickly.

'Sounds of footsteps along the passages, when everyone else should have been asleep. They generally came in the early morning.'

'What was he doing?'

'Ah, you know! But it surprised me when I looked out the first time, and saw the young master. His face was so full of sorrow that I could have cried for him. Then I thought there would be trouble in this house.'

A raging pain was throbbing across my forehead. 'There was no cause for fear,' I muttered.

'But he was walking again this morning. It was just past three o'clock. I looked out and saw him.'

'If he wishes to take exercise at that time, why should you interfere?' I said testily.

'He could not sleep because of some sorrow. But you say everything has been explained. What trouble can he have now?'

'None,' I said. 'He has none.'

'Then his manner of moving about the house of late. His step was nervous, and he would start at any sound. I have seen him looking at you when you didn't know. It seemed to me as though he wanted to speak, yet didn't dare open his lips. I'm an old woman, I know, but my eyes are still good.'

I burst into a loud shout of laughter. She started back, affrighted, when the mocking sound rang upon her ears.

'Can you not see? He has something weighing heavily upon his conscience.' And I laughed again.

'There can't be anything now,' she said.

'We cannot read the heart,' I replied. 'For all you know, I might have trouble hanging over me now.'

See how my brother had taught me cunning!

It was her turn to laugh. Then she said, doubtless with the idea of diverting my thoughts, 'But doesn't he look well? I've never seen him so good-looking as at present.'

Her words of misplaced affection stung me grievously. In my foolish self-pride I had never given thought to a serious comparison of personal appearance, an attribute which must of necessity go far in winning the affections of women. 'We are alike,' I muttered angrily.

'No, no,' she said reprovingly, with the privilege of her position. 'Only a woman can judge there. The young master was always the beauty, even from the cradle. You are never without that ugly frown upon your face, a bad habit I could never cure in you of a child. You have the money and the property. You can't grudge the young master his good looks.'

I made her leave me, for I could listen no longer. Ignorantly she had stirred up so much pain and anger within me, that, had she remained, I might have disclosed my secret. I was alone again, and the knowledge that the mask might be dropped for the time afforded me relief.

I crossed to a side-table, where a mirror flashed in the sunlight. I gazed into its liquid depths, and finally cast it upon the floor with a groan. The truth was there; the most prejudiced could not call me passably good-looking. My appearance was even forbidding, nor had I any charm of manner to compensate for lack of face beauty. Just then, certain evil longings, coupled with the wild light playing across my eyes, rendered me even repulsive. My false brother had all in his favour, everything, except that single possession of wealth, which can procure a man all, save the one thing which alone will make life worth endurance. His poverty had bought that prize which my riches could not even bid for; he had made the purchase by a foul, underhand stroke, by the miserable process of deceit. He had placed his affectionate smile between me and his treacherous heart.

Up and down the room I paced like a caged beast, my fury melting into a profound grief, then changing again to a wild despair.

I made my way downstairs. Everything was silent, and strangely motionless. The sunbeams lapped across the carpet, and played like falling water upon the white walls. Merciful God! How frightfully I felt that loneliness.

Almost the first object that met my gaze was a small frame, which contained two tinted photographs, one representing myself, the other him who had until recently been my brother. I sprang towards it and tore it from the nail. Scarce knowing what I did, I broke the frame up in my hands, cast it into the fireplace, and set a lighted match to the whole.

The wood crackled, the faces twisted up in the heat and shrivelled away, curling into fantastic black shapes, which I dispersed up the chimney with my foot. Nor, until my sudden anger cooled, did I realise what I had done. I had burnt my own portraiture with his; in figuratively destroying him, I had inflicted a like injury upon myself.

I turned suddenly, to find my uncle standing in the centre of the room. He had entered in that noiseless fashion, which with him betokened the highest rational state he was capable of attaining.

At first he said not a word, but came forward to poke at the glowing embers with the stick he always carried. Then he looked at me sharply with his small eyes.

'A fire, nephew! On such a day as this!'

'I was burning some papers,' I said; and then, with a new desire to assert my power in that place, 'I can do what I like here.'

He lowered himself with stiff motions into a chair. 'I have been looking for you. There is something I want to tell you.'

'What?' I asked.

'I forget now. Sit down—there, opposite me. I shall remember soon.'

He leaned his white head upon a shaking hand, while for a time there was silence. Certainly he was in an unusually sober frame of mind.

'Ah—ah, I have it now. Yes, it was last evening. I saw it in here then.'

'What?' I called. He was probably about to disclose to me one of his fantastic dreams.

'I came in from the garden, and sat down beside the open window. The sun had disappeared, and it was beginning to grow dark, when—'

'Yes, what?' I cried fearfully, well remembering the nature of my occupation at that particular time.

'A spider ran down the wall and across the floor.'

'You killed it?' I shouted, the words wrung from me by an excess of fear.

'It was a stranger to me,' he said madly. 'It was not one of my subjects, and unlike any of them. When it got half-way across the floor, it stopped and turned round to glare at me. Ah, its eyes!'

'You let it escape?' I gasped.

'I had no choice. Nephew, I was afraid of this creature.'

'Such a being is a creation of the devil's. It is a thing made to be killed.'

The old man drew his body forward in the chair. 'It was an evil spirit,' he muttered in a grating voice. 'There was a time—I was a different man then—when I studied such things. If the evil nature of a man could be released from his body, and given a separate existence, it would bear some shape which is naturally horrible to the eyes. There is no madness in that idea, nephew.'

'It may still be here. It may be hiding away in some dark corner.' I shuddered. 'It may creep forth any moment and drive me into insanity. I might fall asleep, and—' I could not finish.

My uncle rose and shuffled away. 'I have told you, nephew. You must grow accustomed to such things. I see many dreadful objects, both by day and night. I am not afraid of many; but this one—'

His voice died away into a murmur, which faded beneath the hollow echo of his receding footsteps.

Yet—had he only killed that creature! Might not its destruction have brought about my peace of mind? But now the evil was to return to its own home, there to work the slow immolation of the body.

For minutes, which stretched themselves out like hours, I trembled at every shadow cast by the warm sunlight through the rose leaves outside, starting and shuddering at each slight movement caused by the soft wind as it played into the room.

But there was no rest for my burning mind. At length my eyes fell upon a large, black-bound volume in a corner shelf, and I rose to fetch it. I glanced at the title and seemed to dimly recognise it. I opened it at the beginning, then realised that I was holding in my nerveless hands the accepted text-book of man's salvation.

Salvation! Eternity! Who can torture the brain with such abstruse theories, while delirious with the fever of life?

My eyes were devouring certain lines—the book was new to me. I read, and I read aloud, at the first chapter of time; but, as

I did so, all the muscles tightened and strained along my body. I discovered that my story, and all my suffering, were as old as the world itself.

'If thou doest well, shalt thou not be accepted? and if thou doest not well, sin lieth at the door. And unto thee shall be his desire, and thou shalt rule over him.

'And Cain talked with Abel his brother; and it came to pass, when they were in the field, that Cain rose up against Abel his brother, and slew him.

'And the Lord said unto Cain, Where is Abel thy brother? And he said, I know not; Am I my brother's keeper?

'And He said, What hast thou done? The voice of thy brother's blood crieth unto Me from the ground.

'And now art thou cursed from the earth, which hath opened her mouth to receive thy brother's blood from thy hand;

'When thou tillest the ground, it shall not henceforth yield unto thee her strength; a fugitive and a vagabond shalt thou be in the earth.

'And Cain said unto the Lord, My punishment is greater than I can bear.

'Behold, Thou hast driven me out this day from the face of the earth; and from Thy face shall I be hid; and I shall be a fugitive and a vagabond in the earth; and it shall come to pass, that everyone that findeth me shall slay me.'

The words became blotted out by a red mist, which floated between my eyesight and the page. I only know that I shouted aloud; that I cast the great book upon the floor, and stamped upon it with loud oaths of fury; that I finally fell across it, choking in the throat, foaming at the mouth.

The awful, fateful repetition of history! The first man, born of woman, was a fratricide!

## CHAPTER VIII

### DECEIT

For it is not an open enemy, that hath done me this dishonour;
for then I could have borne it.

PSALM lv. 12.

Monday, 12th May.

I COULD not fail to profit by the sharp lessons which my brother had
unwillingly taught me, so now I was his equal, even his superior, in
the art of intrigue. For I watched him at all times; I became persistent as his shadow; whenever he turned he found me, ready with a
light phrase or careless jest, perhaps even a word of affection. For
what did it matter? I hated him, but it was my duty to speak, and
my wish to deceive. When there is no feeling at the heart, what is
the difference between the expression of love and hate?

During the long days of opening summer, I was never silent,
though always lonely. Nor did I allow a single event of note to roll
over my head unmarked. I was watchful as the tiger, garrulous as
a parrot. This latter comparison I use advisedly, for I thought little
of my choice of expressions. His black deed of treachery was the
skeleton always present before my vision. Yet this was a dismal
object only to be looked at and pondered over in seclusion.

My brother became manifestly impressed by the friendliness
of my actions. My loud, almost furious, conversation at the din-
ner-table, my uproarious shouts of hoarse laughter, when we sat
together at night, not only puzzled, but actually alarmed, him. He
could not fail to perceive that my humour was unnatural; my jests
were founded upon slow deaths by torture, upon deeds of dark
murder, and silent acts of horror. There were times when I would
hold up the great destroyer himself as a fit subject for my mirth,
and treat the end of all things as a pandemonium of delights.
While he sat speechless, shivering, sometimes faintly smiling from
sheer nervousness, sometimes shrinking away, but almost always

silent, because he feared to trust the power of speech, and dared not to reprove me.

None could have failed to note an alteration in my appearance and manner. The servants put their heads together in low whispers whenever I passed. My old nurse brought me daily her carefully prepared compounds, thinking, foolish woman, that my body needed strength. Physical force! I was full of it; I overflowed with energy. But to what end was this strength, which would enable me to bear the struggle against mind for many weary years? I cursed it, and envied the weak, the sick, all who were slowly tottering from life to death, down the rugged path of pain towards the sluggish solitude of the grave.

There was one shrill cry, which rang at all times into my ears, like the sharp blast of a storm wind. In the whispering of the wind through the long grass, in the plaintive melody of the birds, in the ticking of the clocks—reminding the happy of the shortness of time, and the miserable of its eternity—came the continual message: 'It is the doing of your brother, the man whom you have loved too well.'

Cold rain was falling heavily from a leaden sky, but I rejoiced to see it. The dreary mood of Nature agreed with my own misery. I had for hours sat in the quiet of the library, half hidden within a large oak chair. As usual I had discovered something among my books to interest me, some story of human suffering and passion, which I might aptly apply to my own condition.

I had taken a book by chance from some dusty shelf, and sat down to read, first with absent mind, then my attention became riveted, while I finally devoured with grim earnestness a tale of more than ordinary life agony.

A man of a great nature, yet sudden in his anger, had lavished his entire devotion upon a beautiful woman, receiving her plighted affection in return. One day he set forth to meet her at their cus-tomary trysting-place, but his horror, when he approached the spot, and beheld how she was occupying herself in his absence, may scarcely be conceived. For she was lying upon a grassy bank, resting with full confidence in the arms of his greatest friend, a man whom he had trusted with all the secrets of his heart. He crept closer, and soon came to realise the entire perfidy of his friend's conduct. She, whom he loved, was stretched upon the ground, her head drooping over the shoulder of the recreant, his lips pressing, too evidently in the mad passion of love, closely upon her forehead.

Can it be wondered that such a sight drove him mad? He seized the villain, unheeding his piteous cries and frantic shouts of explanation. Too surely was this an evidence of guilt, so he drew his weapon, lusting now for the blood of the man he had loved.

The other could but defend himself. The fight raged long and fiercely, for they were well matched in strength, but at length the false one sank to the ground, with blood gushing from a mortal wound.

Then the victor turned towards the faithless woman, to upbraid her for inconstancy. But, behold, he found himself addressing reproaches to a corpse.

From the dying lips of his friend he gathered the truth. How that he had walked by mere chance along that way, and had come upon the lady sleeping against the grassy bank. Disturbed by his footsteps, she moved, but, in doing so, had aroused a venomous snake, which had curled within her hair for warmth, as she slept. This creature had bitten her furiously upon the brow. She cried forth, and he perceived the reptile gliding away through the grass. There remained but one thing for the brave man, who set his friend's happiness before even his own life. He caught her in his arms, applied his lips to the wound, had commenced to suck the poison from her veins, when the other arrived with the madness of a wronged lover.

Then he fell back in death, while the wretched survivor, murderer of the two beings he loved best in the world, went into a wild frenzy of madness. Finally he ended his earthly miseries by his own hand.

The startling facts of this narrative impressed me not so much as the weird power of the description, which portrayed, with the wonderful vividness of actual vision, each succeeding stage of that terrible disease of insanity. With fearful detail, the unknown author of a long past age described the wearing away of the mind, the gradual rotting of the brain, the slow evaporation of reason and drying up of moral energy, all leading fearfully up to the final culmination, when the hand could not understand the meaning of its action, and when the heart longed only to be stilled. I read to the end, then dashed the book aside.

This man had no doubts, for he saw with his own eyes, yet he cast away his happiness and life for an imagined wrong. A friend may be relied upon at time of need, a relative never, a brother least of all. I had not only seen, but actually heard. My brother's love-speeches were still hot upon my ears. These in themselves condemned him.

My fury, which had melted into sympathy for the sufferer of fiction, burst forth anew. Despite the cold damp and the anger of the elements, I must go forth, to cool my brain, to feel the soothing touch of the pure wind. This stifling room, large though it was, bound me down with its roof and four walls, like a prison house—almost as a tomb. There was more space for my passion, more scope for my superabundant activities, beneath the lowering and spreading canopy of the sky.

Oh, my brother, my companion, my friend! Had I not loved you so greatly in the past, the hatred of the present had been less. Had I not treated you with such generosity, this wrong would be the easier to bear. If I had driven you from my home, closed my purse to your needs, then I might have looked for your animosity. But what have I done for you? We have dwelt together on a perfect equality, when all was mine. More, at times I have allowed your voice to prevail over mine, and this is your return. I would have given with open hand, resigned everything gladly, except that one thing you have stolen.

I staggered along the grass paths, hatless, my garments disarranged, my fists clenched in the air. I was drunk with my passion, nor in my present mood did I care who noticed the condition of my mind. I was the wild beast, ravening with hunger, come forth to seek my supper.

The sun was vanishing, where the west was clear from mist, and the blood-red bars of splendour shot into my eyes and blinded me. I shouted to the dead leaves, as they rained in sad showers upon my head; I ploughed my feet through them, laughing at the music they caused, like dry bones rattling in the sepulchre; I shrieked back to the mournful birds of the sea, who wheeled above, making the

air piteous with their cries; with my own groans I strove to silence
the hollow murmur of the waves, ebbing upon the rocks beneath,
and still I went on, raving at the wild nature around me, surely the
scapegoat of all human misery.

I had reached the moor. Over the dark surface I hurried in my
aimless course, my body scourged by the slanting lines of rain,
the wind hissing against my teeth. No description may convey
any idea of the sombre nature of my surroundings—the bleached
sedges, bent and lined with shivering tear-drops; the moss-grown
rocks, black and slimy with moisture; the blasted oaks, dark and
awesome in decay; the broken, furrowed ground, steaming with
grey mist. Before, lay the weird circle of the sun, sinking in a
blood-red bed to another world of misery. Here and there flashed
pools of water, flickering mirrors of scarlet hue, where dead leaves
floated, like lost souls seeking Paradise. I pressed along a miring
track, pouring forth wild words to the keeping of the elements. At
times I fell, but rose instantly to continue my wild journey, with
hands and clothes besmirched with mud. I was aiming at no goal;
no limit had been mentally appointed for my wanderings. I must
only go on—on. What mattered the question of an ending? All
eternity lay ahead—I could not, cast aside the hours as I might, I
could not drain even an infinitesimal portion from that unfathomable ocean of oncoming time.

A black shadow loomed up between my body and the sunset.
It advanced rapidly, with sharp clicking sounds, as of metal upon
stone, and presently resolved itself into definite shape. Then I saw
a man, riding hard, with back to the wind, and face lowered before
the driving clouds of misty rain.

I stood in the centre of the path, and shrieked with my entire
force. The beast snorted and half stopped. The rider raised
his head, and I noted with pleasure his fright at the manner of
interruption.

'You madman! Would you ride over one who has done you no
harm? Go back! You shall not come on. I tell you this moor is my
property.'

'What! it is you! Great heavens! but you frightened me.'

Then I recognised the doctor, returning homeward from some
visit.

'You were trying to kill me,' I cried into the wind. 'Would you be a murderer, you fool? I have heard that such men, even if they escape the law, die by their own hands. They kill themselves, doctor. The victims see to that.'

He reined in the horse to a standstill upon the oozing pathway. 'What are you doing here at this time? Has anything happened in the house?'

'Have I not a right to be here? May I not walk over my own property?'

'But in this rain?'

'The weather brought me out. It suits my mood.'

'Your face is splashed with mud—so are your clothes.'

'That is my concern; I can do as I like. I tell you I *will* do as I wish with my own.'

He regarded me with a shiver. 'I'm not preventing you. Professionally, I would advise you to return home. Your health will suffer.'

'I have the strength of a hundred men,' I shouted. 'Come down from your horse, and fight with me. You shall learn whether I am weak.'

But he only touched the horse's flank with his whip. 'I can't afford to stay shivering out here, whatever you may do.'

He would have continued the journey, but I sprang forward and held the animal back by the rein.

'Let go!' he cried angrily.

'A second. I have something to tell you.'

'I want to get home. I am chilled already.'

'Listen to my discovery first. Doctor, have you ever owned a brother?'

'Yes; some years ago.'

'He is dead then. You killed him!' I cried, pulling at his knee. 'Tell me, did you kill him?'

He shuddered again. Perhaps my voice may have sounded strangely in that solitude.

'Kill him! He was drowned at sea, poor fellow. What do you mean?'

'There is no enemy like a brother. I found a book the other day. It was called the Bible. Perhaps you have heard of it?'

He only laughed grimly, so I continued, 'What do you think I found there?'

'Well—what?'

'The first man, born into this world, was a murderer. He was something more—a fratricide. He killed his own brother, doctor.'

He shook off my excited hand, and moved away. 'Read further,' he said. 'And do your mind good by such reading, not harm.'

I scoffed at his foolish reply. 'This man Cain set a good example. We cannot do better than follow it.'

There was no reply. Only his horse's hoofs clicked away through the white mists. But I raised my voice to shout after him once again.

'There is no enemy like a brother. There is only one way of silencing the enemy. The first man, who called a woman mother, was no fool!'

My strength swept over me again. An uncontrollable impulse attacked each sense, to race and outstrip the flying horse. So I ran, sped furiously over slippery turf and jagged stones, in pursuit of that indistinct shadow which flitted away ahead. Yet I failed in the superhuman attempt; the shadow grew fainter, then the merest of outlines, then disappeared altogether.

Breathless and perspiring, I reached the rustic gate which led to the garden, then made my stealthy way up to the loneliness of my own room. There I managed to compose myself to the customary dignity of master of the house, and prepared for the ghastly formula of dinner.

By the time a summons called me to the dining-room I was calm. With my uncle I sat down, and later my brother entered, still with the smile upon his face, and the glad laughter in his eyes. He came to my side, while I dissembled after a mighty struggle, and answered him question for question. But I did not glance at his outstretched hand, because I guessed whose fingers it had lately held.

When the house was silent, and others had retired to that sleep which we are told the body requires, we sat together beneath the lamplight. But now our positions were reversed. He was the one to pace the room, talking fiercely, as though to still the sharp biting of an angry conscience. I was the one to shudder, whenever his hand lighted upon my shoulder. Earlier than usual he departed to his bed, while I had no wish to stay him.

We were unusually affectionate brothers, for, though grown men, we had never from the early days of infancy neglected a certain custom—a kiss always passed between us, when we separated for the night. After he had stated his intention of retiring, he came slowly to my side. I was seated upon a low chair, half lying, with my head resting back. He paused for a moment, while there was silence, then stooped down to press his lips upon my forehead.

I did not move; I did not speak; I made no sign.

But as his face came down, his wide-open eyes caught the snake-like glitter of mine. Again he paused, while we looked at each other with faces almost touching, and he drew back, also like the snake that is about to strike. Then he closed his eyes, and feverishly touched my forehead with cold lips.

Not a word had passed between us, and the next moment he was gone. I still lay in the same position, laughing to myself in bitter hatred.

I continued to sit there, while the night hours passed, wrapped in a sombre contemplation. I had no wish for sleep, rather I dreaded it. Besides, my brain was active and did not require rest.

I was aroused from reflection, as the lamp flame began to sink down, and the chilliness of night crept into the apartment. Then I heard footsteps descending the stairs, and remembered the words of my old nurse. Presently the door opened with a weird creaking, and my brother was with me again.

'You here!' he faltered. 'I thought you were in bed.'

I gave him no answer. I looked at him quietly, until his false eyes dropped.

'I could not sleep. I have come down for something to drink.'

I waved my hand towards a table whereon stood several different brands of liquor. 'You will find there what you wish for,' I said, then watched him, as he slunk along the wall, with averted eyes.

He poured forth some liquor, while I resumed. 'All that is mine is yours. We have shared alike, since the death of our father left me master here.'

I paused, and he saw that a reply was expected. 'You are right,' he said. 'You have always been generous to me.'

'I have withheld nothing from you,' I went on, with increasing bitterness. 'Why did I not keep all to myself, as I might have done? Why?'

He looked up at me then, and there was a dull light in his eyes.

'Because I loved you. Because I knew how well and truly you loved me.'

The glass trembled in his hand. He could not face me, he dared not look me in the eyes. I was deliberate and very calm.

'You would hold no secret from me. Still less could you think of practising deceit upon your brother. You would die rather than treat me with injustice. I know it, and I have a right to expect it. This, and more, I would have done for you.'

My cunning references to the past he did not observe. He only slunk towards the table, muttering hoarsely, 'Why are you speaking in this manner?'

'Have you ever doubted me?'

The hot flame within surged up fiercely at this hypocrisy. I rose to my feet, and, while the lamp flame ebbed and flickered within the blackened globe, I spoke furiously, while he listened in the semi-darkness, with white face and trembling limbs.

I spoke discursively upon traitors of all ages. I declared it was a subject which had grown suddenly attractive to me. I spoke of the arch traitor Judas, and gloated long over his fate. Many another, less known to fame, did I mention, and I harped especially upon the miserable end of each, until my heart warmed, when I saw him slinking against the wall, his entire appearance transformed.

My mood changed. As the light dropped lower and dimmer, I dilated upon the charms and accomplishments of her whom I loved. I told him how entire was my adoration, how sincere was her affection for me, how closely we were bound together, with many another lying tale besides. While speaking, I could gratify myself by listening to his hard breathing.

As the light darted out in a cloud of evil-smelling smoke, I explained how firmly she had bound herself to me. I went on to expatiate upon the awful consequences of the broken vow—the misery and the curse. I dwelt at length upon the fate of that man who should attempt to seduce her affections. And I pictured in glowing letters the fate which must also fall upon him.

We stood together, yet separated by the darkness. During the time that my words raved forth, I could note, with exquisite pleasure, his groans beating through the curtain of gloom.

Then I groped to the door, and we reached the light of the hall.

'But what have such things to do with us?' I cried, and my voice may have been even cheerful. 'You have no trouble which can disturb your rest.'

'There is none,' he muttered. His voice was scarcely audible.

He was about to depart, but I had not yet done with him. I placed myself at his side, and spoke. 'You have forgotten to wish me good-night.'

He turned, and, for the love I had borne him once, I could have pitied him, when I saw the agony struggling across his features. He came up to me, while I bent forward, and down—I was much the taller—to greet his salute.

Again his lips lightly touched my forehead. I shuddered. They were as the rigid pressure of ice.

## CHAPTER IX

### CHOICE

The moaning of the sea!
How it rushes! How it swells!
Upon the beach, upon the strand.
How it fills the heart with longing;
And the sad heart with a sighing,
For the sorrows of the past.
How it fills the mind with bodings,
Grim and sad,
For the future, and the morrow, and the
days that are to come.

Saturday, 31st May.

Lately I had displayed a power of histrionic talent, which had startled even myself by its completeness and its profundity. I had recommenced my visits to her, who had passed away from me; I came often to her house; I made constant and numerous appointments, nor would I be denied. All this was a portion of my plan. I would be with her as much as possible, to lessen my brother's opportunities.

That day I had set out for her home, holding a bunch of red roses in my hand. Unexpectedly I had come upon her on the way, and had joined myself to her, without asking her consent, for I felt myself entitled to the position of her escort. I gave her the fragrant blossoms, and presently asked her to explain, if she could, that subtle power of attraction which draws all men's sympathies towards the flower. Like others, she could not tell.

'What is a flower?' I asked sharply.

'A flower—well, a flower. It is a thing of brightness and beauty—'

'Scented and lovely one day; dead and shrivelled up the next—like woman's love.'

She started, while a frown crossed her delicate forehead.

'Woman's beauty is like this rose, perhaps; but woman's love is an everlasting flower.'

'That artificial bloom, which drops dark and tawdry in the garden, when all others have gone. I know it. The insects flee from it; nobody plucks it; Nature herself seems to frown upon it.'

We walked along the road in the open daylight. I was no thief, no coward, that I should allow my heart to perform its work in the darkness, or beneath the shadow of the dark pines, where the sad moaning of the sea came as a continual reproach.

'You must not look for everything in the single bloom,' she said. 'In the everlasting flower you find endurance; beauty and fragrance belong to others.'

'But the end comes so quickly. There is a bud in the early morning, a blossom at night; the next day a shower of falling leaves. This is too much like life—and death.'

'Perhaps that is why the flower is the favourite emblem.'

'Of life?'

'Of everything almost. The poets sing of it; myths are founded upon it; the painters depict it; all wear it.'

'Yes,' I said eagerly, my morbid nature asserting itself. 'Life is nothing but a wearing of flowers. The child plays with them; the bride carries a white wreath upon her brows; and it is a white wreath that is placed upon her coffin.'

'We are under the spell of Nature all our lives,' she said.

'And the flower is that Nature idealised. Is it not so?'

'I suppose it is.'

'The flower represents joy and sorrow: to the sick it brings hope; to the weary rest; to all it brings remembrance. The lover gives the myrtle to the lady of his heart, to signify his love.'

She drooped her head at this, but no richer colour visited her cheeks—her eyes were invisible. She had looked full into my brother's face. Why did she not do the same with me?

'I have gone forth in the early morning, to look at the flowers as the sun was rising,' I said. 'I have parted the closed petals with my fingers, and within I have found pure pearls of dew. It was as though trouble had come to the flower by night, and the tears were not yet dry from its cheeks.'

She looked up at me then. 'You speak like a poet,' she said, yet there was a carelessness in her manner of expression. Then she buried her small face, itself like a flower, within the mass of scented blooms she held in her gleaming fingers.

'You know I am not,' I said quickly, and there may have been tears in my eyes, for I could not see her plainly. 'I am an ordinary man. You may call me, if you wish, the everlasting flower. Scentless, lacking in beauty, ungraceful—but enduring.'

I was in a different, a softer, mood. But then I loved—I loved exceedingly, though I dared not speak.

She was confused. At length she said, 'One should not judge the heart by the face.'

Unwittingly she had played into my hands. 'Yet many do, and almost all women,' I said loudly. 'A handsome appearance will win them, while they cast thought of heart aside. You cannot judge the pearl by the shell of the oyster. Yet you would try to do so.'

'I!' she cried. Her voice was frightened, while the red roses shook in her hand.

'I spoke of your sex in general.'

'I do not think so,' she said presently. 'We women look for that which is best in a man; we seek strength of mind and nobleness of purpose.'

'And when you fail to find these things?' I interrupted, the bitterness growing upon me.

'You are disparaging your own sex,' she said, smiling faintly.

'Tell me this,' I cried. 'Does man ever appear to the woman as Man? Does he not rather stand to her in the light of a mere representative of such things as power, riches, or a position? Does she not take him for the gifts the world has allotted him, rather than for those Nature has provided?'

'There are some—shall I say many?—who would do this,' she replied.

'But you are not one?'

'No.'

I could not refrain from asking this question. Now I longed to go further, and sound her heart, but I reasoned that my brother would certainly hear of this conversation. Man has one advantage over the woman—he possesses the power to place a bridle upon his tongue.

'You do not then believe in the doctrine of "bought souls?"' I continued.

'What do you mean?' she asked.

'In the world of society, where men are puppets and women are dolls, there is a market of exchange—so at least I have heard. The dolls are placed for sale upon the market, where the puppets bid for them. The highest bidder takes the best constructed doll, and calls her a wife. And this is done under an outward title of love.'

'Which is a thing no money may procure.'

I groaned at the trite maxim, the truth of which was becoming so fearfully apparent to me. 'I have shown you that it can buy woman.'

'No,' she denied, almost fiercely. 'It cannot do that. You buy the person, not the being. You purchase a waxen effigy, which moves, speaks, and eats. But you cannot so win the heart. When you lead such a creature to your home, you admit misery.'

She was reading me a sharp lesson, for I now understood that I was dealing with that exceeding rarity—the woman with a heart. But there was more that I wished to learn.

I drew one of the drooping roses from her hand, and began to pluck forth its blood-red petals.

'Many consider riches and position principal factors of life's happiness. In this lottery of sex union a woman might find herself attracted by a man who possessed these things.'

'That would be to her advantage,' she said slowly.

'There is no reason why love should fly about penniless. It should be practical, as well as sentimental.'

'Up to a certain point—yes,' she admitted, yet with some doubt.

'Where would you set that limit?'

'If a woman, herself poor, should find herself with two suitors, one in the same condition as herself, the other rich—'

'Yes—yes,' I cried, for my eagerness could not be restrained. She was, unconsciously, citing her own case.

'If she liked both of them, and felt that she could live happily with either, she should certainly take the man with means.'

'That is what you would do yourself?'

'Yes.'

Then my heart leaped within me and, for the last time in life, I enjoyed a fleeting moment of happiness. She would marry me, provided that she felt she could live with me happily. Could there be any doubt on that matter?

'For a beautiful woman the choice of husbands must be a difficult task,' I resumed. 'There are so many ways of reading the heart, and it cannot be easy to find the correct reply.'

'But on the other hand, there is usually no doubt at all,' she said quickly.

'Except when the choice lies between two,' I ventured.

'It is the same as a multitude. For a woman, who knows her own mind, there should be no weeding out.'

'Yet you have admitted that there may be doubt.'

'Now I am speaking of myself,' she said proudly.

'As a woman whose mind is irrevocably fixed.'

'Yes.' The monosyllable fell from her lips defiantly.

She had made up her mind, and—I knew this woman now—nothing could turn her from that determination. She had either mentally chosen me and rejected my brother, or she loved him and despised me.

The question I desired to hear answered was this—What was my brother to her?

This longing gradually overmastered determination. I turned to her again, this time with the intention of learning what there was to know.

But, before speaking, my eyes fell upon the half-despoiled rose in my hand, with its few remaining petals curling sadly. As I looked, there was a strange motion, the entire bloom seemed to vibrate between my fingers, and finally what appeared like speckled hairs endowed with life, made themselves gradually visible. I gazed transfixed, but the words I was about to speak resolved themselves into a shout of great fear, when a small, horribly-marked body crept forth from the heart of the flower and lay motionless before my eyes. It was a spider, small certainly, but none the less horrible.

I dashed down the blossom, and trampled it into the grass with my heel. Afterwards I saw the girl at my side, with a disdainful smile upon her fair face.

'You are afraid of that—that little insect!' she said.

'Afraid!' I shouted. 'Are you not afraid of the horrible and the unknown? That creature is the embodiment of all that is vile.'

My anger had passed over me again, and I was a different being. She moved aside, and in doing so dropped the roses I had given her. It was, of course, an accident, though she expressed no desire to regain them.

'Are you going?' I called. 'No, you will not leave me yet! Or, shall I come with you?'

'I must go,' she replied fearfully. 'I should not have stayed so long. No—no. I will go by myself.'

'But we have much to talk about. We had only commenced our conversation.'

'Another time—but I must be leaving you now.'

'No!' I shouted, with all my fury. 'Oh, that spider! That damned spider!'

She slunk away, as though I had struck her. That fearful red atmosphere again surged up before my eyes, until I scarce knew what I was doing. I sprang to the spot where the bunch of roses lay, and stamped them into the soil. She was moving away, trembling, with white face, and quick coming breath. I wondered who, or what, had terrified her.

'Stay!' I shouted. 'You do not know me yet. My God! but you shall know me. It is time now. Come back!'

'You are not to come with me. You must not follow me.'

'I will! You cannot prevent me. I have a right to go with you, and I will.'

'You have no right,' she cried hotly.

'I have. You do not know what you are saying. You have given it me.'

She clenched her lips. 'What right?'

'The highest, the best, the noblest. You know well enough, but perhaps you wish to hear again. Come here, and I will tell you.'

'What?'

'You belong to me. You have told me so. I have listened to you saying it many times. But I can listen again, and you can speak again.'

'Leave me!'

'I know it all well enough. You love me, but not so much as I love you. Come, and tell me so again.'

'You fool!' she cried sullenly.

'Tell it me again. You will be true to me always. You know how I worship you. I will give you everything. I love you. How I love you!'

'Fool!' she only muttered. 'Oh, you fool!'

'You have your choice between two men. One is poor, the other rich; you could live happily with either. So the rich one has it—ah, the rich one. He wins you.'

I sprang forward with furious motions. I came up to her, panting like a beast, and would have caught her in my arms. But she conquered me. She struck me, weak woman though she was, with a weapon there was no resisting. Yet she merely raised a hand and pointed. Her mouth was a thin red line, while her eyes flashed and burnt me. She merely spoke,—

'I have never loved you—and I never shall.'

Grovelling, I sank to my knees and shouted wildly. I tore up handfuls of grass in my frenzy, and scattered the fragments of the bleeding roses in the air. I cursed and I raved against all things living and dead, seen or unseen, against my own destiny, and the fate which had called me into life.

At length my brain cleared, and I came slowly to a fuller understanding. I had sought for the truth, and it had not been withheld from me. Now there was nothing for me in life. I could only wonder at the mystery of existence, the meaning of its inscrutable end.

In this world there had been two beings whom I had loved exceedingly.

My brother had been guilty of vile treachery, and therefore I hated him. The woman abused me, while sharing in my brother's deceit.

But her I could not hate.

## CHAPTER X

## DEATH

And it came to pass, that Cain rose up against Abel his
brother, and slew him.—GENESIS iv. 8.

Sunday, 1st June.

DURING the long hours of darkness sleep had not visited my eyes.

On returning to my house, I had shut myself in my room and
admitted nobody. First came the old nurse, but she fled away in
fright, when I cursed her through the closed door. Then came
my uncle, to beat upon the panels with his trembling fists. When
I shouted at him in my fury, he cried back with a wild mirth of
excited laughter. Until midnight he continued to pay me periodical
visits, and after that there came silence in the house. But there was
one who had taken no thought for my welfare. He was the man
who loved me.

For the first hours of that night I was distracted with my grief.
I paced wildly up and down, taking a savage pleasure in destroying pictures and furniture of value. Then my mood changed; I
sat motionless, in almost a statuesque rigidity, starting only when
a leaf tapped upon the window-pane, or some weird night-bird
screamed in the garden without. Biting my fingers, and trembling
with nervousness, I crouched there, dimly realising that work lay
ahead for me, until shivering lines of a raw greyness shot behind
the curtains and slanted into the dreary room with the message of
a new day. An hour or so later the sun burst through the shadows,
the dawn broke, the misty clouds rolled up; Nature awoke and
uplifted her flushed face towards heaven; the world became noisy
again with the motion of life.

The new day found me still crouched within the chair, yet
entirely cool and calculating. I was again a practical being; my
brain was at rest; the heart throbbed with scarcely perceptible
motions. I was prepared to act.

Sounds rose above and around me. Presently there came a scratching upon the door; I moved through the wreck of furniture and opened it. Only my uncle, kneeling upon the carpet, rubbing his weak eyes.

'I have been looking for you all night, nephew. I want you to come down with me.'

'Good morning, uncle,' I said quietly.

'Morning again! Why, I have been asleep here as I waited for you. Didn't you hear me knocking?'

'I slept too soundly,' I said grimly. 'Nothing could disturb me.'

He laughed loudly. 'Come along with me. We will have breakfast together. Then we will go out. I have a new mixture to give you.'

'Presently,' I said. 'You go down now, and I will come later.'

'Then you will taste the mixture?'

'Yes.'

'I left it covered up in the blue chamber. It should be there now, unless the big toads have taken it. There were a lot of them there yesterday, and they drove me out. Perhaps they will have gone away by this time.'

I closed the door and he retired, muttering as usual thickly to himself. Later I was again disturbed by soft movements, and, on looking out, found some breakfast spread upon a small table. I groaned at the sight, which convinced me that there were still some who had thought for me. I felt this to be an injury. It was the duty of everyone to hate me now.

I partook of the food mechanically, then made my way downstairs, like a thief in my own house. Suddenly I encountered my old nurse, dressed in her best, with a black book in her hand. When she saw me, she started, and placed a hand to her bosom.

'It is a fine morning,' I said calmly. 'Are you going out?'

'Ah, sir, but you frightened me. Yes, it is Sunday, and I am going to church.'

'What for?' I cried. 'What will you do there?'

'I am an old woman now. Perhaps my time may come soon—'

'So you will enter a musty building, to cringe and mutter in the hope of salvation. Tell me, do you believe in prayer?'

'It wouldn't be any use my going to church, if I didn't, would it?'

I bent towards her. 'Then pray,' I muttered. 'Pray for my happiness.'

'I do,' she said piteously. 'God knows that I do.'

Then I looked upon her, and saw that her eyes were red, as though with weeping. For whom had those tears been shed?

'Does my brother go to church?'

She shook her head. 'I don't think so. I have never seen him.'

I smiled grimly. 'Then,' I whispered, 'pray for him, too. He may need it.'

She crept away from me silently, while I passed on laughing. Yes, I laughed, until my uncle caught the sounds, and came forth to loudly join in a mirth he could not understand.

I went with him into the blue room, and drank with him there. The fiery liquor I imbibed had little effect upon my senses. It was afternoon when I left him, and again returned to the solitude of my own room.

And here I sat until evening came on, still calm, still collected—only a little nervous.

Then I found the Bible again, and turned to the place where I had ceased reading on a previous occasion:—

'And the Lord said unto him, Therefore whosoever slayeth Cain, vengeance shall be taken on him sevenfold. And the Lord set a mark upon Cain, lest any finding him should kill him.'

I dropped the book, but this time with a new understanding. Light dawned within my brain, the clear light of knowledge.

This man had committed no sin in killing his brother.

Vengeance should be taken on him, who killed the murderer, sevenfold. Therefore Cain had done nothing to merit punishment. A mark was even set upon him, a distinctive mark, which meant to him immunity from injury. He was rewarded for his act, not punished. He came under the special protection of God! With such a thought in my mind, I walked forth into the silent garden.

My feet guided themselves along the path to the gate in the yew hedge. Through this I passed out into the pure, glorious air, that was tinted with colour by the approach of evening.

I stood within the wood of pines. Their dark tresses hung

overhead. The fragrance of their perfume flowed upon my mind; my feet pressed lightly upon heaps of springy pine needles and small browned cones.

I came to the whitethorn bush, now but sparsely decked with a few bunches of drooping blossom. Here I fell, my face upon the ground, my entire body rigid with determination. How long I was thus sheltered behind the bush, I am unable to say, but, after a space, which must be measured by other things than time, I heard footsteps; I heard the soft sound of voices. I could have laughed aloud for sheer agony when I recognised the authors, but again I exercised that surpassing power of self-control, and waited for the two to come up.

Slowly they drew within my sight, true type of faithful lovers, and she was lovelier than ever.

Was it because of the love-light in her eyes? or was it the full happiness of her heart? Beautiful she had always been, yet she had never appeared like that to me.

There is no monster upon earth which may surpass in fury the man whose limit of endurance has been exceeded. Had my brother known where I lay, surely he would have refrained from giving that frightful blow upon the heart, which drove all the higher instincts of the man from me; but he remained in ignorance, therefore he placed me upon the rack, and applied the tension which broke my soul.

They were not more than two yards from me. I could plainly detect that well-known odour emanating from her hair. I could hear the thrill of her soft laugh. I was able to listen to the trifling catch she always gave to her voice before speaking, a most enchanting fancy, which had allured me from the first.

So near were they to the whitethorn bush that at their every movement, white petals rained down like snowflakes.

They spoke softly, in such low tones that I heard little of their conversation; but if I listened to little, I saw much.

'When shall it be?' she murmured.

'Darling! I do not know yet. . . . I shall have to face him, and see what he will do for me. . . . Then we can go away and forget this dreary place.'

'Let it be soon. . . . I am afraid of walking out now.'

'You mustn't do so any more without me. Dear one, I cannot have you hurt.'

'I thought it best to keep in with him, for your sake. . . . But surely you can win him over.'

'I know he is suspicious of me.'

'But you will try—for my sake?'

'Dearest! Anything for you, my sweet one.'

As she lay in his arms, he drew her round towards him. Her head fell back upon his shoulder, while she smiled at him, with a beauty like a ray of sunlight floating upon pure water. His head dropped, and she closed her eyes. All this I could see plainly. He kissed her with a great love, while the devil entered into my heart and took up his abode there.

I was calmer now, for the cunning was returning. It is true that there was blood upon my hands, where I had bitten them; that my lips were hot and raw, but I had to preserve complete silence, while there was much to listen to, and not a little pretty love-making to witness. No man is ever complete master of himself.

'I must go now. It is getting dark.'

'But I am with you, dear.'

'Still *he* comes out in the evenings. I don't want you to meet.'

'It would be best not, perhaps—just yet.'

'Take me home, and I will see you to-morrow.'

'But first—darling!'

Her head drooped over his shoulder again, and this time I closed my burning eyes, else I must have shrieked aloud—For she was kissing him.

At length they moved away. I rose and walked out into the open path. The certainty of my footsteps surprised me. There was no hesitation, no wavering. I walked firmly over the dew-tipped grass, until the little gateway lay but a few paces ahead. Then I sat down, close to the line of the path, to wait with patience and a still determination, for I knew that one other traveller would pass along that night.

I sat there, as the moon came slowly up, and the stars spangled the mysterious sky, to glitter again in the sea. During that period I thought of many strange secrets of the hidden sense, but I cannot set down these thoughts, none of which survived that night.

The night was chilly, but calm—calm as myself. Now and again a drop of soft rain came with the wind, or a dry leaf whispered against my cheek; below, gulls floated, or hung screaming before a dark cloud, like moving snow patches. The stone, upon which I had seated myself, was slippery with dew, save where the ancient moss afforded a protection. I could scarcely note the sluggish pulsations of my heart.

It was when the rising moon flashed a white fringe along the rugged edge of the cloud bank, and the water began to glisten in angry patches of black and silver—the colours of mourning—that a traveller came.

I could hear his footsteps from afar, the cracking of dry twigs, the brushing movement of the wet grass, even—so preternaturally acute were my aural faculties—the motion of his body through the still air. My mind was strung to a pitch at which that of another must have broken.

He started when he saw me, and half stopped. When I turned, so that the moonbeams played across my face, his own went white, while the swinging motion of his footsteps ceased. I called to him, and my voice was so hearty that he approached my side with as easy a mind as the traitor can possess.

'It is a raw night,' I said; and I laughed noisily.

'Yes—it is,' he replied guiltily, though he found no reason for a smile.

'You have been for a walk,' I cried. 'This is a lonely spot, and a dreary time. Surely you have felt the solitude greatly?'

'I have only been on business,' he faltered. 'I have been to see a friend.'

'A friend!' I shouted into the night. 'Would you inconvenience yourself for the sake of a friend? Beware of them. The closer connected the friend, the greater his selfishness. He imagines he may prey for ever upon your forgiveness; but there is a bar which may not be crossed.'

I watched the suspicion crawling into his mind. I had laughed anew at the countenance he turned towards me. 'Where have you been to-night?' he panted.

'I have been enjoying the beauty of Nature. I have seen the day decline, and the moon rising up out of the waters. There has been much to interest me in this lonely spot, and it is my property. I have not closed it up. I allow the people to use it as they will. Lovers meet here, I am told—I have seen some myself. Doubtless, many a vow has been sworn beneath yonder trees.'

Fear was growing upon him. 'It is getting very late,' he said. 'Had we not better be going home?'

'We!' I cried. 'What do you mean?'

His eyes sought the ground. 'You and I. Who else?'

'Why not your friend? Why did you not bring *him* to share my hospitality?'

I saw him wince at that.

'My friend,' he said blankly.

'Yes, why did you not bring *him*?'

Again he looked at me, while his shrinking eyesight beheld my uncovered head and dishevelled garments, with the blood marks upon hands and chin. Slowly he began to understand what his perfidy had done.

'Home!' I continued. 'It is a lonely home; yet we have been happy there. Look through the branches of the trees, and over yonder bushes. If your eyes are as good as mine, they cannot fail to perceive a dull glimmer of light. This is caused by the lamp, which burns in that room, where we have spent many a happy hour. You can see it, can you not? There will be a fire, with two chairs drawn up. The tables are arranged as we always have them; refreshments are awaiting us, according to our custom. Everything is ready. Shall we go now? Presently we shall be sitting there. We shall talk on many things; perhaps on friendship, perhaps on the treachery of others, perhaps even on love.'

Then he cried out, and I saw that his hard heart was touched with sorrow. I had risen by this time; he sank upon his knees to the dewy grass, and raised his hands above his head. There was to be no further misunderstanding between us.

'Forgive me,' he cried. 'I have been unworthy of your kindness; I could not help it. I struggled against the temptation. I suffered more than you can guess. I have been base, a treacherous brother. Forgive me.'

There were cones lying round us on the peat, large cones, green and heavy. One of these I picked up, and hurled into my brother's face. He fell back, half stunned. I shouted like a maniac, when I saw the blood flowing from his nostrils.

'We have never quarrelled all our lives,' I cried, the blood rising before my eyes. 'We have loved each other well, and I could not strike the man I love.'

He was upon his feet again, and came up near me, his fear scattered by the pain and shame of the blow.

'What are we to do?' he muttered, in a deep voice which seemed to arise from the moaning sea.

'What choice is given us?' I howled back. 'Hark at the wind sobbing above our heads. Listen to the water lapping the base of the cliff. One of us is being summoned from hence.'

'No!' he cried, blenching from the naked face of death. 'We are brothers, and though I have wronged you—'

'Will you refuse, traitor? Must I call you coward as well?'

At that the light of anger surged up within his eyes. He took his stand opposite me.

'The sea calls us,' I shouted, in a mad glee. Then he put up his hand and stopped me.

'I am still your brother. Let us part in this place. I will go away and never trouble your life again. Pity me, for I dared not confess the truth. I have not willingly injured you.'

'Fool!' I howled at him. 'Do you think I will be twice deceived? Shall I give you an opportunity of tearing open the old wound? I have learnt under a good master. I have caught the spirit of your actions. You have taught me cunning and deception. You have taught me hatred. Now we are man and man together, with the grave beneath, and destiny overhead.'

He bowed his head and turned aside. 'I will not fight with you. I call God to witness that I have striven to make reparation, that you have refused it. We will part for ever. I will collect all that I am entitled to call my own; then I will leave you, and you may forget.'

I followed him with words of hatred. 'Coward!' I howled. 'Traitor! thief and liar! You well say that you will leave my house; you know that after this night there will be no place for you there. Tell me this, traitor; tell me this, coward—will you leave here alone?'

His entire anger was aroused at last. He spurned me from him like a dog. 'Do you think I would leave her here?'

'Will you do that?' I shouted.

'And leave her exposed to you and your assaults!'

He moved away in a rage, but he did not know that there was a greater fury behind. He despised me now. He did not hear my stealthy footstep. I followed him like a gliding shadow.

As I reached him, he turned. I gave a frightful shriek, and smote him full upon the temples.

He staggered forward, groaned fearfully, and groped into the air. He lurched towards me, then dropped upon the grass.

I bent over my brother, while the devil in my heart rejoiced. He was breathing thickly, in strange fashion, and was entirely insensible. He was plainly delivered into my hands.

I bent over the silent figure, with the ghastly face and rigid limbs. With my small knife I stabbed the eyes which had looked into hers, the lips which had been pressed upon hers, the hand which had fondled her, even the heart which had throbbed for her. Then I rose, and dragged the body to the edge of the cliff.

The wind had risen, and white spray flew into my face; great birds circled round my head with frightful cries; the huge waves leapt up the cliff face, muttering in a thousand tongues of strife; the pine trees rocked together, and groaned before the presence of death; cold shadows swept along the ground.

The body of my brother fell from my arms, and was drawn down into the unfathomable abyss.

I looked around on all sides, and shrieked again. I missed my brother. Where had he gone? Again I looked, with hot, sore eyes, but there was no trace of him. Yet, he had lately been with me. Where—where was he now? The grass around was trampled down, as though with a struggle, and there was—yes, I could certainly see strange markings, long red lines and patches. How did they come there? What had caused them? Was the gleaming object yonder responsible? What was that object? I strained my eyes, and at length made out a knife, the blade dulled, sticky and red with—Oh, merciful and pitying God! was it blood? could it be human blood?

Where was my brother?

From below came only the wild jubilee of the sea.

I staggered forward with awful cries; I reeled and fell upon the downtrodden and sodden grass. Then the light of the stars went out.

## CHAPTER XI

## REACTION

How is't with me, when every noise appals me?
What hands are here! Ha! they pluck out mine eyes!
Will all great Neptune's ocean wash this blood
Clean from my hand? No; this my hand will rather
The multitudinous seas incarnadine,
Making the green—one red.—*Macbeth*, Act II., sc. I.

Midnight.

I DREW my stiff body from the grass, and gazed upward at the peaceful heavens, wondering, even then, at the unseen powers which control the smallest human action. The night was very still. It seemed to me as though I had destroyed all the beings upon earth, and was myself the sole survivor. It was only one, one only, a mere unit out of countless millions. Surely the single grain of sand could not be missed from the shore, the unimportant life which was cast off in a second of time. Surely the slight addition to the myriads of the dead across the dark, ever-thronged barrier of eternity could not be marked. Only one more, when there were already so many. This one had died as the others, in the natural order of fate. No question would be asked, no examination could be possible, in that ever press of fleeting souls. It would pass on, to what place was not for me to say, and lose itself in the endless circle of other like forms, and none would ask, 'Who are you?' or 'How came you hither?'

Fear was therefore foolish. What is the loss of a life? This had throbbed away suddenly into the infinite, leaving no mark which eyes could note, no gap in the ragged phalanx of humanity, no sign of departure. The world would roll on as before: there would be no change in the appearance of anything, no ears would be troubled, no minds distressed, outside an extremely narrow circle. These would listen then forget in the trouble of their own life.

Surely then, the one man who alone knew of the time and cause of that life's departure might well forget the action of his hands. Surely—the span of life being so exceedingly short, and the world populated so thickly with evildoers—those Realising Eyes, which scan the motions of the universe, might—nay, must—have over-looked so insignificant a scene.

But what of that? Let us suppose the world is left in ignorance; let us suppose the searching Glance of Fire has disregarded; what do we know of the course of action upon the opposite side of Time's gloomy bar? There may be no questions asked, no reason sought, but are the ears of those guardians of the gate closed to cries from passing souls? chief of all, can, and may, those same souls raise voice in constant prayer for mercy—and for vengeance? If the victim *can* speak upon his woes in that nether world, then is the murderer lost.

A mournful soul would come through the night to seek admis-sion into Purgatory. Would it not, throughout the entire course of its long journey, raise the loud and perpetual cry, 'My brother has killed my body, and dismissed me here. Give me, O God, ven-geance on my brother?' Would it not weary Heaven and Hell with prayers for my destruction?

My greatest terror was for the vengeance of man. None had passed that way, or my body would certainly have been recovered from its perilous position. It was possible that a belated wayfarer might suddenly arrive, to bear away a tale of guilt. When this thought occurred, the criminal cunning returned. I set to work with busy hands to obliterate all traces of the struggle. So care-fully, so methodically, did I toil, that none could have suspected me to be an alien, an outcast, one set apart from the rest of men by the red mark of blood upon my forehead.

I cast the blood-stained knife from the cliff, and sought a path which I had often climbed as a light-hearted boy. I descended at a pace I had never approached in the most daring moments of youth, scarring my legs against sharp points, and cutting my hands upon rough edges. A false step, a chance slip, and I should have gone to join *that* which rose and fell upon the black water beneath. Down, still down, the loose stones rattling along the smooth face of the rock, the birds dashing aside with frightened cries, until the pine trees lessened and the damp breath of the waters met me in the face.

So the rocks, glimmering white in the moonlight, were reached. I looked down upon the grim face of the dead, gently rising and falling like a child being rocked to sleep upon its mother's bosom. It was long before I found courage to touch it, for the solemnity of that immortal presence overmastered my resolution.

At length I dragged the stiffening limbs upon the hard rock bed. When this had been accomplished, I felt easier, knowing that the worst of my task was ended. There were large stones piled up around my feet. Some of these I selected, and bound to the body of my victim, lashing them closely within his own garments, until the weight was sufficient to carry him down to his cold grave.

But as I was about to return him to the dark abyss fear returned, and I wept with horror. Wept, when, alas! it was too late to mourn, now that the hour when forgiveness might have served had become nothing but a recollection.

With that hot scar upon my brow I dared not, though the thought occurred to me strongly—offer a prayer at this strange burial. This would have been a mere mocking of the God, Who was even then inclining an ear to hearken unto the wild cry of the brother's blood ascending from the ground, which was now to throw her curse around me. But I called aloud to the dead flesh, relying on a frantic hope that the ever-living soul might listen. My calmness departed, as I prayed wildly for forgiveness, as I entreated for a remission of part, at least, of that inevitable approaching punishment. Finally, I had the courage to bend my head and press a kiss upon the cold forehead of the past.

A strange thing happened, or appeared to my nervous imagination to take place. At the moment my lips touched that icy brow, a sudden vital energy animated the body with the electric touch of new life. The arms shot forth to drive me back; blood spurted anew from the wounds; a furious frown of hatred contorted the ghastly features. Before I could move, or even cry out, it had forced me back upon the wet rock, and had plunged itself into the inky water. The swirling chasm closed, bubbles and foam boiled upon the heaving surface—and I was alone.

Thus I bade farewell to my brother.

As I stood there in the loneliness which my fury had created, Nature revolted against my existence. The elements shrieked at me with the tongue of hatred; the wind beat round my head and feet, with a just desire for my destruction; the dark water sprang upward, hissing like a thousand serpents; the moon disappeared; the sky grew overcast; heavy drops of rain began to fall, while the tempest rose higher and fought in the air above.

My knees shook, and the cold sweat stood upon my brow. But again I reflected that here there was no cause for fear. It was not the indefinite punishment of the unknown, not the vain threatening of natural powers, that I had cause to shrink from, but the immediate vengeance of man. So I turned from that spot, and fled along the rocky path to the gate in the yew hedge. Here the yellow light dripped faintly and tormented my eyesight. Everything was familiar, yet—had my vision been affected?—they were all strange settings in a novel environment. Before me was a tree, beneath which I had whiled away many an afternoon. Beside me was a shrub, which my own hand had planted. Yet they were not the same. I had lived here all my life, but now I was a stranger. I groped my way along like some intruder, not knowing where this path would lead me, yet venturing along it with a doubting hope. I was like the man who has seen a certain landscape in a dream, and who many years afterwards is suddenly brought into contact with the scene his fancy has depicted.

The walls of the house towered blackly before me, and I took courage when I sighted my place of refuge. Things began again to assume their natural shapes, yet the familiarity, which they inanimately resumed, was frightful in its intensity. Each plant, every dew-tipped flower, each leaf quivering on the overhead branches, possessed a far-seeing eye, which glared upon the murderer, as he passed, with a look of hate. Each also owned a voice, loud and terrible, with which they proclaimed the deadly secret to the wind, as it whispered in their midst. 'Go,' they shrieked, 'go forth quickly, and tell the world of this. Let not this man escape the penalty of blood. Go forth, and let all men hear of the deed.'

This was the garden, where I had sported as a child, in the loved company of one who had now passed beyond my knowledge. Here had we played the laughing games of youth, and forged the early links of a chain, which had now been broken. Here had we walked as grown men, with passions hot within us. Here had we sought and given friendly counsel. Here had we learnt how ennobling a thing is love!

'Your brother—where is he?' they cried forth, until my ears were deafened. 'Does he seek your assistance? You were always ready to give it. How is it he is not with you now? He cannot be in danger, or you would be at his side. No brothers ever loved like you. He is late in coming home to-night.'

Then, as I stumbled across the threshold, these voices rose together into a great and vengeful shout, the echo of which followed me fearfully into the dreary house,—

'What have you done with your brother?'

Unconsciously I cried forth, and answered them. 'What is this to me? Am I my brother's keeper?'

'What is the meaning of this cry of blood rising from the ground?'

'I have but punished justly. Cain was more guilty than I, and he was preserved against injury by God.'

'*Thou art cursed from the earth. A fugitive and a vagabond shalt thou be.*'

The door closed behind me, and shut out the hollow voices. I blinked my hot eyes feebly in the artificial light. There came a nervous tread, and the rustling of a trailing skirt, and I beheld the old nurse. I re-animated my cunning, and cast again the lying smile across my features.

She was trembling, while her face was drawn and haggard. 'Where is he?' she called. 'Hasn't he come back with you?'

'Who? Who?'

'The young master. Where is he?'

I answered her easily, though my body was frightfully cold. 'He is in his bed, sleeping. I am sure he is sleeping well.'

'He is not,' she cried.

'It is past midnight. He sleeps well.' I scarcely knew what I was saying.

The door of the blue chamber swung open solemnly, and a ghastly light streamed into the hall. There were movements, and a cracked voice called, 'Nephew, nephew.'

'The old gentleman would not go to bed. He has something to tell you.'

'What?—what?'

'I don't know. But where have you been? There is blood upon your face!'

'Blood!' I screamed, while a fearful laugh rang weirdly from within. I calmed myself with a supreme effort. 'Why are you up at this time?'

'I have been waiting for you and the young master,' she said. Her voice was strained and frightened. 'Night after night, these many years, I've listened for your footsteps. I'd hear you moving about downstairs and talking. Then there'd come the footsteps of first one and then the other, sometimes, maybe, you'd both come up together. I'd listen to you coming up the stairs, and then I could get into my own bed and sleep peacefully. But I've missed those sounds to-night. I got troubled, as an old woman will, so I came downstairs to see if I could find either of you. Now you are here, but where's the young master?'

I was shuddering like a leaf in the storm; but I did not fail at the moment when cunning was required.

'He is in—upstairs. He went to bed without disturbing you.'

'I looked into his bedroom—the door was open. It was dark and cold, and there was nobody there. I can't tell what time he left the house, but I'm sure he hasn't come back.'

My hands and feet were ice blocks. 'It is strange,' I muttered. 'There is rain falling now, while the wind is rising.'

I groaned inwardly. Then she threw open the great door, and admitted an awful tide of blackness, which surged inward, like the grim shadows of my approaching fate.

'Shut the door,' I cried in an agony of terror.

'There is nothing,' she called. 'It is cold, and the wind is blowing.'

'Will you shut it? He will not return to-night.'

Mechanically she repeated my words, then obeyed me.

'Nephew! Come here, nephew.'

I cast back a wild reply, and the bent form of my uncle appeared.

'Come inside, nephew. I have seen wonderful things to-night.'

'What?' I muttered, my brain writhing.

'The black spider—the big one. Ha! ha! It was a fine sight.'

I could only stare furiously at his wizened countenance.

'Ho! ho! I saw them plainly. It was a fierce fight.'

'A fight!' The monosyllables dropped forth in a single gasp.

The old woman came between us. 'Leave him alone. It's near morning, and time you were a-bed.'

'Go away! My nephew is coming with me. I am going to tell him about the black spider.'

I staggered toward the door. My hands were dripping with blood. The drops were falling all over the white carpet. Surely they must see the dreadful markings.

'You had better go away to bed,' she said tenderly.

She placed her wrinkled hand upon my arm, and tried to draw me away, but I could not move. The very silence was suggestive of unnatural sounds.

'Can't you hear those footsteps?' I shouted. 'They are getting terribly loud and close.'

I saw that she was shivering. 'It's nothing. You're not well to-night.'

'There is somebody. There *is* someone at the window. Oh, God! Can't you see that face?'

My uncle caught at my arm with his crooked fingers.

'Go away, old woman! Can't you see what's the matter with him?'

'What do you mean?'

The dreadful echoes of that lonely house were awakened by his shout of unnatural laughter.

'He is mad, I tell you. Go away, and leave us together. Mad, both of us. Ha! ha! Mad!'

## CHAPTER XII

## REMORSE

Ecstasy!
My pulse, as yours, doth temperately keep time,
And makes as healthful music; 'tis not madness
That I have uttered; bring me to the test,
And I the matter will re-word; which madness
Would gambol from.—*Hamlet*, Act III. sc. 4.

1 o'clock a.m.

HE pushed me within the blue chamber, and closed the door. He dragged me to a seat, and forced me down with excited hands. Then he took his stand opposite me, his face working dreadfully, his eyes wan and blood-shot.

'It was here. Perhaps it is in the room still,' he muttered.

'What?' I cried. My tongue was blistering.

'It has escaped behind the draperies. You will find it lying somewhere against the wall.'

'What have you seen?'

'The spider,' he said, with a weird chuckle.

'Where?' I shouted, rising in my terror.

'It was in the centre of the room that I saw them—'

'Them!'

'Let me speak, nephew. I saw them plainly.'

I was burning inwardly. At that moment I feared my own tongue might betray me.

'I came here early in the evening. I sat here for a long time. Night came on, and I grew sleepy. I was aroused about two hours ago. The great clock had ceased to work.'

It was *that*, then, which caused the weird sense of loneliness in the room. On entering, I had missed something; I now understood that the feeling of desolation was induced by the complete, almost stifling, silence. There stood against the dark draperies of the wall a massive clock, ancient in design, and of great size. Usually the pendulum of this great timepiece swung, with long steady sweep, metaphorical of the time that flies, while the throbbing of its continual beat echoed at all times, and with fearful impressiveness, throughout the room. But now it was silent.

I glanced towards the dark pointing hands. There was no animation there, no sign of mechanical life.

My uncle was tapping me upon the knee. 'Listen, nephew. There have been strange things here tonight.'

I turned my face towards him. I knew that it was cold and ghastly.

'I waited here, after the clock had stopped. I was in good health, nephew. I have seen no toads all day. As I sat in the chair that you are in, a shadow passed across the floor near my feet. It was like a black leaf swept along by the wind—'

'It wasn't—'

'I saw a huge spider, black as ink. It was dragging itself along hurriedly. I recognised it.'

'Not the one you saw the other day?' I shouted. I was fearfully cold, though my throat was burning, and my lips were dry.

'Ha! ha! It was the same one. I am old, and mad perhaps, but I know something. That insect was not altogether an insect. No— no. I know something, nephew.'

'Where—where did it go to?' I whispered.

'Listen, nephew. This creature had an object in view. He was tracking down some enemy; he was in danger of his life.'

'Why do you say *he?*'

He only grinned at me. 'Ha! ha! I know something, nephew. They call me mad, but I can understand.'

'Where did you see it? What time?'

'The great clock had stopped. It was not very long before you came in.'

I gnawed my hands, while hot fingers tore at my brain.

'I watched him, nephew. He rushed forward. Another shadow darted across the floor. It was another black spider, but not so large, not so fierce. I watched more closely.'

'What—what did you see?'

'I knew what the first spider was after. Directly he saw this one, he dashed after it, and overtook it.'

I was bent together in the chair; my knees were tapping one against the other; ice drops were coursing down my features and dropping upon the carpet.

'They fought before me. It was terrible to watch them. They were writhing together silently. I was trembling, for the struggle was awful, and the creatures were very loathsome. But the smaller one wanted to get away. He watched for his chance, then he began to slip away. But the larger one—he was cowardly, nephew—ran up behind, and attacked him.'

'Did he kill him?' I moaned.

'I did not see. They ran under the table there. I went to sleep, until I heard you talking.'

I startled even him by my scream of terror. 'My God!' I shrieked, clutching at his arm. 'Did you hear that?' For a hollow echo sounded round the room. A hand was knocking upon the door, with nervous touch.

It was only the old nurse who entered, with fearful footstep. 'He has not come in,' she said. 'There is no sound outside.'

No sound! The whole place was alive with fierce voices, with cries of hateful laughter. No sound! The very universe was torn into shreds by the shrieks of lost souls.

My uncle staggered across the carpet. He tapped the clock with his bony knuckles, and spoke to it, as though it were a thing of life. A solemn, metallic ring issued from the invisible interior when his hand descended.

He looked round with a dreadful smile. 'It won't speak, nephew. The clock is dead. It will never speak again.'

'It will go presently, uncle. See! open the case and swing the pendulum. That is all it requires.'

But the old woman put in her word. 'No! It will not go. The spring is broken.'

'You hear, nephew? It is the heart of the clock that is broken.'

The silence was appalling. 'That is not much,' I cried. 'Merely the breaking of a spring. What is that?'

'You do not understand, nephew. It is *the* spring on which everything else depends.'

'Another spring may be put in, and then it will live again. Mechanism is not like human life. *That* cannot be restored. Merciful God! It cannot! It cannot!'

'Eh? The man may live again, but we haven't learnt the arts. It may come, nephew. In the meantime we must be content to die. But it is a pity that so many fine machines should go to rot. For man's a fine machine at his worst, a wonderfully fine machine.'

'Ah, sir, won't you go up to bed?' put in the anxious, old woman. 'It will be morning light presently. Won't you go up, while I wait here?'

'Wait! What for?'

'The young master, to be sure,' she said mournfully.

'He is safe,' I cried. 'I swear that he is—very safe.'

'Yes, yes,' chuckled the old man. 'He's safe enough, especially if he's dead. A closed box, and four earth walls. Safe! Ha! ha!'

She shuddered. I was tortured by passing waves of great heat, then by excessive cold. I longed to get away to the peace and privacy of my own chamber. There I could think—and sleep; sleep—and dream. But dream!

I was about to depart, when my uncle gave a cry, and dropped upon his knees. 'I have him, nephew! I have found him!' he exclaimed.

That nerveless dread again came to poison my body. 'What?'

'Ha! ha! I have found the dead spider! Here it is; curled up upon the floor. The cowardly one killed it after all.'

I could not, I dared not, speak. Distinctly I could hear the sounds of slow, approaching footsteps along the gravel walk outside.

'Dead!' he howled. 'This is a night of death. First the old clock, then the spider.'

I fell to my knees in the centre of the room. There was a great hand at my throat, choking the life from my body.

Then the old woman was at my side, with an arm around me. 'What is it, sir?' she cried pitifully.

'Ha! ha! Only mad, old woman. That is nothing.'

'He's so anxious about his brother, but he wouldn't show it before. They are so fond of each other.'

The footsteps came nearer. There uprose a confused revelry of sounds. I had never heard my brother talking so loudly. And she was with him. They were laughing together. Now they were kissing. Why could they not go further away, and leave me alone? The wind was frightful; the noise of the sea was deafening; the lash of the water, as it leapt up over the smooth rocks, was ice cold. And that ghastly body was still floating—still floating. The face was awful in its rigidity. Why was there blood upon it?

'Bury it! Why won't you cover it up?'

My brother again! How fearfully he was shouting! And how merry he was, how light-hearted! He was winding his arms round my neck, and trying to kiss my forehead.

'Traitor! You shall not touch me!'

I was upon my feet, while the room rocked and heaved in a fierce glow of lurid blue light.

'Stop them! I am master here. There are fingers of bone rattling against the glass. Pull aside the curtains and look. You will see a face. It is marked with death. Can't you see it? Oh, God! It is hideous! It is hideous!'

The wind was raging, while the trees were bending and crashing. Green cones flew, like live shells, through the furious air. One of these struck my brother in the face. Surely he was not injured. I loved my brother. I could not bear to see him hurt.

'Hark! Listen more carefully. The footsteps are treading lightly; they are crossing the grass. You can hear the bushes parting. The body is pressing them aside. There they go, back again to their former position. The footsteps again. They are much louder, for they are on the gravel again. They have reached the front of the house. They have almost reached the door.'

Ah! She was smiling. They were both together. I could catch glimpses of them both as I whirled round with the universe. The pace was fearful. Still there were great hosts of lost souls. Cain was quite close. I could recognise him by the mark on his forehead. There she is again! I just saw her, by the pines, as I was hurried past. She was by herself—he was not there. Her face was fearfully pale, and full of anguish.

'It is here! It is at the door! Are you mad? Its hands are reaching out for the knocker. Are you blind? Its fingers are searching for the bell handle. Are you deaf? Rush to the door! Open it! Drive that away! I tell you, it is about to raise a clangour, which will disturb the sleep of the dead!'

Arms were clinging to me, but I broke away, and leapt outside— out, into the hall, across the tiled floor. The lights darted up before my eyes; my forehead struck terribly upon the oaken door. I sank to the ground, with the frightened screams of a woman ringing in my ears.

# PART II

## The Under-Shadow

CHAPTER I

ON DRIFTING CLOUDS

Around, on all sides, . . .
Are filmy forms, half seen, whose numbers vast defy
Our utmost reckoning. These are the watchers, then,
Of Life—the Drama of the Mighty Mind. . . .

Monday, 7th July.

IN the raw gleam of the early morning I stood by the death-bed of my old nurse. Since that fatal night of the first of June, she had been afflicted by a disease to which I could give no name, beyond that of a gradual wearing away. Since that night, I say, her energies had been impaired; she became suddenly weak and wild in appearance; stranger still, she avoided me, or started with fear whenever we chanced to meet. About a week back she had taken to her bed, and now, at this early hour before the sunrise, she was to be called away.

'Stay, nephew; I'm coming with you.' It was my uncle who called at me, as I made my dreary way up the stairs, which were thronged with shuddering shadows of the dawn. He sprang after me with strange motions through the breaking light, like some uncouth animal.

'They say that the old woman is dying. Ha! ha! We'll go and bid her good-bye, nephew. It is a great jest to see people die. They curl over on their backs and they turn blue. Come along, nephew.'

I pushed him away. 'I am going in by myself. She is nothing to you.'

Dog-like he obeyed. I left him sitting regretfully upon a lower stair, watching me as I entered the strange-smelling apartment.

Even so, I was only just in time. The doctor had gone, because his services could no longer be of use. A small man in clothes of an ominous black stood near the bed. I bade him leave us, and he did so, though he remarked vaguely that it was a priest's duty to remain by the dying until the end. Still he thought that the old woman could not revive from her unconsciousness. He added that he would keep near at hand, and be ready to receive a summons.

Left to myself, I looked upon the still figure and trembled. Here was the full solemnity and awfulness of death for the second time before my eyes. Strange odours filled the room; all those various artificial aids to recovery were scattered upon chairs and tables; a tall candle cast yellow rays upon the bed and its occupant. I fixed my eyes upon the spear-like flame—it was absolutely without motion; I listened, with senses painfully acute—silence, complete and awful. But no, there came a gasping groan from the bed, a sound full of grief and pain, yet to me welcome, for it spoke of the present life.

I came nearer and bent forward. The face was livid, pinched, and deeply marked with long furrows; the eyes and mouth were tight closed lines; the passing of the breath was imperceptible. Thin hands were clasped upon the cover, over the region of the heart. I saw that they clutched some small object, so I pulled the candle nearer and looked again. It was a brown wood cross, alike in colour and appearance to the grim mark stamped upon the back of Nature's most hideous creation.

I would have torn the symbol from that death clutch—I cannot tell what gave me the desire—only I dared not violate that gaunt and departing presence. Outside voices were disputing weirdly. My uncle had followed me up, and was endeavouring to force his way inside, but the man they called a priest was holding him back. Presently there came heavy blows of his stick upon the door panels. It was a strange death scene.

'Nephew! Let me in! Is the old woman dead?'

I made no answer, and the struggling continued.

'Give her brandy, nephew. There's new life and eternity in brandy.'

The dying woman stirred upon the bed and groaned again.

'Give me the cellar keys, nephew. I'll bring up a big bottle.'

The door fell back, while the small man in black entered. 'Is this a Christian home?' he said, in a half whisper, 'or is it an abode of madmen?'

This deliberate insult aroused my full fury. 'Madman!' I shouted at him. 'You come into my house, unasked! You dare to call me mad!'

'I do not. But the old man outside most certainly is.'

'Beat him, nephew!' cried a howling voice. 'Kick the black dog.' Then the speaker himself appeared with upraised stick.

'For the mercy of God!' exclaimed the preacher solemnly, 'remember where you are, and control your passions. We stand in the presence of the dying.'

'You called me madman!' I shouted.

'You called me madman!' repeated my uncle, at the same moment smiting the small man heavily upon the shoulder with his stick. 'Ha! ha! See the dog jump! We will kill him, nephew, shall we?'

The priest was white-faced and shivering with fear. We shouted together in a burst of loud laughter. But, while the sounds of our mirth still echoed round the room, I heard a deep sound from the bed. I turned, to behold the two eyes of the old woman opened widely, and fixed terribly upon my face.

My mind calmed at once, because I remembered what she had done for me during the life that was then passing away.

I compelled the two others to leave the room. I dropped some keys into my uncle's eager hand. 'Go,' I said. 'Go, both of you, and drink if you will. Only leave me here alone.'

The preacher protested angrily, while my uncle chuckled with glee. Again he thrust his wizened face back through the doorway.

'Good-bye, old woman. I shall come to the funeral. I'm going to drink your health. Ha! ha! Drink your health! Ho! ho!'

I slammed the door in the faces of both, and returned to my post at the bedside. The eyes of the dying woman had closed again, while a singularly restful look settled down over her features. Peaceful and happy at the moment of death! How could such a thing be?

I stood by the side of this old woman, who formed the only link connecting me with a happy past, while the daylight intensified, and swallowed up the yellow blot cast from the dim candle. She was so entirely motionless that I imagined she must be dead. I bent forward, and touched her hand. The electric fluid of my superabundant life flowed from the finger tips into her rigid body, and called it back to consciousness. Again the eyes opened. She beheld and recognised me, yet she did not speak; she had no smile. That ghastly pallor, which overspread the features where the death film lingered, could not have been mistaken for sign of gratification. Yet I must speak to her.

'I have come, nurse—to say good-bye.'

Her eyes grew more fearful. The thin lips stirred faintly. 'My poor master! Oh, my poor master!'

'Why! What is it? I am here, beside you.'

'Good-bye. I will pray for you. Oh, good-bye.'

Then her eyelids wearily sank together, while she fell back in the unconsciousness from which she was never to recover.

I wondered at this strange manner of farewell; but there was more to come. Though her mind was torpid for ever, there was still a duty left for the tongue. Before dissolution, I learnt from her involuntary lips an awful tale.

When I saw the blue mouth stirring, I bent my head to catch that last message. But every word that dropped and thrilled into my sense of hearing, awoke that already awful memory to more vigorous and vindictive action.

'I suspected on that night—the next day I knew. . . . On the shirt he had cast aside were blood stains . . . small, but visible to eyes that sought. . . . I have kept this secret . . . though it has killed me. . . . I have guarded it so carefully . . . the strain has been too great. . . . Now he is safe—in this world. . . . Perhaps I was wrong . . . he was my dear master . . . as a child I nursed him—his innocent arms would go round my neck . . . his little heart would beat against mine. . . . I loved him the best—I pitied him . . . he was always nervous, while the other was so good-looking—the favourite of all others. . . . My poor . . . young master. . . . Had I known—'

The sounds rambled into senseless mutterings as death stretched forth a clutching hand. I stumbled into a chair, and poured forth my useless sorrow to that dreadful silence which follows the passing of death's footsteps.

What a consummate and perfect villain I was! I had slaughtered wholesale, innocent and guilty alike. What must have been the misery of that faithful old woman, while that hideous comprehension was biting at heart and brain? When she forced a smile at my approach, her thought must have been on my unutterable vileness; whenever she touched me, she must have hurried to cleanse her hands from the pollution. Yet she had remained heart-true; more, she had actually preferred a broken heart to my public shame. She refused to speak those damning words which would have consigned me to the hangman. She had chosen death with a burden upon her conscience, to life with sorrow upon her mind. Truly the love of a great-minded woman, whatever be her station in life, is a priceless treasure, and one which no riches may acquire.

I bent myself over the stiffening shape. The woman, who had given me of her best and noblest, was where she could understand. Only in the raw light of the sun-rising were the two wide-open eyes, fearfully and reproachfully staring upon me.

I spread aside the window curtains to admit the glory of the day. I turned towards the sickly candle and quenched its flame. A thin cloud of blue smoke uprose and vanished—suggestive of the mysterious passing of a soul. Then I departed from the room, without sparing another glance for the dead.

How fearfully quiet was the house! At the first landing I spread forth my left hand, and inspected the palm. The first gilded rays of the cloud-breaking sun darted through a dusty pane, and licked that open hand with hot menace. I shivered at the sight. The scaffold sign was certainly very distinct; every line writhed and bent its sinuous course, like a blood-red worm of fire, across the flesh. The fingers bent over slightly, as though anxious to conceal that repulsive spectacle. Fresh light played along the blunted tops, and presented to my vision another omen of dismay. The nails were buried, hidden almost, by pillowy phlanges of wax-like flesh, which protruded upward, and curled over as though to meet.

This was none other than the hand of the murderer, the criminal, the man predestined for sin.

Dismay passed speedily from my heart, and I laughed at the fatuous beliefs which scientists have conjured for the fear of others. In this mood I went to my morning meal. I ate heartily, and afterwards walked forth into the bright morning, along the road by the pine wood, and down towards the bare fishing village beyond. Yet I was not alone. The dim image of my fate stalked close behind, dogging me with the persistency of my own shadow. Sometimes the hollow footfalls sounded so loudly, that I would start round with hands upraised to repel the blow.

Down in a damp, secluded valley, stood a small stone church, wreathed over with tangled ivy, and surrounded by ancient yews. In this peaceful spot my ancestors lay buried. Impelled by a certain curiosity, for I had not visited the spot for years, I trod along a moss-grown path, and finally approached a lych gate covered with yellow lichen, and hanging together in the last stage of rottenness.[1] I was about to pass through into the enclosure beyond, when a figure rose suddenly from amid the heaving grass mounds, the graceful figure of a woman, who swung a small basket in her hand as she stepped forward to unconsciously confront me. I started violently, for it was she.

She flushed—whether with pleasure or anger, I could not determine. 'I did not expect to see you—here.'

I smiled. 'It is not my usual walk; your magnetic influence must have drawn me here. What are you doing?'

'I came to put flowers upon my mother's grave,' she said simply.

Then I remembered that we were both orphans, and commenced to vaguely wonder in which part of this dreary field of death the bodies of my own parents lay.

'Flowers again,' I muttered, then came towards the grave side. Here I noticed something. 'These are poor blossoms. I sent you finer yesterday. You do not use them.'

'No. I give what is my own to my own. These grew in my own little garden, and I cannot afford better.'

Her words brought satisfaction to my mind. She preserved my gifts for herself exclusively.

'It is a strange custom, this spreading of flowers upon graves,' I continued. 'What connection can fragrant blossoms have with the rotting flesh or brown-dried skeleton beneath?'

She shuddered at my words. 'I do not look at it in that light. These flowers are but a mark of affection for those who have

---

1 Lych (from Old English *lic*, corpse) is a roofed, wooden, churchyard gateway, also known as a "corpse gate," under which the funeral party, with the deceased, awaited the arrival of the clergyman.

gone. They remind the dead that they still have a place within the memory of the living.'

'Dead'—'Memory,' two horrible words those. Their significance became intensified by the presence of those silent stone memorials, cross-formed, which uprose on every side.

'But those dead!' I cried. 'Can they see? Can they appreciate? Can they understand?'

'We cannot tell. We only know that they live.'

'And even that is nothing but a surmise. Is it not so?'

She turned aside a little wearily. 'I will not discuss such things with you. For one thing, they are beyond both of us.'

'But you believe, though you cannot prove.' Then the tones of my voice changed. 'Pardon me, I would not trouble you. The dead are the dead, and we are the living. This is our space of light and enjoyment. Let us leave this horrible place.'

Without demur she came with me, while we passed together out by the lych gate. Again I was close to her side; again I felt the subtle essence of her being communicating itself to my hidden sense in those slight touches of her wind-blown skirt. Again there surged up within my heart the overwhelming torrent of love.

Why should I not obtain that, which the humblest dweller upon earth may enjoy?

I looked down upon her face, and perceived that her dark lashes were moist. 'You have been crying?' I said, with attempted cheerfulness in my voice. What cause could she have for grief?

'Yes. I have my sorrows, like everyone else—as you.'

She passed a handkerchief across her eyes, then accidentally dropped it.

We bent quickly together. Our fingers touched the piece of cambric—I felt her warm young life circling through my body; her silken hair brushed upon the dark wrinkles of my forehead—the delicious contact maddened me.

For a moment I could not speak, while her cheek grew hot. How I longed to press my lips upon that peach-like flesh! But deliberation and forethought were necessary. I fought down the rising impulse, and spoke again,—

'You say we both have sorrow. I have no right to pry into yours. But what is mine?'

For the first time she looked me straight in the eyes. The rich stain died away from her face, which was now firm and resolute, almost fierce.

'You have lost your brother,' she said.

We were all by ourselves within the glorious sunshine, with the wind sweeping upward from the sea. That sea, so tranquil and smiling, which was yet the grave of so many.

'My brother!' I gasped.

Again that memory, which was now commencing to accumulate substance, raised its hideous face between me and her I loved. It pursued me, most faithful of satellites. When I bent forward, that I might look again into her face, I saw not her, but—It.

'You loved him,' she continued, while her voice was cold and hard.

'But he is dead,' I cried. 'Surely he is—we have heard nothing. You cannot know what I have suffered for his loss. I loved him—yes, I loved but one better.'

'And for the sake of that person you would do anything?' she asked.

Did she know? but that was clearly impossible. This was meant for no accusation, as her head was bent, and her posture that of sorrow. She was but trying to plumb the depths of my heart.

'Yes,' I answered wildly. 'Anything that might not be barred by the laws of justice. Anything else.'

Her lashes lifted slightly, and I noticed the direction of her glance. It was towards the clenched fist of my left hand. Why did she look there—why? Then I remembered the sign, the red lines, the entire configuration of that hand. Again—had she cause for suspicion? But the deed had been committed with such complete secrecy. Nobody could have guessed the author, except the old woman who had just left the earth. At that moment I could feel glad that she was dead.

We had reached a spot where the road branched, and here she stopped. 'I must leave you now. Please do not offer to come with me.'

'But there is one thing,' I said. 'You have guessed my sorrow, am I not to learn yours?'

A faint smile crept round her mouth. 'Perhaps it might not interest you. The heart is selfish, even on questions of grief.'

'Anything that concerns you interests me. Will you not tell me?'

'Perhaps some day, but not now. Good-bye.'

She held forth a small hand. How fragile she looked! Truly, in a woman's weakness lies her great strength. I grasped and held the delicate fingers.

'May I see you to-morrow? I have something to tell you, something which will not keep longer. Shall I see you?'

She hesitated, while I watched the colours chasing one another across her features. Her bosom rose and fell, while her breathing came strangely. At length she spoke, yet with the manner of one who had just formed a mighty resolution.

'Yes. I will see you to-morrow if you wish it.'

I positively laughed aloud in my new-found pleasure. 'In the afternoon,' I cried happily. 'I will come along the cliff, at four o'clock, in the direction of the pine wood. Shall I see you there at that time?'

Again she paused, again, after an interval, she replied, with a strange coldness in her voice, 'I will be there.'

She raised her face to mine half defiantly, and I liked her the better for her womanly pride. 'Then I will not say good-bye now,' I said. 'We are soon to meet again. I will send you flowers—I will bring them myself. You shall have anything, everything, I can give you. Do you wish for anything? Ask me, and you shall have it, if it lies in my power to give it. You will let me give you some proof of my affection.'

The red atmosphere was swimming around me again—I scarce knew what I was saying; whether, indeed, I was speaking aloud at all.

She drew a little away. 'I will come,' she repeated dreamily.

'You have promised?'

'Yes,' half impatiently. 'I do promise.'

I came up to her, and took her arm. 'As proof of that promise, as a sign that you are not offended with me, may I kiss you? Ah, do not say no.'

She did not, though I saw and felt her tremble—from nervousness. She raised her face and parted her lips. The last person I had kissed had been my brother. She closed her eyes, as I placed my arm around her. Only the solitude of the wind surrounded us.

I had conquered my brother at last! I could have shrieked aloud in the overflowing ecstasy of my mind.

I pressed her closer, until I almost fancied I heard her moan. I brought my head down, with a delirious smile upon my face.

Then I kissed her.

CHAPTER II

THE WARNING

The sobbing of the sea!
From its bosom how there pours,
With a shudder, with a whisper;
From its dark depths how there wanders,
With a heaving, with a murmur,
Message from the dread unseen!
While a spectre winds forth slowly,
White and drear;
Passes slowly with the sobbing, passes from
these eyes of mine.

Tuesday, July 8th.

THE morning I spent in the blue room, poring over the yellow parchment of the Norse manuscript. That my uncle had been there before me was at once evident. For there were numerous glasses, containing weirdly coloured compounds, on almost every table. Later, I looked out and saw him in the garden, springing wildly from spot to spot, shrieking in loud notes of anger or fear, and aiming terrific blows with his stick at inanimate objects, which bore, for him, an appearance of foul living creatures.

But at noon he came in, and presently joined me at table. He swallowed his food with the senseless voracity of a beast, and took but little notice of me, until I rose to leave. Then he drank off a glassful of rich port, and blinked at me with small, bloodshot eyes. He nodded and chuckled, making desperate efforts to form intelligible sounds.

'Well, uncle,' I said, and I was surprised at the cheerfulness of my manner. 'What have you been doing to-day?'

He grinned, showing his broken teeth. 'It was a hard fight, nephew. The garden is full of rebellious spiders. Great creatures as large as bears. They have gone against me.'

As usual, his words had their effect upon me. 'You were fighting, then?' I said wildly.

'Yes, yes. I attacked them with my big stick. Their bodies were
like indiarubber. They only curled up a little when I hit them. But
I kept them off, nephew. Ha! ha! I was too much for them. I must
go out now and restore order to my kingdom. You will come,
nephew, eh? You will come with me? We will fight them together.'

He reached for another bottle, and grunted as he pulled at the
cork. A strange heat uprose within my body. It was terrible to
listen to him.

'I have other duties, uncle,' I said, with forced calm. 'I cannot
come with you.'

He swore fearfully at the bottle he could not open, then dashed
it to the floor. He lurched unsteadily to his feet. 'Come and see the
old woman, nephew. She must be hungry by this time.'

'She is dead,' I cried blankly, though I recoiled at uttering the
word.

'Ha! ha! Dead and cold. We will go together and have a look at
her.'

He came forward and hung to me. I broke away from him in
horror. 'No!' I cried fiercely. 'Go back to the garden. I will come
out to you there.'

He was satisfied by a fresh thought. 'I'm going to look for
the black dog—the one who insulted us, nephew. He called us
madmen. Did you see how he jumped, when I hit him with my
stick! Ho! ho! It will be great sport if I can find him.'

'Yes,' I said. 'Go and look for him.' I only desired then to free
myself of his company.

He was satisfied. 'Ah—ah! If I can only find the black dog, I'll
drag him back here. I'll give him to the spiders. Ha! ha!'

His weird laugh died away, while I hastened to my room, there
to compose myself for the great act of my life.

I attired myself in the dark clothes which I felt best befitted me;
I carefully arranged my somewhat long hair, and shaved my chin
with unerring skill; after that, I sat before a mirror and applied
cosmetics to my face—to detract from its natural pallor. Finally,
I pulled a sprig of myrtle blossom—remembering that it was the

symbol of love—into my coat, and buried the line disfigurement
of my left hand beneath a tight-fitting glove.

With all this, I shrank from meeting my own eyes within the
mysterious depths of the mirror's surface. I would shrink at times,
with a still-born cry of fear frozen upon my lips, when I imagined
a hand had touched me lightly upon the shoulder, or the muffled
whispering of an unseen presence had surged dimly round the
room.

The afternoon grew, so I presently left my room, hoping to
escape from house and garden unperceived by my uncle. On my
way downstairs I was compelled to pass a solemn door, which separated me from the presence of the dead. Here I paused, because
the dark curtains made dreary shiftings, as I came near. In these
lifeless objects was animation, which was denied to the mortal
figure within. The wind had risen considerably since noon, and
was now sweeping and groaning round the house, while loose
branches lashed the masonry, and tight rosebuds drummed, like
human knuckles, upon many a misty pane.

It occurred to me to enter, since there were so many sounds of
unnatural life in the worm-marked woodwork, beneath the heavy
hangings, and along the dim-lighted corridor. Perhaps the old
nurse had revived again from a cataleptical fit,[1] which had borne
but the semblance of death; even then she might be groaning with
the horror of her awakening, at finding herself oppressed beneath
all the grinning ceremonial of the dead; she might, furthermore,
be vainly striving to call upon the one whom she had saved from
the execration of a world.

I laughed aloud into the echoing recesses, as I turned aside
from the dim flickering of the curtains. This was indeed a shallow
phantasy. I would not open that door, not because I feared to face
the cold matter upon the bed within, but that my intrusion would
be motiveless.

Then I recollected the nature of my approaching appointment,

---

1 Catalepsy is a state of seizure, trance, or unconsciousness induced by hypnosis
or schizophrenia; it is characterized by a failure to react to stimuli and by sudden
muscle rigidity in which the limbs cannot be voluntarily moved. This may be one
of numerous echoes of Poe's "Fall of the House of Usher"; Madeline is buried
alive in a cataleptic state.

as I discerned the faint odour of the sickly flower which gleamed before my downward glance. I was a lover, in the full hot passion of manhood. This was no time for morbid thoughts at the gate of the tomb. I was a lover!

My body seemed to melt within the liquid infinity of a long mirror ahead. Therein I perceived the marked contrast between my white-gloved hands, sombre clothes, and the prominent colour along my high cheek bones. My forehead shone wax-like beneath a heavy mantle of black hair. But I was a lover. So I smiled, while my brow rippled up into long lines, and the teeth flashed each one into view.

The next moment I shuddered and turned from that glass, which was beyond doubt defective. For the smile, which should have been symbolical of the heart's rising happiness, resembled more closely the grinning agony of a skull. And outside the wind shrilled louder, while I could plainly note the lashing beat of water against rock.

Even then, the future mistress of my house was awaiting me.

I hurried down the stairs, and along the dim hallway, where blurred faces of ancestors gazed down with many a depicted frown—out into the garden. Above, the stormy sky was covered with fleeting rack; below, the tree branches lashed the air. Still on, through the wavering light of the avenue, where a great beetle scuttled fearfully before my footsteps, and then to the cliff gate, where the whin bushes shivered beyond.

Suddenly a figure sprang forth from one of these bushes. It was my uncle, and his grey locks streamed dreadfully in the wind. His face was white and wizened. He pushed at my advancing body with trembling hands.

'Go back, nephew! Go back! You shall not come this way.'

The health-laden touch of brine that whipped upon my face invigorated each sense.

'What, uncle,' I called. 'Let me get by, for I am in a hurry.'

'I know. I know. You are rushing to death. Come here, nephew. Come back. It is within the wood. I have seen it.'

'What?'

'The tiger. The white-clawed tiger. It is lying in wait.'

'What do you mean, uncle?'

'See my stick!' he cried, shaking it before me in the wind. 'See the blood on it! See the black hair. I have beaten the great spiders, nephew. They will not rebel against me any more.'

He panted for breath. His excitement was terrible. There was a line of blood along his forehead, as though he had fallen and cut the flesh.

'I looked along the road for the black dog. I couldn't find him. I saw someone else. Her skirts were blown round her, but she walked strongly—yes, she walked fiercely.'

'Is that all? What is there in that?'

'I turned to follow her, for she did not see me. Her head was bent against the wind. I came after her. She went to the other side of the wood. I thought I would speak to her.'

'What did you say?'

'I came after her through the wood. She didn't see me, for the wind crushed against her face. She didn't hear me, for the wood was shrieking all around. I crept behind. Ha! ha! I could see the soft shaping of her ancle, and the delicate curve of each leg. Ho! ho! I see such things. She is a fine woman, nephew. I see more than others think.'

'Is that all you have to say?'

'You are a fool,' he shouted. 'Let me go on. I am not mad now, nephew. No—no, not mad. Listen.'

His long fingers hooked round my shoulder, and we staggered together before the gale.

'It was a fearful journey, nephew. Long green snakes, covered with slime, hissed away among the bushes. Huge spiders, black or brown, each bearing a great cross upon his back, shivered in the centre of a network of thick web, and clawed at me as I passed. Great toads squatted at my feet, with hideous eyes, and spat poison. It was awful, but she didn't seem to mind. She came out upon the cliff, and I heard her talking.'

'Who to?' I cried, again in the fury of jealousy.

'Herself. The words were thrown back against my ears by the wind. Now you are hurrying, with your gloves and your white flower. You are a lover! Ha! ha! A lover!'

'But what was she saying? What?'

'A woman has a pretty mouth, and a loving heart. I know,

nephew, but cross her will, rob her of that she loves—that mouth will curse then, while the heart will turn black with vengeance.'

'What did she say?'

'I heard her angry words of hatred; I listened to her oaths of vengeance. She would sacrifice herself, her soul, that she might win. Ha! ha! I heard her, as I knelt by the whin bush, with a great toad winking into my face. Now you are coming along to meet her, dressed as a lover. Go back, nephew! Go back!'

I tried to get away from him, but he struggled with me. 'What have you done to her, nephew? What have you done?'

'I will tell you later. To-night, when we are sitting together; but let me go now. I tell you I must go.'

'The tiger will drag you to pieces. She will drink your blood, and eat away your life. Her face was awful. Come back with me, nephew. We will drink together, down in the quiet cellar. There are only small black spiders there, and I will order them not to come near you.'

'I am late now. We will talk presently. You are excited, uncle.'

'I am sane,' he shouted, drawing his strange figure upright. 'My brain has cleared to save you. I am not the madman now.'

'Am I?' I shouted. 'Back from me, uncle! I am stronger than you.'

'You are the madman.' Then his note changed to a wheedling tone. 'But I love you, nephew. I always liked you better than that other one. We are relatives, and we are friends. Besides—ha! ha!— we are both mad. Let's go back to the house together. Leave the tiger alone. You dare not face her claws and her teeth.'

My poor uncle was more insane than usual. I struggled with him there, on the wind-beaten cliff-top.

'You fool!' he shrieked. 'I will throw you down to the sea.'

These words recalled a past scene, and made me tremble. With a mighty fury of passion I threw him to one side, then sped away.

But his howling words pursued me. 'Where is the other one? Do you know, nephew? Does the sea know? *Does the tiger know?*'

The myrtle spray in my coat fell to pieces in the gale, leaving but a dry, withered stalk. His dreadful laughter beat round in that shuddering atmosphere, and followed as I hastened away.

'Does the tiger know?'

From the dim distance, where water and wind met and struggled together, came the reverberating signal of a ship in agony.

The muffled knell of a lighthouse bell tolled solemnly through the storm. While my brother slept beneath.

Plang! Plang! Plang!

## CHAPTER III

## THE WINNING

The horror of the sea!
With the colour on the waves,
With the light upon the waters.
How the mem'ries riding gaily,
Passing on each crested billow,
Writhing madly to the strand,
Cast their mist and damp around me,
Wild and cold,
Cast their dampness forth to mingle tears of
spray with tears of mine.

4-15. p.m.

THE heavy booming of distant guns rose louder, while a rumbling answer was cast upward from the rocks beneath. It was growing more misty, and a dull red eye flashed from that spot whence came the riotous scream of the iron bell.

I crossed by the border of the pine wood, where already the principal portion of my life's dream had been laid. Upward I went—the path was steep and stone-covered in places—on, as though I would reach the heaving clouds ahead, and lose myself within the mystery of their stormy depths. Bunches of foliage leapt along the ground; the whins cracked in their tortured writhings; hollow echoes of the wind beat with conflicting voice about my ears.

I was a man with an object. My uncle, with his mad ravings, was left behind; before me spread the goal of ambition—happiness, respite from memory, a calm life of painless ease. Little wonder that I hurried, without thought of the spreading passion of ocean and air, not heeding a hidden sense of warning, which stirred within and called my footsteps back.

Sheltered from the anger of the wind, behind the protective shield of a gaunt pine, appeared a figure. The mad strength of the elements gave me courage and perfect confidence. I shouted aloud, while a thousand tongues shrieked back reply. Then the figure resolved itself into a slim shape of beauty. A line of spray rose and shivered between that and my eyesight. I wiped it away and looked again. There was a face, flushed with a lovely red beneath the sting of the wind; parted lips, as the breath passed in short, quick gasps; eyes, moist and radiant, flashing an unspoken challenge of love up to mine.

We had met together at the appointed time. And this was the tiger! Where were those white claws? They were sheathed for me. The teeth, that he had feared, glittered, when the soft mouth bent into a smile of welcome for me. To him she had been the tiger, but to me she was the white dove of peace.

·   ·   ·   ·   ·   ·   ·   ·   ·   ·   ·   ·   ·   ·

'This is a glorious wind!' I cried. 'It is grand to battle against it, and feel yourself the winner.'

She had changed. She was not the half-cold, half-suspicious woman of yesterday, nor was she the proud, defiant being who had before spurned my affections. All that time she had held a mask to her face, and, for some secret plan of her own, had chosen to cloak the true feeling at her heart.

'I am glad we agree,' she said, with a light laugh; 'I, too, like the wind.'

She had never before looked upon me like this. Her face was glorious, with the rich stain of health mantling boldly upon her cheeks. Her eyes flashed upon me with alternate gleams of joy and love, yet with a soft moisture between the long eyelashes. I had seen her like this, and in that very spot. So she had stood at my brother's side, and glanced wonderfully up into his face. So she had spoken to him, with the delicate catch in her thrilling voice, with a lingering caress upon each sweetly-voiced syllable. Uninvited, she slipped her hand into my arm, like a bird fluttering home to its nest, while her wind-tossed skirts swept about my legs. I felt that arm shiver, and knew that it was caused by the ecstasy of love.

I felt the subtle fire of passion consuming me inwardly. I was drunk with my unutterable joy. I clasped her closer to my body, and held her, until I felt the warmth of her being passing and circling within my frame, while the storm swept above, and God spoke aloud from heaven. I had fought my fight with the hidden powers, and I had won—I had won! The entire reward of victory had fallen at my feet.

'Shall we go back a little?' My voice was wonderfully tender. It must have been, for she started, as though with surprise.

Then she looked into the green-tinted shelter of the wood, which was alive with strange sounds. 'Yes—it will be easier to hear. Besides, I'm afraid my hair is loosening.'

Suddenly there came a sonorous blast from the sea, a raging, snatching hand of tempest, which swept away the last clinging hindrance of the half-supported tresses. Down tumbled a black cloud of scented mist. Wildly it tossed, and enwrapped my face in its soft, enervating embrace. Only for the moment, while I pressed my hands upon the warm, wonderful fabric. It was maddening, intoxicating. The delicate odour permeated my entire being; the voluptuous waves curled over each feature, caressed my neck, blinded my eyes, and filled my gasping mouth. I caught it in my fingers; I kissed it; I bit it even, when I realised the full significance of love. Then the marvellous mist faded away with a last caress, and I could see the lovely face of its owner regarding me with a glorious smile.

'I told you so,' she said almost pettishly. 'You see, such long hair as mine is not always an advantage.'

It was surely with such clinging vesture of hair that the spirits of mythology appeared, to allure and conquer priests of old; it was with such golden cataracts of wonder that the silver-tongued Siren lured the hapless wanderer to his fate; with like glistening web of shimmering delight do the mermaids arise from the moonlit sea to sing their ever-old tale of love.

'It is by the vision of such hair,' I said, 'that warriors conquer those stronger than themselves.'

Her body nestled softly against mine; her hands struggled to capture a portion of that drifting mist.

'Let it remain,' I pleaded; 'it is lovelier so. See! it is sheltered here.'

Even as I spoke, that dark shadow of remorse, like the silent skeleton of the Egyptian feast, like the solemn voice of warning spoken into the ear of the Roman hero at his triumph, rose before me, with a double question upon its pallid lips. 'What have you done? What are you doing?' it muttered, then fled back into the wind with a dreadful laugh.

I conquered the weakness. I led her on, by a well-known path, for I wanted the satisfaction of feeling how complete was my triumph over the dead. Yet I could not restrain a cold shudder, when we came up the brow of the cliff, and I could see the dark tresses fighting in the wind.

I drew her along, as *he* had done; I led her to the whitethorn bush, where the curled brown blossoms had fallen and green berries were taking shape. I imagined a tortured figure, crouching in the dark shadow, biting his hands in the fury of frustration. Only it was my brother's body which lay there, while mine was in the place he had usurped.

Would she, who had professed to love the brother, consent to cast in her lot for life with his murderer?

She could not suspect what my hand had accomplished on that fearful night. Still I might question her.

The storm swept strongly round the wood, while the distant bell still throbbed with startled cry. But here it was almost peaceful, and her long hair only rippled gently against the hand which held her waist.

'I saw you,' I began, after a strange pause, 'with my uncle the other day.'

'Yes; I met him at the iron gate, and walked in with him. His strange talk amused me.'

'I thought you were afraid of him?'

'I was—once. You told me he is harmless; now I have come to see that for myself. After all, he is to be pitied, poor old man!'

'Your conversation must have been a strange one.'

'It was,' with a quick laugh. 'He is very fond of you.'

'What did he say about me?' I asked, with sudden fear.

'Nothing worth repeating.'

'But what questions did you ask him?'

Then she broke into open laughter. 'That is my concern,' she said archly.

So I had nothing to fear from her. My great secret had been

known only to the old nurse, who had carried it with her to the grave. I was still free, with the world open before me.

'Yes; she is dead,' I said, not knowing that I spoke aloud, until the wondering question came,—

'Who?'

'My old housekeeper. She died yesterday.'

The lovely face became sorrow clouded. 'I had heard nothing. I am very sorry. You will miss her greatly.'

I assented. 'She was old, and inclined to be foolish. It was her time to go.'

'No consolation can diminish the sadness of death,' she murmured, and for the moment I suspected there was some hidden meaning in those words.

'She went that room might be made for another,' I said, throwing the entire effort of my heart into the words. 'Her work was done.'

She looked at me fixedly. 'Yes,' she murmured.

'You know!' I cried. 'You know what I mean.'

Then her head went down.

The hollow clang of the lighthouse bell became appalling, while the grey surges shrieked upon the rocks.

'You know why I asked you to meet me here. You know I must ask you a question, which is to alter the lives of both.'

Her head was still down, but her bosom was heaving. She was greatly agitated at this portentous moment, while I remained calm.

'Tell me,' I cried, pressing her shapely form more closely to my body.

Then she glanced up, and I saw a wonderful light in her lustrous eyes. This melted into a smile, as she spoke in a tantalising whisper,—

'But—you haven't asked me any question yet.'

Then I remembered that women delight in tormenting the men they love with such pleasing fancies. So I laughed myself, and gathered her yielding body to me again.

I bathed my hot face in her cool, fragrant hair. 'Dearest,' I murmured, while a mocking voice made echo to my words. 'Sweet star of my soul—you know what my love for you is—'

She shivered again. How she loved me!

'I have loved, I could love, none as I worship you. You have always been before my life as a—'

I was astounded, for she broke in upon me with a strange voice, wherein lay the shadow of a sob, 'Let me finish—may I? From what you have said, I may conclude that you are about to ask me to be your wife. Am I right?'

I could no longer restrain myself. I bent over and kissed her passionately. She did not draw back, while I began to pour the vows of my eternal love upon her ear.

Again she interrupted me. 'You ask me to marry you. You are waiting for my answer?'

'Yes, dearest, loveliest of all—'

'*I will.*'

.   .   .   .   .   .   .   .   .   .   .   .   .   .   .   .   .

I bound her within my arms; I madly kissed the quivering mouth that my brother had once kissed, the eyes which had looked up into his, the ears which had listened to his treacherous words of love. But she drew herself softly away, and declared she must leave me.

I noticed that her face was white—she was tired. I felt that she shivered, as though with sickness—the excitement had been overmuch.

My arm holding and protecting her, with the heartfelt words of love still falling from my tongue, we came to where the cool wind lashed upon our faces, and the world seemed to break off into space at the edge of the cliff.

We stood together on a grass patch, where the fresh young blades of green shot strongly upward. But, even as I looked, the ground seemed to wave beneath my feet, and each sharp grass-tip became a small spear-point dipped in blood.

It was here that my brother and I had finally separated.

Unknowingly my footsteps had been led there by the inscrutable power of my overshadowing fate, that my happiness might be marred at the very moment of success.

I was free now—surely I could cast aside the fearful thought. I had mocked at all these hidden powers, but now I had strength to cast them aside, and claim my freedom. I had conquered my brother; I had won the fair woman at my side; now I had to struggle with the hidden sense of Memory.

The base of the cliff was tottering. Doubtless it was the hot glare of the departing sun that cast a fearful glow over the boiling waters, which marked a human grave.

Maddened by thought, I determined upon a frightful action. To utterly destroy the hateful foe, to defy it to its utmost, I would ask her again, though in that dreadful spot, to be my wife. I would drain my sweet cup of vengeance to the lees.

I spoke, yet I could not hear the mutterings of my own voice. I asked for her lifelong affection, though a hand of fire clutched at my heart, a white-hot iron writhed into my brain, lightning flashed from the lurid sky across my eyes, and voices laughed horribly round my head. The sun withered into a black mass of decay, as it sank into the water from the western clouds; snatching hands darted from the angry sea beneath; the waves rose and boiled hungrily up the side of the rugged cliff, higher, higher, until they seemed to clutch at my feet. The grass was wet and slippery. Once I glanced down to learn the cause, and found it red and sodden, like a field of battle. Then I was listening to a distinct voice close to my ear,—

'What is the matter? You seem to be speaking, but I can hear no sounds. What are you thinking about?'

My excited fancy made this voice appear vengeful and heartless. This was the tiger—but, no, my thoughts wandered. My uncle was mad. This was the woman who loved me, who was about to become my bride.

I shrieked aloud, for an ice-cold hand grasped my shoulder. I started round, with sweat dripping from my forehead, but there was nothing there, though two reproachful eyes seemed to float along down the wind.

Again came the hard voice, seeking an explanation of my strange conduct.

The blush had died away from her cheek; the lustre had faded from her eyes; there was no added elation in the graceful pose of her head. She stood a little apart from me—while the dead filled up the interval between. That ever-present memory touched me again with an icy finger. I saw the girl (who now stood near me gazing wistfully over the sea), with a wonderful light in her eyes, with a drooping grace of affection in every line of her body, with the complete abandonment of self to the protecting care of another. And I could see a tortured figure crouching beside the whitethorn bush.

This phantasm burnt out, when I reflected that all this would come for me in time. Complete love, I argued, may only be matured by the loving influence of another's heart. Everything in Nature must be trained and reared into affection. So the ivy must grow a certain length, before it may be brought to trail round the oak. Affection is born with none—it must be evolved and matured carefully, until it may be finally wound firmly round its life support. Yet it may not be forced aside from that inclination which it raises up for itself.

For the plant, which has been wantonly torn away from the pole it would reach, returns, or dies in the attempt; the creature, removed from its native element, strives to regain it, but upon failure—perishes; the human heart, bent by force of stronger will from its life-appointed path, merely suffers. But I have learnt that such suffering is greater than the actual pang of death.

Again I cast aside that whispering demon, and came across the slippery grass towards the woman I had won. Again I held her to my side, and when I spoke my voice was calm.

I bent over her. 'Promise me again—once more, that you will be my wife. Let me have the sweet answer from your lips again.'

She lifted her small head, with its glorious wealth of flowing hair, and looked fearlessly into my face. The two words thrilled forth—'I promise.'

So the sun went down on the fringe of the storm, and darkness came shivering up along the ground. I turned to embrace the woman I loved—whom I had won. But she was not there. I came nearer, and looked more fiercely, while a face was tilted upwards. But it was not hers. There was a figure near me, and one that I could recognise. But it was not hers. There were eyes gleaming out of the shadows. But—oh! maddening, persistent and pitiless memory—they were not, they could not be, hers. For they were cold, furious, vindictive.

And the lighthouse bell still tolled.

CHAPTER IV

MARRIED LIFE

Not poppy, nor mandragora,
Nor all the drowsy syrups of the world,
Shall ever medicine thee to that sweet sleep
Which thou ow'dst yesterday.
*Othello*, Act III. sc. 3.

Wednesday, 27th August.

THERE had been no delay in our marriage, which was celebrated
mournfully within the damp, moss-covered church down in the
valley. I understood that her guardians objected to the union, but
she was of age, and could act as she wished. Only a few villagers
and fishing folk clattered into the echoing edifice, and gaped at
the ceremony. My uncle stood beside me as best man, shivering,
clutching my arm, biting at his fingers, and muttering discordant
syllables of fear. The bride was in cold white, like a snow mantle,
and her face was whiter than the clinging dress.

The binding words had been uttered; the blessing, which
sounded like a curse, had melted into air; we turned to depart.
But, as we came from the chilly atmosphere of the crypt-like building, out beneath the rotting woodwork of the porch, my uncle's
madness rose. He hung to my left arm, until his shoulder shuddered against mine. 'Nephew,' he whispered hoarsely, 'come away.
Leave the tiger. There is time—still time.'

I frowned at him and told him to leave us, but he only clutched
at me the more. 'I know the tiger. She will kill you. She will suck
your blood. Come away, nephew.'

I felt a slight movement at my other arm. I looked. Curved
upon the blackness of my coat sleeve were claws, long, slim and
clutching, bending round their prey. Discordant bells clashed a
blatant revelry overhead. I was looking at the soft fingers of my
wife.

My uncle's fear redoubled. He broke away, and staggered through the rank grass, tumbling over splintered tombstones, and muttering fearfully.

I turned, and looked again upon the face of her whom I had won. She was smiling—yes, smiling, as she gazed at the crooked figure beyond. But there is a parable and a mystery under the smile of women. I realised for the first time how chilling is the influence of the smile, when the heart is bitter, and the mind is dead to happiness. She did not love—not then, for everything was strange. Yet she would. The linking of life to life must involuntarily create that passion, which is love. But—the thought occurred to me only after the final exchange of vows—does this joining together of two separate human bodies constitute also the blending of soul with soul—which is love, apart and distinct from the crude passion of the brute? Oh, my God! my God!

Flowers were cast upon us—red and yellow blossoms, that fell to the ground hopelessly, and shed their petals to the wind. Feet trampled upon them, and left their beauty mired and bleeding, until the path became compared, in my mind, to a purgatory of hopes broken eternally and hearts destroyed. The chime of the bells altered to a single, solemn knell.

We passed on, and met a funeral waiting at the lych gate. I saw the pall, and there were flowers there. The faces of the mourners were pale—as the countenance of my wife; doubtless their hearts were heavy—like mine.

We sat within the carriage, while the horses dragged us from the close atmosphere of the valley. In a moment of courage I grasped my wife's hand, and essayed to speak, but words were wanting. At length I exclaimed, with a cheerfulness most unreal, 'This is a bright morning for our wedding.'

'Yes,' she said, yet without turning. 'The sun is bright.'

Then our hands fell apart, and we spoke no more.

Only a few days—a period of inexpressible dread and bitter awakenings—sufficed to convict my heart of its life error. I knew then that my uncle had been in the right. Against my inclination, I was compelled to perceive that this frightful marriage had exaggerated my sufferings, instead of bringing alleviation, as I had so wildly hoped. I had introduced into my house a close watcher of my actions; one, moreover, who fell far short of the ideal that my mind had built up for itself; one, who moved silently, who spoke little, who yet watched me like a detective, noted each of my changing moods, analysed my feelings, deducted facts from my despondency, formed suspicions from any occasional unguarded phrase.

Yet she was my wife. I had bought her body. I had given her my name—the name indeed she had sought after. I had longed, with the full passion of heart and mind, to hold her in my arms, to embrace her slender figure with all caresses known to love, to kiss her lips, her hair, her neck, to whisper burning words of devotion into her ear, to warm my cold body with her blushes of affection. All this I had now a right to do. She had given me that right, yet I made no use of it. I did not come near her. Why? I could not; I dared not. I sought even to evade her; I shrank in dread at her approach.

. . . . . . . . . . . . . . . .

It was the evening of our wedding day. We sat together, yet apart; strangers, though husband and wife. The darkness came up, wrapped itself round the house, blotted out the shadows, and brought the night. My wife stirred, and with a sudden movement cast from the folds of her dress a bunch of white blossoms which had been my gift. At the other end of the room I sat, trembling like a man on his death morn, awaiting the executioner and the fatal toilet. Yet it was my wedding day.

The darkness conjured up shapes and scenes of horror. After many efforts I spoke. 'Shall we have light?'

The sounds ran in a ghostly troop of echoes round the room, and presently a distant voice replied, 'If you wish it. I am satisfied with the darkness.'

'It is growing late,' I said.

She caught at the opportunity. 'I am tired.' Then she rose, and came across the room, like the spirit of my lost life.

The grey folds of her dress flickered across my knee. This subtle contact drove away my fear. I sprang up and caught her in my arms, when she would have passed.

'You are my wife,' I cried exultantly. 'Let the world say what it

will, we are man and wife now, and may not be separated.' Then
I laughed wildly in the pride of possession, laughed loudly, until
her eyes closed, as though she would hide from them some object
terrifying or repulsive.

'Yes,' she said at length, with a strange quiver of the lips.

'We shall be happy together, you and I, shall we not?'

'We cannot foretell the future. Perhaps we shall.'

The flame of my sudden passion burnt down. She tried to draw
herself away.

'One more thing,' I said. 'You love me—your husband?'

She opened her eyes. They were large and luminous in the
darkness, and their gaze pierced me. 'Did I say so?'

'You told me. You swore it at the church. You gave me the
promise in the pine wood.'

'You asked me to be your wife. I consented. You forgot to ask
the one thing—whether I loved you.'

'You do. You would not have taken my name, unless—'

'I had loved your name. You are right.'

Then she laughed as I had done; but when I heard the sound of
the laugh, that in the morning had been a smile, the room seemed
to me cold and bare.

For over an hour of weariness I paced up and down. Then I
remembered that I was married, that my bride awaited me. So I
came along the passage, where the thick, yellow light dropped like
a tangible presence, and stood at the silent door. Within was light,
warmth—and love; outside was gloom, despair—with fear. And
fear is almost synonymous with hatred. But my wife was awaiting me within that chamber, and her, at least, I loved. So had my
brother, fiercely, bitterly; but his love had led him to his death.

My hand dropped from the door handle, while I shivered. I
should enter that room, and, as custom ordained, should rest with
her whom I had won. While I slept, she might lie awake, and watch
my insensible figure with those piercing eyes. In sleep my tongue
might be released. I might speak of things I had done in the past,
of frightful fears I entertained for the future, while she would lie
awake, and listen—and understand.

Again my hand went to the door, again it came back with
the sweat upon it, for my uncle's wild words intervened—'The

tiger. . . . Her oaths of vengeance. . . . She will drink your blood. . . . Does the tiger know?'

Was this some frightful snare? I should lie at her side. Would she, during the still night, put some fearful plan for my immolation into execution? Would she, under the seal of love, draw away the life from my body? Was love to ruin me, even as it had ruined another?

Shadows came up the passage at the thought, and hung round the door. I fled, with a cry of fear, a cry of pain. I had fought, but I had lost, and my brother had won. I could not enter that awful bridal chamber, and face the ordeal. For he was there. He lay in my place in the form of Shadow. I was still his slave. My wife was his. The vengeance of the Shadow was settling upon me.

So in the morning we sat together, as strangers almost, while she asked for no explanation, and I offered none. Too well I knew that it was not needed. By my action I had made a fearful and silent confession. Both of us understood, but neither dared to speak.

During the following days suspicion grew on one side and fear on the other, until, when we sat together, we would look anywhere, towards any object, rather than at each other. Our words became fewer, more strained; our short walks less frequent. We finally took even our meals apart, though we met perhaps in the drawing-room during the evening for a short time, when I generally took care that my uncle should be with me, or in the garden at the middle of the day, when she might be gathering flowers. Even so, each quickly found the presence of the other a burden, and hastened to escape on the first opportunity. And this was the woman whom I had so madly loved!

It is true that, during the earlier days of married life, we held the masks of self-deceit before our respective minds, until Nature snatched them away with fiendish glee. During that first week we talked together—though even then she did little but feign to listen. We drove along still roads, where constant rattlings of wheels afforded excuse for silence. We sat together in the evenings, and sometimes she played to me soft, wailing melodies that touched some secret chord in my heart, and drove me well-nigh to distraction. But in all this we never laughed, nor even smiled, nor did any light phrase pass between us. Often did we sit down to a meal, and rise at the end without having uttered a word or exchanged a look. Yet these were to have been the happiest days of my life!

. . . . . . . . . . . . . . . . .

One evening—and this was shortly after returning to my home by the sea and the wild moor—we were alone together, and I proposed a game of chess. This was a game I had been fond of once, having during the long winter nights frequently fought out with my brother the burlesque of a human life-passion upon the chequered board. She consented, and we sat down silently at the table. She drew the white, and opened by playing out her queen's pawn to the fourth square.

I put out my hand, but it shook over the board. Her head was bent, and so low that my eyes fell upon the gleaming nape of her neck with the thick coils of hair above. She never looked up, but I could hear her quick breathing, while her head went still lower, as though she would have kissed the inanimate object that she had just touched. Why had she done this? Why had she played that opening known as the Queen's Gambit?[1]

My God, as I looked upon the silent piece it seemed to swell to the size of a man; the ivory turned to human flesh; the face took form, and turned towards me with livid lips and sealed eyes. It was my brother, and the white queen stood behind.

My hand fell down of its own action upon the king's pawn. I cast aside the whole theory of the game, in my madness, my fury at this haunting shadow, my one desperate desire to free my soul from its avenging hold.

'Why did you play that?' Her head was still down; her voice was very low, but firm.

Speech came readily in my then mood. 'It is not the game, you think? I tell you it is. I assure you that it is a good move—a very good move. I know, for I have worked it out—carefully, thoroughly, often at night, and I have found it sound. It is a good reply to your opening. You shall see that it is. I shall beat you. Yes, I shall beat you in the end.'

She shivered, for in the fever of my rising excitement I had allowed these words to express my innermost thoughts.

---

1 This is the name for a line of opening moves in chess, allowing the sacrifice of a pawn to set up a later advantage.

'I do not think that it is good,' she said, and I longed to see her face. 'But we shall see.' Then she replied to my move.

She moved her queen's bishop pawn to the side of the one that was my brother.

'You have not taken my pawn,' I almost shouted. 'You have let it go. You shall not have another chance.'

Then she looked up. 'Are you going to take mine?'

The sight of her face made me mad, for it was white and full of hatred. It reminded me of her victory over my desires; of my brother's triumph in his sea grave; of their love for each other; of my impending fate. And it recalled to me my own blasted life.

The red pawn that was myself seemed to bend forward and leer at me. It looked a horrible, a monstrous thing, as it reeled upon its black square. My fingers worked towards it, but missed their aim. My hand fell with a heavy rattling among the pieces. Then the grim horror of the situation came over me, and I burst into ghastly cries of merriment.

'I must take it,' I cried, rocking my body backwards and forwards. 'This is the game of human life, in which the one strives to get the better of another. I know, for I have played it often. I must take the pawn prisoner—prisoners are killed sometimes, are they not? Killed, you understand, not murdered. We have criminals who are executed, but that is because they have done wrong. They deserve their fate. But it is not murder. No—it is justice—justice.'

She had drawn her chair away, and now stood upright, tall and calm. I had no fear of her now, for I was drunk and besotted with this horrible rehearsal of my life's tragedy.

I bent gloatingly over the board, like a miser at his money chest. Her voice came dimly to me from a great distance. 'I think we had better not continue this game.' But I only laughed and shouted the more, for I had something there that strangely suited me.

'You see them standing together? The red pawn is going to take the white one prisoner—he will punish him perhaps. See? Ah! I have him. I shall put him from the board, and lay him aside, where he will soon be forgotten. Ha! ha! The white pawn is vanquished. Now I will take the other—my pawn. I will set him in the place of the white one. Do you see? Can you understand all this?'

But there was no strength in my hand to raise that deep-red

image, for I dreaded lest the ivory should become hot flesh to my touch, lest the entire figure should palpitate with passion in my grasp.

'Look!' and my voice rose to a scream. 'You see the pawn with the red running down all over him? That deep, dark, horrible red. Do you know it? Do you see what it is?'

She made away from me, towards the door, while I rose staggering to my feet.

'I tell you, it is blood. It is strong human blood, that once had passion in it; but now it has been spilt so long that it is caked and dry.'

I stared round, screaming in my mirth, but I was alone. I dashed over the table and destroyed it. I leapt upon the ivory pieces, and shivered each one to fragments.

I sprang from the window, and rushed out upon the moor, where rocks and dead trees stood ghastly in the moonlight, and sullen waters heaved with mysteries of the night.

And at that time I was lusting, with all the fury of the most furious of beasts, for someone to kill, someone to stab or strangle—whether man or woman.

.   .   .   .   .   .   .   .   .   .   .   .   .   .   .   .

After this, the cold barrier of hatred grew between us stronger, more impassable. We shunned each other, and sedulously avoided spots where it was likely, or even possible, that a meeting might take place. In the house sometimes, we would enter the same passage from opposite ends. Here a crossing was inevitable, but on such occasions we would each speed past, close beneath the friendly shelter of the wall, with eyes fixed sternly ahead, as though each were an incorporeal spirit invisible to the other. Wandering aimlessly in the gardens, we would now and again almost collide in some secluded spot. After much confused speech and embarrassment of manner, we would retreat behind the protection of some clump of bush. Sometimes she would preserve silence; at other times she would murmur a few words, or I might by chance stammer forth meaningless apologies; perhaps again our eyes might actually meet for the second, each blasting the vision of the other. Then we would part, in a manner strangely dissimilar to the cold precise steps which had brought us involuntarily together. So she kept on her way, while I kept to mine.

On my part it was a restless dread, that held me upon the hot thorns of anxiety, lest some incautiousness should reveal my damning secret. She, in her physical weakness, was so far superior to me in mental ability, that I had no hope of being able to successfully cope with her. Her feminine peculiarities, the catlike tread, the calm, almost wearied, manner in which she moved and spoke, the sudden penetrating glance from beneath long lashes, the cold, inscrutable bearing—all these were suggestive of deep-rooted suspicion, a secret probing of my mind, a subtle searching for some opportunity to trip me up in an unwary moment. Such conduct inspired me with an ever-present terror.

I had thought to marry the pure, high-minded woman, who would bring balm to my ever-open wound of conscience. But what had I obtained, in place of the loved brother of my youth, and the fond, faithful nurse? A woman indeed, yet one invested with all the sleek cunning and latent ferocity of the tiger.

Tuesday, 19th August.

I hurried across the moor, returning to my silent house and the heavy memories it contained. It was an evening of weird colouring, in which every object brought to my mind some resemblance, some undefined shape of the fantastic. I was alone, fearfully alone, in a solitude that was greatly intensified by the frightful shadow that haunted my footsteps. Often I would start round, with hands upraised to repel an expected blow. I would turn with an agonised cry for mercy. I would grope blindly towards the horrible essence of the unseen, and pray it to depart. Still, there was nothing behind me—nothing, save all the concentrated horrors of hell and crime combined.

A sombre gloom pierced through the shivering haze of colours. Everything was motionless, peaceful, yet with the gloom of the tomb, the statuesque quietness of eternal death. The black trees, blasted and bent into frightful shapes, stood as emblems of tortured souls; the rank grass, with bleached heads hanging droopingly, represented life in its nakedness, stripped of its smallest pleasure; the black mirror of the lake, with its noxious miasma of bursting gas bubbles and fetid herbs, spread before me as a symbol of the unknown that confronts the soul beyond death, and the continual horror of that same phantom over life. The gaunt rocks were tombstones, that sealed down the crumbling bones of a forgotten past.

As I came onward, it seemed to me that all shadows separated themselves from the solid cause of their origin, then sped in riotous revelry from spot to spot, between the wood of pines and the sun balancing on the horizon. I watched my own. For a time this amorphous, this dark, devil of my body sprang around me, pointing and gibing with horrid mirth. Then it dashed away, over narrow hillocks and the grass ridges that looked like human graves, to finally plunge with wild motions into the dark waters beyond. Here it vanished, without ripple or sign, while weird laughter uprose and fled in echoes from rock to rock.

I sped from this haunted waste, nor did I pause in my flight, until I came upon the terrace that lay along the back of the house. But here I stopped with suddenness, for I met my wife face to face. In her hand she held a basket, which was overflowing with fragrant herbs.

'You here!' I exclaimed. And then, 'Where is my uncle?'

My eyes were upon the lichened walls; her gaze was fixed towards the wild and wonderful cloud-rack that sped and broke across the west.

'Your uncle?' she repeated, in the monotonous voice I had grown to hate. 'He is in the blue room, I think.'

Even as she spoke, screams of fear, with loud oaths of fury, burst from the house. I knew then that he was engaged in fighting with the horrible creatures with which he was so frequently surrounded by madness and his imagination. I was left entirely alone with my wife.

'I have been for my evening walk,' I said. 'As you perceive, I was hurrying back, for it was growing dark.'

She looked upon my dirt-marked clothes, and the cuts upon my hands where I had stumbled against the rocks. She said nothing, but began to more securely arrange the herbs in her basket.

'Have you wormwood there?' I asked sharply.

'No—I have no wormwood,' she replied. 'But here is rosemary.'
'Rosemary! Once I heard a quotation.'[1]
'For remembrance.' She lifted the green bunch to her lips, and I think she groaned.

Memory again. The frightful spectre that accompanied me always, and refused me rest.

'What is that?' I asked boldly, touching a crinkled leaf.
'That? It is balm,' she said.

I tore the sprig from the basket and drank in its sickly odour, but its charm was not for me. There was no drug, no creation of nature, no invention of science—nor could there be—of sufficient potency to lift from my mind even an infinitesimal portion of its burden. I, also, groaned at the foolishness, the futility, of hope.

She made as though she would leave me, but, in the very act of motion, stopped, and looked with fearful eyes into the mysteries of the sky. I turned also towards the west, when I beheld her lips part in a half sigh of amazement. The tragic picture of the heaven was portentous and charged with mystic intensity.

The sun had long gone, while the last colour had been erased by the black fingers of the inscrutable night. Far above the horizon spread a mountain wilderness of dark purple cloud crags, ragged, and fringed with a luminous glow of faint blue. Beneath lay a long, heaving line of sulphur-coloured light that leapt and flickered in lambent waves. Above spread many forms of greenish-grey matter, passing, as it were, over the dark mountains of despair towards the boundary line of doubt and sensibility. This was—what?

I stared and strained my eyes, but on either side the heavens were black—hung with the dark veil that cuts body apart from soul—and frowning.

As I knew not from what bourne of sorrow these cloud images had set forth, so I was unable to learn on what dark shore of despair they were destined to touch and rest—or not to rest.

For a moment my wife had drawn close to me unthinkingly. Then she remembered who I was, and again dropped back. But there was wonder upon her face, and there was fear.

'It is like death.' Her lips parted, then closed, with a shudder along the voice.

---

1 Shakespeare, *The Winter's Tale*, 4.4.74-76.

'No—it is the hereafter,' I broke forth violently. 'Our souls do not moulder, nor do they foster the undying worm. They wander forth into the air, of which they become part. They watch the deeds of mortals, and mock the passions which once ruined them, to which they are dead.'

'It is death,' she repeated. 'See the strange figures that pass along and vanish behind the dark cloud mass. They are never seen again. They are lost for ever.'

'There are mysteries beneath and above,' I whispered in my fear. 'They lie beneath the water and writhe above the clouds. The body is bound down to crawl along the earth, but the soul may follow these mysteries, may pursue—'

'May search,' she cried, and there was passion as well as hopelessness in her low tones. 'Souls are immortal. One may follow another, that has gone before, and search—search for eternity, but never find. For space and time are both beyond calculation and appointment.'

She spoke on strange things, but I scarce listened, for I had something to engage my closest attention. There was a procession of corpses passing overhead, above the purple crags. They were clad scantily in fantastic cloud garb, while their flesh and faces were still livid with the paralysing touch of the destroyer. One by one they drifted to the rugged line and plunged into the invisible. These were all beyond the craft of priests, or dim, religious ceremony of the Church. Each had been convicted, sentenced, and was now being hurried to its perpetual and particular prison pit.

Even then the sullen fire broke forth in the centre of that black veil behind which they were passing, while the deep note of wrath shuddered and beat through the throbbing air. The aerial mountains began to shift and clash together, while great tears of rain dropped and hissed upon my fevered countenance.

My wife had left me—it was the last time that we spoke together beneath a semblance of friendship. I watched her spirit-like form gliding through the darkness, and saw the sudden burst of light as she opened the door, then I turned again to the western picture.

There was still a plain of sulphur-tinted light, and yet one more corpse to pass across. It came along slowly, while a tinge of red shot across the yellow and entered my eyes. The vision paused and waited for another to come up. Then the purple veil fell, and smothered them up, while the whole sky grew overcast and ominous.

The first figure was that of a murdered man, while the second was like unto the first.

One was my brother. The other was—

The incarnation was coming, and soon. Pitiful and unerring God, it was coming, and quickly.

Within the house I found my uncle mad, while a servant told me that my wife had fainted, and was still unconscious.

.   .   .   .   .   .   .   .   .   .   .   .   .   .   .

A month elapsed with its gigantic periods of light and darkness. Then came the time when the hushed sound of my wife's footfall, or the light rustling of her dress, made me shudder and drive the nails into my hands; when the mere sound of her voice addressing some servant caused me to shrink back into a corner with fingers pressed against my ears. I knew that the storm must break, yet, with the explicable weakness of humanity, I postponed the inevitable as long as possible, blenching from the explanation of my conduct towards her, dreading to listen to her questions, each one of which would fall like a hot knife into my soul. Only one single, one agonised, prayer fell from my lips a thousand times in the course of each infinite day,—

O my brother—you are surely avenged. Rest now; for the love I bore you, rest, and leave me.

## CHAPTER V

## THE COMING OF SETH

And God said, Let the earth bring forth the living
creature. . . . And it was so.—GENESIS i. 24.

Friday, 5th September.

FOR some days there had been a great calm in the atmosphere. In
early morning I would walk out, when the dew pearls still hung
and glistened, to find the silence complete and stifling. Later, when
the day rose to strength, and shook off its sleep garments, the sea
surface spread like a smooth plain of oil beneath the hot sunlight.
Not a breath of air disturbed the feathered branches of the trees;
the flower heads stood erect and motionless; gossamer-like seeds
fell to the grass and found no wind to raise them into the overhead currents; the tall grass stems remained fixed in set pose. Thus
it would continue all day, while at night I would venture forth,
and gaze upon a deep blue sky, cloudless, and covered with innu-
merable spiculated eyes of splendour, that regarded coldly a dark,
dreary landscape over which brooded, like some mighty genius of
repose, the illimitable silence.

'Is it peace?' the sky vault would then address the earth; while
the earth would reply, 'It is peace.'

My spirit refused to be bound down within the house. Even
the mysterious night beat upon my body, and well-nigh choked
each sense with its peculiar oppression; while the startled throbbing of my heart, more, even the hot bubbling of my blood along
each particular vein, raised of themselves a sufficient clangour to
disturb this unnatural sleep of Nature.

Day after day this stagnation in earth and sky endured, until
six of those mighty periods, known to some by the name of night
and day respectively, had passed away. On the seventh came the
change.

The day came in with rain and a close mist. I did not leave my bed until past noon, then quickly made my way to the blue room, that one place which my wife never entered. I wished to reflect upon this woman, and upon her actions. By this time I hated her, even as I had once loved my brother. I desired to consider how I might best free myself from her malignant presence. There was still the cliff path, with the hungry, rock-lined sea beneath. Could I persuade her but to walk along that way again, to stand once more upon the spot where my brother and I had each made confession of our love, then I might perhaps return free and alone, while she might seek, with the soul, him whom she had loved when in the body. I had thought out such a plan deliberately, with the cold precise acumen that belongs only to the completely sane, and my reasoning showed me that peace to my mind, security to my body, lay only along that road.

In the blue room I came upon my uncle, busy, as was his wont, on some strange experiment.

'Ha, ha! nephew,' he chuckled, when he noted my presence within the livid light. 'We don't meet so often now. You have to be busy with your wife—I know. But we are good friends, nephew. Ho! ho! Good friends. There is a mixture for you on the table. A fine mixture. Drink it, nephew.'

I lifted the glass he pointed out, and drank a small portion of its contents.

It changed my brain into flames, and my blood into streams of molten lead. My eyes started, while strange phantasmagorical figures leapt forth upon the sombre wall-hangings, vile reptiles that twisted in slimy coils, and spun round on an ever-increasing circle.

'Ha! ha! You see them?' The wizened form of my uncle darted from side to side, while the room became filled with hissings and alive with diabolical motion. 'You see them, nephew? Are there any toads? They squat, and they look at you with red eyes, but they don't move. Drink some more of the mixture, nephew. Then you will see the toads. Ha! ha!'

The spinning motion ceased. My head seemed to return to me and settle back slowly upon my shoulders. The furious heat within cooled gradually, while the noisome creatures disappeared. I became again a rational creature, and sought to learn the nature of my uncle's occupation.

There were many glasses and vessels of all kinds in front of him, while around lay great clusters of choice flowers that had recently been torn from their parent stems.

'What are you doing with the flowers?' I asked.

'I found a book in your library, and I began to read. Ho! ho! It said that flowers were living creatures, and fed like men. I thought I would try them, so I made up some mixtures. I went out for the flowers. Ho! ho! There was a man, and he wouldn't let me touch them. I hit him on the head with a spade. Then I hit him again, and he lay quiet. Ho! ho! I took the flowers.'

'What are you doing with them?' I asked again.

'Take care, nephew, take care. There may be spiders there.'

I fell back in horror, while he went on,—

'I am trying the flowers with these mixtures. See! These have not been in long, and they are already falling about. Ha! ha! They are like us, nephew. Those have been in for some time, and they are quite drunk. Do you see, nephew? They can't stand up. Flowers are like men. Ho! ho! The book was right. I am going out for some more, nephew.'

'Stay, uncle,' I cried, catching at him. 'I have something to ask you. Have you seen my wife?'

He stopped, and blinked up at me. Then we sat down together in the blue light.

'You have lost her? We will go and look for her together. Perhaps she is along the cliff path. Ha! ha! I don't see you there when I take my walks. You don't come out to the pine wood now.'

'I have not seen her for a long time. Listen! I hate her, uncle.'

His wrinkled face grew smaller and more strange. 'I told you, nephew. I told you to come away from the tiger. You hate her, nephew. Ha! ha! That is very good. And she hates you.'

I seized his bone-like knee. 'How do you know?' I asked wildly.

'I see many things. I am not so mad as they say. Once I liked her, too, for she came up and talked to the old man; but now I see it, nephew. She asked me about you. She thought I was mad, that I would not remember what she said, but I remember many things. Ha! ha! She knows about the other one, nephew.'

It never occurred to me to ask how much he knew. I could think only of her.

'Uncle,' I shouted, 'why did she marry me?'

He doubled together and laughed, laughed, laughed. The horrid infection seized upon me, until I bent with him and screamed in frightful mirth.

'Ha—ha! Nephew, I am an old man. I have seen many good jests, but this is the best. I am not so mad that I cannot see such things. She wants to kill you, nephew. I heard her oaths of vengeance. I saw her on the cliff, when you were a lover. She is going to suck away your life. That is why she married you.'

He leapt up and dragged me away with him. 'Come, nephew, we'll go and look for her. I'll take my big stick, and if we find her I will hit her, like I hit the black dog, nephew. Ha! ha! We'll have great sport together, you and I. Come into the pine wood now.'

So we came out on the mist-veiled cliff, where the damp whins were overhung with gossamer, and the heather was grey with rain slime. But we returned without having sighted any figure that was familiar, while my uncle left me in the garden, and returned to his pastime within the house.

I walked along the crumbling paths, between lines of moist bushes, until close upon evening. Here there was certainly nothing to attract, yet in the house there was much to repel. By reason of some occult presentiment, I dreaded entering and entombing my body behind the black walls that frowned upon me, as I came within their shadow, with such entirely living malice. I shrank, indeed, from my own ancestral mansion, with the same vague feeling of terror that impels the traveller by night to turn aside from the route which would take him through some ancient graveyard, or which causes the wayfarer to prefer a cold bed upon the grass to the comparative shelter of some lonely ruin of ill repute. I repeat, I dreaded making an entry to the house where I had been born, where generations of my ancestors had lived, sinned, and breathed their farewell to life and passion. There was no other sense of definite alarm, no separate aversion or repugnance of any clearly stated object. I simply shrank from the black mass of masonry, as from the horror of a silent sepulchre, where I was convinced that my bones would be placed in due course to their decay.

Still, this was weakness, this merely human fear of a vague

possibility, so I came forward to the steps, while the mist behind broke, and a wind sighed upward from the sea with a low utterance of distress. I opened the door, and gazed within at the semi-darkness, while the strange, oppressive odour of old woodwork hung heavily upon my nostrils, suggesting, as indeed it had done before, some gloomy vault, with its marble slabs, its leaden coffins, and the grisly burdens these contained.

Even as I stepped across the threshold a cold wave of fear wrapped itself round each sense. It seemed to me that somebody, with whom I was, or once had been, most intimately acquainted, yet who was then disguised under a strange and terrible form, somebody, moreover, who had been given dire cause to hate me, and who was even then searching for some opportunity of wrecking my life, had passed in ahead, and was climbing the flight of stairs that lay directly in front. So completely had I fallen a victim to my own frenzied imagination, that I was barely able to distinguish false from real, and this impression, this supposition, was so evidently, so unmistakably, false. Yet surely the flickering and watery sunlight cast a strange shadow upon the wainscoting—the shadow of a being with searching feelers and reaching tentacles of an octopus-like hideousness. Most assuredly a presence had recently withdrawn itself in subtle manner, like the dying away of a distant echo. At what point had it disappeared, and where had it departed? Also, why was it that I could most clearly feel the irresistible and paralysing magnetism that drew me onward and forward continually along its wake?

Outside, the wind was growing in strength, but here there was no sound, no motion. The servants were either out, or collected beneath in their hall. Where my wife was I could not tell, and had little wish to know. I had not set eyes upon her for a long time, not indeed since the commencement of the strange atmospheric calm, which was now being broken and dispelled. This seemed to me to be ages ago.

She must be an old woman now, I thought wildly. Toothless probably, deformed with age, and face lined with wrinkles in place of beauty; bent, without a trace of her former lithe grace, the light gone from her eyes, and the spring from her footstep; she would be faded and worn. But then my glance fell upon the hand which I had just rested upon the balustrade, and I started with a violent surprise. For certainly it should have been shrivelled and dried up by age; the destroying years should have sucked all strength out of its muscles. Yet I noticed that it was still rounded, still perfect, of good shape and colour. Then I recollected again that for me the flight of time had been stayed. I was a young man, with my life before me.

Up the wide stairs I proceeded, and along the passage, until I came to the door of the room where I was accustomed to spend the greater part of my time. In deference to my peculiar order the walls of this apartment had been whitewashed, but not covered over with paper; the carpet was also colourless. When the nature of my overwhelming nervous affliction has been considered, the reason for this fancy becomes at once apparent. Beneath a strong light I could always perceive at a glance the bodies of any frightful insects that might be crawling along floor or walls. I could see them at a distance, while I had still opportunity to withdraw into safety, for, as I have explained, the mere touch of an insect's leg upon my skin was of itself sufficient to render me insensible.

I pushed back the door with firm hand, and entered the apartment.

Let a man come innocently within a room, which has been heavily charged with a poisonous gas. As he makes a first inward step, the evil blast strikes him full upon the face, gradually stupefies the nerves, and finally conquers the body. Yet he sees nothing, he feels no resistance of a solid presence, there is apparently nothing to hinder him from escaping. For all that, the invisible bar of poison stretches between himself and liberty. He may not to able to cross it. He may struggle, fall and succumb—a mass of soul-charged matter overpowered by impalpable vapour. Let the odour be slight, the effect of poison weak, then the natural feeling of repugnance would probably be vanquished by a stronger sense of curiosity, and he would seek to make investigation.

Some such subtle power fearfully attracted and held me the instant I breathed the atmosphere of that room. I was drawn in, not out of morbid curiosity, but by a hand irresistible. A breath of air passed behind me and closed the door, while I stood a prisoner—to what? To my own fancies, my vivid, tortured imagination, or what other conspicuous image of my fear?

I seated myself in the centre of the room, and drew from my pocket the small black book, which now I always carried for a certain sense of protection it was said to afford. It opened at the first pages, where the leaves had been worn and thumbed, while I began to read:—

'And the Lord said unto Cain, Why art thou wroth? and why is thy countenance fallen? If thou doest well, shalt thou not be accepted? and if thou doest not well, sin coucheth at the door; and unto thee shall be his desire, and thou shalt rule over him!

The atmosphere grew more suffocating. I rose and forced open the window. My head was on fire; my brain writhed like a fiery serpent. This was merely the effect of the fearful compound my uncle had given me to drink.

'And the Lord said unto Cain, Where is Abel thy brother? And he said, I know not; am I my brothers keeper? And He said, What hast thou done? the voice of thy brother's blood crieth unto Me from the ground. And now cursed art thou from the ground which hath opened her mouth to receive thy brother's blood from thy hand!

I groaned fearfully, while cold sweat burst out upon my body. The mist was pouring in at the window, or was it shadow, and not mist? The wind was still rising, for moans came frequently from the house angles, while the tree branches began to rise and fall. The raw light gleamed fitfully upon the white walls of the room. Again I turned my eyes down to the threatening text.

'And Adam knew his wife again; and she bare a son, and called his name Seth.'

I shrieked as the word burnt into my brain, and burst there like a shell. I cowered back into the chair, my whole body quivering and wringing with the agony. Seth! The shadow; the avenger. Oh, Memory! Oh, Remorse!

I stared wildly, before, around, yet, with joy inexpressible, perceived that I occupied the apartment alone. There was none other, and yet what was there? Something—the essence, that had passed up before me, that had drawn me along by a fateful magnetism, that hung around in the shape of foul air. That was present, but where? Only in the form of a mocking spirit, or as a probing finger of reproach? No; that it had been for long. It was time for the change, time for the fate, time for the end.

It had come, but I could not, I dared not, I had not strength again to look up.

'Avenging God!' I gasped, in the choking accents of death—Cain had spoken to God, so why not I?—'blast me now with lightning, pulverise my frame to that dust from whence it came, consign my body to the worm, and hurl my soul to hell—but, spare me, spare me, this last horror! Shield me from the punishment of the Shadow.'

There was no reply, save only the vague mutterings of the elements, and the sobbing of the sea. My body shrank together still more, into a shrivelled husk of terror. I became the minutest atom fixed in a limitless space, yet a living, breathing atom, which might suffer, which could understand, which must see.

By that superhuman effort, which enables the criminal to walk with upright step from his cell to the scaffold, I raised my head with a sudden convulsive movement. My gaze fell directly upon a mirror that hung from the opposite wall. Here I beheld delineated the shocking countenance of a fiend, who sat grinning towards me in agony. A more hideous face surely had never passed into life from Nature's mould, for the features were pinched and diabolic, the lips a twisted blue line, the mad eyes were filled with blood. But presently I understood that I was gazing upon myself.

My weakening reason told me that I was beyond all doubt environed by some presence. I felt instinctively, by that same perception which had drawn me so far along a fearful and painful path of inference, that this object was visible, that my eyes must soon fall upon it, that it would be a spectacle of most terrifying form. Yet, with all this occult knowledge burning within me, I sat motionless, drawn together in a contracted mass of agony, never daring to turn my head from the mirror towards the white walls on the left and on the right.

There were beings all around me: they stood between me and the door; they cut me off from the window; they lined the walls, their hellish blackness contrasting fearfully with the whiteness behind and around them. Each bore a different bestial shape, yet in each the controlling soul was the same; each was the stirring representative, or rather the attendant satellite, of that agonising memory, which had lived within me since my brother's death; to each was given life, hatred, and power of motion, by the eternal spirit of that very brother, who had now returned to furiously avenge his unnatural death. Each was a child of that Shadow which Crime had made.

This conviction seared my brain, as I crouched within the failing light. At length I turned my head slowly towards the right wall, which was gleaming in the full glare of its whiteness, turned and gazed, while my hair went white and hard with the motion, my body shrank up to a dry husk of grovelling agony, the blood froze and settled in my veins, animation and reason ceased to be, as I lay almost a corpse, galvanised only by one feeble spark of the electric power of life.

I would have shrieked aloud, but the faculty of voice had left me. I would have shut the lids upon my burning eyesight, but the muscles no longer owned me as their master. I would have fled, but all strength had been snatched away. I would gladly have sunk, a crushed heap of quivering flesh, upon the floor; I would have hidden my head and waited for the doom, but I was held by that inconceivable, overmastering terror, rigid—immovable—hopeless.

A huge scar of incredible blackness rested upon the shining wall. It was gazing fixedly at my quivering body with red eyes of most malignant hatred. So still was it, that it might have been sculptured from black marble, only that no human hand could have moulded such an unspeakable form, or have devised such a shape in the coolness of the brain.

The anguish and the horror of my fate burst upon me in a mighty and overwhelming flood. Clearly I saw the death which had been prepared for me by the ingenuity of an overshadowing destiny. Here was that awful creature, which for a long time I had known must assuredly be born, and placed upon the circle of the world. Here it stood in flesh and blood, invested with a human soul—that soul which I had cast forth to wander through space. Here were my hitherto invisible torments amalgamated, and endowed with a living personality, a breathing individuality. And the form of it. Was that well chosen? Was it of a shape likely to inspire me with any extremity of dread? Would the mere touch of a portion of its frightful body drive me beyond the border line into grievous madness? Surely my brother himself had prayed that his soul might return encased within this unspeakable, this hideous, tabernacle.

The object upon the wall was a spider—monstrous in size, and of a most incomparable blackness.

CHAPTER VI

THE STIRRING OF SETH

Take any shape but that, and my firm nerves
Shall never tremble. . . . Hence, horrible shadow!
*Macbeth*, Act III. sc. 4.

6.30 p.m.

YET the colouring of that vile body was not altogether black. Two marks, two thin bars of an intense whiteness, passed respectively along its length and width, marking out upon the ebon background a sign, the symbol borne by the most hideous of Nature's creations, the startling configuration of a silver-hued cross. Around this sign spread the utterly vile blackness of the still viler monster.

I cannot tell how the minutes passed in that dreadful silence, which remained so ominously unbroken, until at length I found a flickering strength ebbing back to my body, a single dull flame of physical and mental energy, that gave me power to reason with an abnormally clear grasp. It was a part of the carefully elaborated plan for my punishment that I should not be deprived of mental consciousness, that the bonds of extreme terror should be slackened and loosened gradually. I was destined to suffer, so the anæsthetic of insensibility was to be denied.

Why did I not rise in this new found strength, and flee from that haunted room? For many reasons, the chief of which rests upon the fact, that strength is not necessarily courage. I dared not turn my eyes aside for a moment. Inconceivable as it must appear, the idea of flight never at that period occurred to me. My mind was so completely overflowing with terror that it had not space to contain any other leading thought, not even the great and natural one of self-preservation. And what benefit could finally accrue to me from flight? I could rush from house to garden, then back again; from room to room; but where would the shelter be? Almost better was it to stand silently in the presence of this enormity, than to feel it was waiting for my return. On re-entering the house, it might crawl upon me, and seize my body unawares; it might even follow and track me from place to place, with horrid motions of its gruesome form. Here I could locate it definitely—the possibility of its being hidden away for a time was frightful, for when and where would it reappear, in what awful manner would it emerge again from its invisible origin?

The approaching night, with its tangible darkness! Here at least the light was strong, though becoming obscured by a gradual opaqueness, yet its whiteness must be finally blotted out, and then—the shadows would creep up, the night would be upon me, the night with—

The mere contemplation was most horrible. More than ever should I be compelled to call to my aid the full resources of artificial light. Sleep could not be mine for a moment. If I dozed, if I even closed my eyes, yonder black fiend might descend from his position, might advance with his silent, horrid legs, and I should wake in an agony to find myself within his loathsome hold. Would locked doors or stone walls avail me? I knew well they could not, or I should instantly have closed the room and sent for masons to brick up door and windows. I would have enclosed the room within a mile of stonework. But nothing that was human could hold at bay this mysterious creation, this living substance of a crime, this awful being that existed solely for my annihilation.

During those earlier moments, when the altered atmosphere of the room first swept upon my face, I realised that my brother was present. The decayed body in its sea grave went for naught. Here was the mysterious *ipse* of his distinctive cypher in eternity. Here was the soul-vapour, and the speechless presence that is spirit. The essence of existence was here, like the omnipotent, yet imperceptible God-vapour that brooded over chaos, invisible and all-mighty over the evident and the evolving, when time began to be. Here was the mystery of eternity, the mystery that lies not for a foundation upon life and the body, nor upon death and alteration, but upon the Actual.

My straining eyesight was concentrated upon the loathsome visitant. I could not remove my gaze, for might he not stir towards me at the first hint of inattention? The darkening light beat upon the ebon body so strongly as to throw into bold detail every portion. Each of the foul legs wrought a bar sinister across the spotless wall. I could note the fine hairs outlined against that gleaming surface. I could see the body expand and contract, as the creature drew inspirations of that same air which also supported my life. Still it remained in the same fixed position. There was not even motion in the red, baleful eyes, nor was there need. For I was motionless, and upon me they expended their power.

When, I wondered, when would this awful trance have its end? I tried to console myself with the reflection that the monster had only appeared as the fleeting reproach of the moment. Presently it would melt away, while I should be free once again. But as I manufactured the still-born hope, I knew that it was unreal, for how could I fail to remember the gradual growth of that black body, from the germ of a mere distressing thought to its present animated and repulsive stage of full evolution? Had I not felt it approaching by stealthy but fearfully perceptible degrees during the full light of day? Could I not hear the sounds of its vile con- struction, with the slow moulding of each horrid limb, beneath the deathly stillness of the night? It had come, and it had come for ever. It would drive me shrieking to my tomb, nor there would it allow me to escape. I should find it waiting beyond the bar of change, ready to torture my shivering soul through all eternity.

The silence grew more frightful, broken only by the wild throbbing of my heart, and my deep gaspings for breath. From the monster came no sound. Could it have spoken only, and assumed the voice of my brother, my suffering would have been less, for then I could have fallen to my knees and have sobbed forth a wild entreaty for mercy. I would have rent the air with my contrition. I would have wearied Nature by the casting back of the echoes of my bitter cries. But no, silence, grim, complete and unutter- able, was to dominate me; the ghastly work was to be performed without speech, without sound; my destiny had come upon me with muffled footsteps and ears insensible; an unbroken peace was to witness my last furious struggles. For Memory does her work quietly, yet none the less completely for that silence.

Chaos entered my mind. For a time my brain swam wildly, and I could reason no longer. I could only crouch, with finger nails digging into my flesh, watching that black excrescence upon the wall, the creature that never stirred even a single one of its many gruesome limbs, that kept its glaring eyes fixed upon my white countenance, freezing me into an hypnotic trance, holding me firmly bound by the invisible chains of terror. The man in the presence of his remorse; the human creature face to face with his crime; the sinner and the avenger. So we remained, while the clock on the mantel counted off the dreary seconds.

And at length it moved. Can any ingenuity depict that cold stab of agony, can any mind conceive the racking shudder which thrilled through every portion of my body, when I beheld each of the sombre legs lifted deliberately, waved in the air, then fastened again upon the colourless surface? It was inconceivable, indescribable. Ripples of animation rose and fell along the entire length of that hair-covered body, the head swayed with slow, regular motions, the pointed legs dug fiercely into the wall, then—how I prayed aloud for the privilege of death—the whole loathsome mass moved, moved, I say, like the first torturing stirring of a stricken conscience, moved a foot upward, then again settled itself rigid, and motionless, quiescent as a black rock.

Was there nobody in the world who would call himself my friend? Out of all the millions of humanity, was there not one who would come forward as my helper, who would strive to relieve me of this hell before death? Could the house be deserted? Had everyone fled, in order that I might be slowly tortured to my end alone? I had a wife whom I had actually loved not so long ago. Where was she now? Why did she not hasten to bear this tribulation jointly with me, to suffer the half of the husband's sorrow as is the duty of the wife, or to aid me in escaping from it? But no— no. There was to be no help, no pity, for the murderer. The hand of every man was against me. Like the first fratricide, I knew that I was driven out from the face of the earth; that I was a fugitive and a vagabond in the earth; that everyone who found me would desire to take away my life. I was the monster whom none might sympathise with. The world would not allow such a one to repent. Death is his portion, cries the world. Death! What is it after all? It is a pleasure, it is a gift, when compared with the agony of the maddened mind, and the remorse of the anguished heart.

The Lord had set a mark upon Cain—the mark of the Shadow, the mark of the eternally damned. And I was Cain.

The agitation came again, the torrent of motion flowed along the hideous body, the black frame heaved upward, and rested on the wall a foot higher.

Was it not a sufficient torment to be compelled to watch it, as it couched malignant and stationary? Why should it further horrify me by its frightful periodic movements, by the dull rustling of its hairy body along the smooth, hard surface, by the fierce glaring of its hideous eyes? Perhaps—and I became delirious with joy at the mere thought—it was about to depart, it was going to desert me. But I had already reasoned that this was impossible. Even were I alone again, would not the horror be increased? What could I do, but to shudderingly await its return, expecting each second to behold a hairy claw feeling over the white coverlet of my bed, or to see the baleful eyes burning in some dark corner? It would not, it could not, leave me, until its mission had been accomplished, until I was at an end.

It moved again, and for the third time. Now it came near upon touching the cornice.

Though I knew well that hope was not for me, I continued to pray incoherently that someone might enter, some counteracting agency who might break the frightful spell. Surely there could be found some priest, who by the sanctity of his life and office could rid me of this plague. I was penitent, assuredly I was penitent, therefore he might absolve me from the burden of my double crime. Could he not shrivel up this hell-creation with power of holy water, or destroy it with his malediction? But no—again that eternal negative. Even in my supremest agony I was able to remember how utterly vile I was, far beyond the ken of holy men or women, cut off by an immense interval from the most depraved of other mortals, below the lowest of the beasts. Even otherwise, where could I obtain the balm of consolation? For though absolution be conferred, penance must yet be exacted, and the endurance of this monstrous portent was the penalty, the heavy price, for merely a partial remission.

Annihilation stared me in the face, death bristling with horrors, but it was better than life, than long life—with this.

I watched the frightful incarnation of crime stir once more. Round the cornice it crept with a horrid rustling, and there remained, pressed squat and awful upon the ceiling, its bloodlike eyes turned down upon my face.

Still I crouched within the chair, shrinking more and more, and powerless to move. Still I lay cringing within the chair, waiting and wondering.

Nor was I to be long left in this maddening condition of suspense, for the next deliberate movement was of greater length, and more replete with dread significance. By slow degrees the fiend dragged its pestilential body along, diverging slightly to the right but never actually pausing, never stopping entirely, until it reached a point where it seemed satisfied to rest. Here it found its destination, here it settled itself, sternly regarding with great eyes the hapless mortal that shuddered beneath.

Where was that stopping point? Why had it turned to the right to creep along the ceiling? Why had it done so? In order that it might place itself exactly above my head.

Faculty of speech flashed back as this unutterable horror wound itself into my being. My dry tongue uncurled and found a borrowed strength, with which it shrieked aloud in pitiable tones that might have drawn tears from stones, frantically giving mad exclamations to a new, a loathsome, a detestable thought.

'Mercy of Heaven!' I screamed, while circles of red light spun wildly between me and that Other while the house rocked and heaved with earthquake. 'If it falls now, it must drop upon my face.'

Silence returned to me from the infinite after the echo of this cry, like the quietness of death settling after the death rattle. With a Samsonian strength I struggled to tear myself away from that accursed spot. But I was held like the tree by its roots. I was chained and bound; I was the most helpless of prisoners.

My head, following the course of the foul tormentor, had fallen back, and was resting upon the back of the chair, with face presented towards the ceiling. By no superhuman effort was I able to stir from that fearful position. I was fascinated and fixed there immovably. At once I perceived that, when the monster dropped, and I could not doubt but that it must drop, it would by the law of mathematics fall sprawling right across my features, with frightful body crushing against my face, with poisoned breath beating into my nostrils, with pointed claws of venom digging into my eyes.

So I understood my fate, and saw the manner of my end.

Of such intensity was my agony that, as I looked upward, I smiled. Smiled, I say, and then laughed aloud with fierce, harsh sounds of terrible pain. Extremities of opposites produce similarity. The bitter cold has effects which may not be distinguished from the results of a great heat. In like manner my suffering became joy, my maniacal frenzy turned to mirth. After the first few moments of dire transition, this loathsome creature became a positive pleasure to me. It was such a rare, such a wonderful, sight in its appalling hideousness. Being a novel creation, it was an ecstasy of delight to watch, to gloat upon its awful shapings, to speculate upon its future movements, to marvel at it as it was.

Gradually I commenced to wonder at the marvellous tenacity of the power that enabled it thus to cling upon the smooth matter of the ceiling with such extraordinary firmness. Here was another pleasing phantasy, with which I delighted myself as the child happy in its new toy. I reviewed the action critically. I dived far into the abstruse depths of mathematics and science, passing from one unsolved problem to another with marvellous rapidity, yet I could find no fitting explanation. A man could not hang thus, in violation of the laws of gravity, neither could a four-footed beast. So here was a creation in the person of this vile octopod, which possessed far higher powers than those allotted to the higher orders.

My brain writhed and twisted, like a green wood stick in the deep scarlet of the fire, beneath the bewildering complexity of my theorisings. I thought upon many deep wonders which perchance had never before vexed the mind of man, or rather glanced lightly against them, never to pause in the gropings of reflection for more than a few seconds, then to plunge afresh into the wild maelstrom of fancy, circling along faster and more furiously into fresh eddies and whirlpools of surmise, borne, swept along by a mad torrent which was not to be resisted. I traced the history of man from the protoplasm to the division into peoples and languages. I deliberated on all the vexed questions that have ever racked the human brain, and dismissed each as trifles easily solved. Theories flashed before me in a turmoil of theosophy, theories that the sane brain could never have contemplated, that the mental grasp in a rational state could never have held for the moment, and these, too, were solved and cast aside, back again into the whirling abyss that had cast them up, like splashes of foam, to be broken upon the unyielding rock of my abnormal reason. I was a fevered mass of heterogeneous knowledge. It was the final upheaval of mind before departure of reason. It was the last mad eruption of calculating judgment prior to dissolution.

My eyes, fixed upon one central point, saw everything within that narrow circle with a most startling distinctness. Saw the black figure, like some ghastly cicatrix, motionless as a rock, lifeless to all appearance, and devoid of all power to harm. Saw each repulsive bristling hair and every hideous line of shape.

And then—

Had I my senses untarnished, I could not write the words.

In the most undiminished silence, without warning, without previous motion, without sign of intention, this monstrous horror—

DROPPED.

## CHAPTER VII

## SILENT WATERS

What, do I fear? Myself? There's none else by.
*Richard III.*, Act V. sc. I.

Tuesday, 9th September.

'You are her partner,' shrieked a discordant voice from afar. 'She is a great poisonous tiger, and she has killed him. She has been trying to kill him for a long time.'

'Go away,' said a steady voice.

'She has killed him, and you have helped her. I will murder you, for you are a bloodsucker. I will murder her, too. Ha! ha! I will murder you both. You have killed my poor nephew.'

'Take him away,' said the steady voice.

A wild shout of rage came louder and clearer. 'Here is my big stick. See it—it is strong and thick. Will you touch me, you small black devil? Will you touch me? Ha! ha!'

'Go away then,' repeated the voice.

'I am going. Yes, I am going, but I shall soon be back. I am going to find a gun, and then I shall shoot you both. The white-clawed tiger first, and then you. I shall shoot you both. You have killed my nephew. I loved my poor nephew.'

The sounds were now distinct and close to my ears. I awoke from the long delirium, and found myself lying in the bed, with semi-darkness wrapping round the room, while attendants stepped noiselessly to and fro. I stirred, and one was by my side in a moment, to ask me how I felt—most mocking of questions. 'Is this hell?' I whispered. Then I found the doctor by my bedside. I clutched at his arm, while my brain awoke again, and the hot life throbbed anew through my body. 'Doctor,' I muttered, 'I have questions to ask you.'

'Yes?' he said. 'You have recovered from your fit. It must have been apoplexy. Can you move your limbs? I see that you can,' he continued. 'Then it is not paralysis.'

'Doctor,' I said, 'tell me this: why have I been insulted with the curse of physical strength?'

He smiled. 'Other men would call it a gift.'

'It has enabled me to revive from that appalling shock. Why did I not die, and put an end to it all?'

His face became stern. 'An end to what?'

I hung to his arm in an agony of hope. 'Only tell me one thing,' I cried. 'Tell me that my sufferings are over, that I am free now to claim the pleasures of life. Can you tell me that?'

He shook his head. 'You had better rest. I will give you something to compose your brain—'

I burst in upon his words. 'My brain is sane. It is as clear as your own, doctor—clearer. Do you doubt that?'

'No, no,' he said soothingly. 'Remember you have been ill, and that you require rest. Excitement may be dangerous.'

'Answer my questions, and then I will sleep.'

He was about to reply, when I burst into an exclamation of fear. 'Sleep! Doctor, stay with me, watch me, protect me.'

'You must not—' he began.

'Cannot you see how impossible it is? Sleep cannot—do you understand?—cannot be mine. It may return any instant. Can you see it now, doctor? Perhaps it is under the bed. It may be in the dark corner behind you. It will come crawling up presently—its black claws will feel for me over these white coverings—and if I sleep—'

A strange cry came from the doorway. 'Nephew! Here I am! Ho! ho! Nephew, are you alive again? Listen! I am going to kill the tiger.'

'Keep it away from me, uncle. You saw it upon the wall of my room.'

'What, nephew? There are no spiders here.'

'It is coming. The great black spider with the white cross.'

The bed that I was in seemed to be circling round the room. I could feel the irritation of a stream of blood along my chin.

'You are killing yourself,' said the doctor simply.

'Yes, nephew. You will be like the old woman then. Never mind the black spider. I will keep it away from you with my big stick.'

'You have seen it, uncle?' I gasped. 'You have seen it?'

'No, nephew. They will soon be going to bed for the winter. I have been through the garden, and a lot of them are asleep; I could not find many flies for them. I've seen no black spider, nephew. There were two lizards upon a chair in the blue room, and there was a green snake upon the stairs as I came up. But that was all, nephew. There was no big black spider.'

The desire to learn more gave me strength. Again I drew the doctor to my side, and asked, 'How long have I been in this condition?'

'Exactly two days. Almost to the hour.'

'Where was I discovered?'

'You were lying upon a chair in the centre of your room, with face towards the ceiling. You were insensible, to all outward appearance, lifeless.'

I nerved myself for the question. 'But what else? Who was there with me?'

'Nobody, so far as I know,' he said, glancing with a look of interrogation towards a servant. 'You found your master?'

'Yes, sir,' said the man. 'There was nobody in the room.'

'And nothing?' I gasped forth.

'Nothing, sir.'

My uncle chuckled, and twisted his dry fingers together. 'They don't see with our eyes, nephew. No, no, they don't see everything. This blind fool couldn't see the lizards in the blue room. But they were there for all that. I saw them, nephew. They were fine fat lizards.'

These answers were incomplete, but in a manner satisfactory. When discovered, I had been alone in the room. The door had been fastened by catch, but the window stood open. There was absolutely no sign of any other presence. Doubtless, as the doctor sympathetically remarked, I had looked upon strange objects during my illness; even at the present I had scarcely awakened from the heavy trance, or entirely cast aside the powerful glamour of my evil dreams.

So emboldened did I become by such assurances, that I actually forced myself to believe that all the late occurrences had been nothing more than mere phantasies. This error was decidedly strengthened by the striking resemblance of the recent terrible scene to the fearful dream of the avenging spider, which had from the earliest years been my peculiar torment. The action had been identical in almost every detail. I became quickly convinced that I had but dreamed again. And what is a dream, but the veriest tissue of unactuality?

And so strength flowed back with rapidity to my usually strong frame. I rose from my bed, while those who had attended me during my illness went back to their several duties.

. . . . . . . . . . . . . . . . . . .

Monday, 15th September.

Beyond all question I had changed. My manner, my modes of diversion, were different. For instance, I would walk out into the garden, and having selected some flower patch, would commence to attack the blossoms with a stick, methodically beheading each one, until all were decapitated. The prospect of such amusement afforded me an unbounded delight. So, as I sat at the table, I would reflect with the most exquisite enjoyment upon the particular bed of flowers I had selected that day for destruction. Already in imagination I was hurrying there through the bright sunshine, with the stick held firmly in my hand; I could see the careful and scientific flourishes through the air; I could hear my own keen note of mirth; I beheld the bruised heads of tinted bloom springing excitedly from their stems and settling to the ground; I could look upon the stiff array of headless stalks. Then I would my rub my hands together in sheer delight.

Sometimes, also, I would take a ball, shut myself up in a lonely room, then play with it against the wall for many hours at a time. I matched myself against imaginary opponents, and fought with them keenly, until the sweat of physical exertion ran from my face. I would spring about wildly, like some electric figure, scarcely ever failing in the sureness of my catch, laughing and talking in the mad exuberance of my mirth.

Until recently I had taken no pleasure in such childish sports. Now, though from a certain sense of shame I executed them in strict privacy, they afforded me the keenest delight. This was a change, yet surely a change for the better, since it proved incontestibly how entirely even was the balance of my mind.

Still, in my wildest moods, I always suffered, and terribly—from a doubt. If the sudden approach of the vile spider had been only a phantasy, where should I light upon the cause of my illness, and this change? If the creature had appeared *in actu*,[1] where was it now? Why did I not see it? Would it return? The inability to find, or even to think upon, answers to such questions drove me the more frequently to my innocent, if unusual, pastimes.

And one morning I arose as it were in a dream. I was a dead man. Plainly I could remember everything that had occurred during the long night. The oppression came over me with suddenness. I would then have shrieked aloud, but a mountain weight pressed my lungs together, while an iron screw, that smelt and tasted of human decay, forced my tongue to the back of my mouth. Then, after a few frightful struggles for more light, more breath, I died.

Gradually I emerged from the pit of unconsciousness to a dim sense of existence that was spiritual and not bodily. So the dreaded death was nothing but torpidity after all. But where was the violent horror? And where the devils? And where—ah, where—was my own appointed place?

Slowly and solemnly I walked down the stairs, with the dignity of my new state heavy upon me. I enjoyed a new sensation—the grim pleasure of feeling myself a disembodied spirit. I would go and haunt my wife; possibly I might terrify her into insanity, and thereby satisfy my own lust for vengeance. And I was fortunate, for I met her upon the stairs.

She turned white, and would have drawn herself away, but I came upon her, and waved my death robes across her face.

'Woman,' I said, 'I have been sent to torment you.'

I saw that her lips were quivering, that her hands were clenched firmly. 'What do you mean by this?' she said.

Then I began to understand that she would not allow herself to be easily disturbed. There came over my body a re-sinking into entire apathy, while my whole troubled soul called for rest.

'Cannot you see that I am dead?' I said impatiently.

---

1 In reality.

She shrank back against the balustrade. 'Dead!' she muttered.

'I felt it coming upon me about midnight, and, just as the day began to dawn, I died. There was no trouble, and very little pain. I passed away quite peacefully. I wish you would close my eyes, for I want to rest.'

But she did not raise her hands, and she did not move.

'So you will not perform even this slight service for a poor corpse that was once your husband? I will go on and ask my brother. Is he down here?'

This simple question awoke all her enmity. A fierce light darted into her eyes, while her body seemed to expand with hatred.

'You vile creature!' she cried at me. 'You miserable madman!'

But this insult did not anger me. 'The dead are not mad,' I said softly. 'And, as you see, I am quite dead. I am cold and stiff now, for I passed away several hours ago. I wish you would tell me where I can find my coffin.'

'Let me go,' she cried. 'This is terrible.'

'I thought I should frighten you,' I said. 'It is very strange—is it not?—how the living fear the dead. Has it never occurred to you what a *very* strange thing it is? Why should you be afraid of anyone in the spirit, when perhaps you have had nothing but contempt for him when in the body? Can you tell me why?'

But she only breathed quickly, and gave me no reply.

'When I was alive I can remember—and I can recall it easily—my extreme terror at any manifestation from the other world. There was one spirit in particular that used to terrify me constantly. So I can sympathise with your fear. I wish you would fasten a bandage round my jaw, to prevent it from dropping—'

She gave a dreadful cry. Then with a sob of pain and fear she pushed by me and disappeared, while a faint dawn of thought occurred to my mental sight. My eyelids quivered, my limbs pricked and smarted, and an electric torrent of blood went surging through my body and rioting to my brain. In grave doubts, and troubled by solemn perplexities, I passed back to the room with the white walls, and there sat down to wonder whether, after all, I had not erred in thinking myself to be completely dead.

I had on entering seen nothing but the gleam of the sun-washed walls and the liquid shimmer of the mirror beyond. I had felt nothing, save only a peculiar lightness in the head, as though the brains therein had turned to feather. I seemed, as it were, to sweep into the room, like a patch of spray borne to the shore on some wave. I was carried along on a tide of mysticism.

I sat there with my new-found strength, until the solitude became again invaded by the presence of the invisible. As I crouched there in the silence, life returned to my body, while shadow rose again and lay across my soul.

.  .  .  .  .  .  .  .  .  .  .  .  .  .  .  .  .  .

Punishment was over now, so I must think calmly on the future—how I should most pleasantly dispose of the best years of my life, and how I could most easily free myself from the galling restraint of the marriage bond. Cain was happy after his crime, since he married and built a great city, and had for issue a son, one who has since been accounted one of the righteous symbols of emblematical history. Never had I been so evil as Cain, for his brother was true to him, while mine had been false. If he had been prosperous, so should I be. But for how long—how long? The shadow was there with Cain throughout that prosperity, and when did it fall? When did that shadow, which is known as Seth, emerge from the Eve-vapour of the earth, and form into substance? How long was it before it came upon him through the periods of day and night, came upon him with its presence, came upon him with its message and its mission, fell across his soul in the awful sternness of its terrible duty, and drove him shrieking to his end? When—ah, when?

I would stay no longer in this dreary, sea-beaten spot, where evil memories crowded so thickly. I would seek some bright country, where the inhabitants walked in gay costumes, where the manner of living was unconstrained. In such a place I could pass away my time, unhaunted even by the shadow of reproach. Perhaps I would take my uncle, to enliven my occasional strange moods with his mad fancies, but I would most certainly leave behind that most hated woman, my wife. She should live in this house if she pleased, by the moaning cemetery of her lover's bones, and should she choose in a moment of despair to join hers to these, the better assuredly for me. But I would live again, laugh again, and call each untried sensation in life to the assistance of my pleasure. I had come back from prison to the world. I had expiated my crime, so the memory must now flee back to the gloomy land from whence it had arisen, while the shadow would dissolve and fail.

My health was magnificent; my limbs pricked and smarted with energy, while the blood danced in exhilaration along my veins. The pulses beat fiercely; the heart throbbed strongly; the limbs pined for mere action—to grapple with some mighty foe, to pour forth a portion of their superabundant strength; in short, to defy the world. This was the glory of returning life with its hot ebb and flow, it was the regeneration of the body fibres, the resuscitation of a muscular strength which belongs to the few.

It is true that there were moments when, as I paused to reflect upon certain solemn subjects, such as the grave and the horror of the final end, shout upon shout of ribald laughter would tear themselves from my being. There were times when, as I suddenly bent myself to intercede before some vague power for my soul's welfare, all the foul jests and damning blasphemies, carelessly listened to, yet mentally recorded, in bygone days, fell from my lips in an eloquent stream, and took the place of the prayer that had been intended; there were moments also when, as I sat in the weird blue light of the livid-hued apartment, strange objects would file into the room, and range themselves on floor, furniture, on walls, hanging even to the cornices, where they might the better grin and gibe at me. These were all small beings, with weird red eyes that continually rolled and burnt, as though in perpetual fright or torment, while their hands and feet were those of skeletons, and their faces were of most abnormal hideousness. I noticed, also, for my perceptive faculty was peculiarily acute, that each bore a curiously-shaped cross mark of a blood red colour upon the forehead. These strange creatures came continually in my loneliness, and sat with me for many long hours, until, although they were hideous and misshapen, I came to rejoice in their company. I felt even that some secret bond of sympathy existed between us, and I was sorry when they gradually faded away, or vanished abruptly, as the mood took them. I could not fail, however, to observe, on passing before some mirror after their departure, that I also wore upon my brow, high up on the temples, a red mark, exactly similar in shape and appearance to that stamped upon the forehead of each one of them.

A strange, unexplained nervousness, combined with a highly vivid imagination, accounted for everything that I did, and all that I fancied I saw. I became assured that both body and mind were perfectly rational, that each sense performed its appointed function, that a clear haven was spreading ahead, on a smooth sea of happiness, and surrounded by the calm winds of peace. This security of feeling I had surely earned.

Thus for the next few days I sank into a pleasant dream, and floated contentedly through the hours, like the wind-borne flower petal on a summer's day.

But the awakening—what of it? What are the sensations of the opium smoker, when he awakes to his squalid misery, his despair and the bare world, from the phantasy, the coloured and scented glories, the impossible beauty and magnificence, of his fantastic paradise of pain?

The awakening—what of it? Merely the difference between the actual life of misery, and a realisation of the imagined glories of an ideal Heaven.

There is madness in the change that follows such awakening.

# CHAPTER VIII

## AVE, TENEBRAE!

When will this awful slumber have an end?
*Titus Andronicus*, Act III. sc. I.

Friday, 12th September.

IT was late in the afternoon, and I walked through the damp
avenue of lilacs in search of some living thing who might spare
me sympathy. But there was nobody, and nothing, save only a few
brown spiders swaying in film-covered webs among the black-
green rhododendrons, so I retraced my steps, and sought elsewhere throughout my lonely property. There was a manuscript
book in my hand—the mystical work of the old Norse saga—and
at times I would seat myself upon the sodden moss that softened
the gnarled root of an ancient oak, to bend my head anxiously
over the yellow parchment with its black-lettered markings.

My mind was distressing. I was unable to realise the full significance of the sudden affliction that had suddenly laid its hold upon
my intellect. This work, which was in the original, had up to the
present been clearly intelligible, since I could read the language
with considerable ease, but now, on this particular evening, I found
myself in a great difficulty. I could extract no meaning from the
characters, which appeared to me new and strange; I had lost all
my knowledge of the tongue, and by some unexplained freak of
remembrance, even the few passages that I was still enabled to con-
strue, rang upon my mind with an entire lack of meaning. Here,
then, was another and more formidable change. Had all my power
of memory been entirely concentrated upon the one supreme
idea, to the jealous exclusion of all else? Had that monstrous creation taken of my best—my reason, my power to understand?
Had he, like the cruel spider of Nature, fattening upon blood of
insects, sucked dry all the sweet juices of understanding? Above

all, could it be that I was not the rational being I had all along supposed? Such questions, with a score besides, came rushing upon me, choking and stifling me with strangling fingers of ice, as I blindly stumbled through the flower beds, as I crushed into the black ground delicate blossoms that were emblems of my past pleasures, as I fell over tree roots that protruded from the mossy turf, but to none could I fashion an answer, for the brain, which should have responded, was cold and lifeless.

I had prayed for the silent waters, and my prayer had been answered—I had been granted the waters of forgetfulness. But what was the effect? Only those things I desired to remember were banished from memory; past happiness, prospect of future peace—these were the things that were gone; the horror of my crime, the presence of the fearfully apparent shadow—these were the things that became intensified to memory by the lack of other remembrance that was consoling—greatly and most fearfully intensified by that same lack.

I staggered into a part of the garden I had so far not visited, and there I came upon a man bending over a small plat, where white and yellow bunches of bloom nodded and shook great ragged heads. I paused, for I thought I would put my brain to the test.

The man started when he saw me. He stood upright, and pulled vaguely at his hat, as though he had some feeling of respect for such a being as myself. I seized a handful of bloom, and crushed it up. 'What is it?' I cried at him fiercely; then, as he gave me no reply, I shouted again, 'What is it?'

The fellow looked round, as though in fear. It was very silent, and moisture was dripping from the trees above. There was a strange odour of decay along the breeze, but that was to be expected. For it was autumn.

'Beggin' your pardon, sir—' began the fellow stupidly.

'Do you think I don't know?' I interrupted wildly. 'I have lived amongst the flowers for years, and do you think I cannot name them now? I tell you these are poppies.'

He shifted his great feet awkwardly, and changed the spade he held from hand to hand.

'Of course they are poppies,' I cried. 'I thought my memory had gone, but I see that I was wrong. These are splendid flowers. There are fine drugs to be extracted from them. Do you not know that? Drugs that give you sleep; drugs that give you insensibility; drugs that give you rest. Do you hear that? Drugs that give you rest.'

'They ain't poppies, sir,' said the man, gathering his courage. 'Poppies don't blow in September, sir.'

'You are a madman,' I shouted. 'You profess to look after flowers, yet you cannot give them their names. I can see that you are mad. Perhaps you do not know it yourself.'

'Beggin' your pardon, sir,' he said again. 'But these be chrysanthemums.'

He mouthed the long word glibly. I tore off a ragged head and pressed it to my face. The white petals fell around me like snow-flakes. I recognised the distinctive odour, yet memory helped me not.

'This is a very mad poppy,' I cried. 'Everything is mad, even the flowers. I tell you it is a terrible thing to be the only sane person alive. But you cannot understand that, because you are mad.'

'I be all right, sir,' said the fellow sourly.

'I knew you would say that. You are not only mad, but you have made the flowers mad. You are a villain to do that. It is worse than murdering a man, and that is a terrible thing. I am convinced that it is a *very* terrible thing.'

'You ask anyone, sir,' he said. 'They'll tell you these 'ere be chrysanthemums.'

'That is because they are all mad. If you were sane, you would understand that they are poppies. I shall come back presently, and I shall destroy them all. Do you understand? If I find you still here, I shall destroy you with them. I cannot have mad people and mad flowers in my garden. I have tolerated the presence of both too long already.'

I leapt into the centre of the plat, and dragged off the heads of bloom by handfuls. 'I shall take these poppies with me. I shall carry them about and I shall take them to bed with me. Perhaps they will help me to sleep. They may give me rest. You shall see me to-morrow, if you are alive, and then I will tell you whether they have given me rest. You understand that I require rest very strongly, for I have been awake now a long time, a very long time. It is quite time I had some rest.'

I left him, and staggered away, while a great wave of heat surged over my heart, and the sky turned red. Presently I bethought myself again of the Norse manuscript which I could not decipher.

This book it was which had first implanted in my mind the possibility of a remorseful memory attaining to the stage of actual life, and assuming definite proportions. There were in it passages—which I am unable to quote, on account of my sudden loss of memory—which exactly represented the terrors I had undergone during the immediate past. This portion only can I imperfectly remember,—

'He who has committed some great crime must await the slow development of his punishment. And this punishment must be through his own body; it must reach and torture his soul through the medium of each one of his separate senses. The hands will be compelled to light upon shapes and forms, living or dead, which are by the process of nature the most horrible to them, while the sensitiveness of the feet will be tormented in like manner. The ears will be assailed, yet not too constantly, for monotony of horror may breed indifference, with direful sounds. Frightful odours will be placed at irregular intervals in proximity with the nostrils, and these will be changed before the sense has time to grow accustomed to the noxious fumes. But it is the eyes, and the eyes especially, that will be the most supremely tortured by objects and shapes of peculiar fearfulness. Separate ingenuity must be left to consider the most fitting plan of accomplishment, since any general plan would require to be greatly varied, to suit the particular aversion of the criminal.'

The sun had almost gone. This much I noticed, for his was the only presence I yearned after. The sad-voiced wind came moaning over the trees, the wind that sobbed over the sea where my brother lay, the wind that brought the loneliness and the desolation home to my sad heart. Long shadows rose and fell across the walls of the house, that dreary mansion which gazed at me frightfully with its dark eye-windows, which warned me *not* to approach, not to commit my body within its prison ramparts. There were many dead windows peering from beneath the frowning eyebrows of the roof, where the mournful ivy trailed in funeral-like festoons. These regarded me with the most ominous stare; these uttered the loudest and longest admonition; these spoke to me in that shrill voice of complete silence—which is so terrible. These represented nothing so strongly as sealed graves, that closed remorselessly upon the decaying flesh and whitening bones of their hapless victims. I came towards them. I staggered up to the house which had been the scene of my birth, where I had come with my bride, where I was—yes, I was, and why not speak the cold syllable of fate?—to die.

I approached with slow steps, and was still some distance away, when the sun, in the act of vanishing for the long night, shot forth a dazzling arm of splendour. This red light flashed and stabbed through the thick trees immediately behind, and fell across one half of the white wall nearest, that particular portion, in fact, which happened to be destitute of trailing vegetation. I lifted my sore eyes, and looked into the heart of this hot, shimmering bath of radiance. I recoiled in utter horror; I fell back with a loud, deep scream of agony; my body shrank together upon the turf; I tore up the grass with my mad fingers, while I hid my burning face within the soft moss bed.

There, upon the bare wall, straddling across the wide extent of masonry, obvious to the most careless of onlookers, stretched a gigantic black spider, twenty feet in length, with huge eyes like furnaces, with the cruel jaws of a shark, with a sable body many times larger than my own, with ebon hairs bristling upon it like ropes. This entire awful apparition I saw shivering and oscillating in the evening breeze. The boldest man in the universe would have gone coward at that sight.

Presently I became aware that the sun had gone, so I ventured fearfully to gradually raise my head and look again. But when I did so, my surprise could only be measured by my relief, for the portentous leviathan had vanished. There was no mark of his monstrous form upon the lichened brickwork; there was not the smallest sign of his late presence upon the time-seared wall. I staggered upright, and resumed the course which had been so terribly interrupted, wondering and calculating until I had almost reached the door. Then, as I gazed back upon the blood-red west, where the light of day was eternally departing, my eyes fell upon the crossed and interlacing branches of the numerous trees, where I found in a moment an explanation of the terrifying appearance.

The sun had cast this direful pattern upon the wall as a last warning to me. But what devilish hand had so arranged, so entwined those boughs with leaves and twigs, to aid him in his design? If, as certain moralists declare, there be no such thing as coincidence, then surely are there many hateful spirits, watching us closely both by day and night, displaying to our gaze, not indeed their hideous selves, but that which follows closely in horror— their frightful handiwork.

The flowers were closing, and drooping tired heads; birds were piping sadly and sleepily in the bushes; dark clouds came rolling up, to blot out the last trace of day; the air became moist with dew, while the first cold evening star shivered in the north.

Then I turned my back upon the painted nature that was lost to me, and the peaceful scene that I was never to behold again. It was evening, a clear, glad evening in the ripe season of early autumn. What was the world doing at such a time?

This was the hour when the old man pushed aside his books, and called the happy children round his knees, to listen to the tale of olden time. This was the hour when the old woman awoke, to listen to the glad doings of the day from the fresh lips of her merry-hearted descendants. This was the hour when friends, who had together weathered the storm of adversity, sat and chatted by the bright fireside. This was the hour when young manhood hurried along the dewy grass paths, rejoicing in the scented shadows of the departing day, to meet one who tripped joyfully towards him with a loving heart and a radiant smile. This was the hour when the aged wished themselves young, and young men sighed to be old. This was the vesper hour of the angelus—the hour of peace, of love, of forgiveness, of mercy.

It was, also, the hour of my fate.

No hand held me back from that black threshold; there was no friendly voice to whisper into my ear that I was stepping into my sepulchre. But the host of shadows within grinned with joy, and fled gibbering in front of me, up and along the wide stairway, in a writhing cloud of mystery. They were all watching the fratricide with their hot, matterless eyes. They saw him step upon his scaffold, with the blood mark on his brows; they watched him enter the tomb by the light of that unholy ray which streamed from his forehead. As I crept up those stairs, tottering beneath my affliction, as the veteran under his hoary weight of years, I could feel them flocking around me. They brushed against my face with an ice-like touch; they derided my weak motions with fleshless fingers; they whispered each other hoarsely, with hollow accents that were plainly audible to my scorching ears,—

'Ha! ha! You see him. He has come.'

'He is here.'

'It is the guest.'

'Bring him out the robe—the best.'

'The best robe—the winding-sheet.'

'Flowers. Bring flowers—many of them, for his head.'

'And his breast. But see that they are white.'

'Strong-scented. Arrange them in the form of a cross.'

'Bring him food.'

'Bring it in abundance—for he is hungry.'

'Ashes—ashes, and dry dust.'

'Ha! ha! Dry dust. There will be much to spare.'

Up the stairs I went, with this wild clamour beating round my head. I could hear the rattling of bones; I could smell the odour of charnel houses; I could feel the clammy cerements clinging to my brows; I could see the worms writhing in and out of a putrescent body; I could see Hell itself, with the souls of the eternally doomed shrivelling with the agony and the shame. I could see thousands of graves, each containing its particular skeleton, semi-upright and contorted with the horror of death.

I was filled with a fiery humour, which increased as the hand of calamity pressed the more strongly upon me. At the first landing, I turned and paused. The weirdly-mixed colours of a stained-glass window bathed my head in the fast fading light. I took up my stand, and waved a hand to the clamouring host beneath for silence. I stood there, and cried aloud with all my power,—

'*Ave, Tenebrae!*'

There came a partial silence, as the fiends gathered upward and around to listen. There were still some that shrieked and jeered at me. So I cried forth again my word of greeting,—

'*Ave, Tenebrae!*'

Then there came silence, great and complete, for all wished to learn the murderer's last message.

I shouted in a great voice, a strong voice. The sound penetrated into every corner; it floated into hidden recesses that my body had never reached; it arrived at realms where my soul might never hope to dwell. The echo of that voice dug the very dust out of forgotten places, like the essence of the dead rising at the last call of time.

'*Ave, Tenebrae! Ego moriturus vos saluto.*'[1]

I gave this wild cry thrice, and satisfied the gibing demons at my heels. Then I resumed my solemn walk towards the grave.

The white room was entered in safety. Here at least there was a strong light, for my instructions on this point were strict. So soon as natural light commenced to fade, the artificial was applied at once. . . .

I sat down to my writing, and spent thus a considerable time. My brain was hot and whirling. Some people might have been so mistaken as to have called this madness. Must I repeat that it was nothing but nervousness? . . .

I suddenly remembered that I was married. But where was my wife? I reflected with pleasure that we should not burden one another much longer. I would go away very soon, and then she might do as she pleased. My hatred towards her had now grown so exceedingly bitter, that I could not even tolerate her presence. I was afraid of her, why, I know not, except that I possessed a morbid dread of all human beings, with the exception of my uncle. But I never saw her, never had to meet her cold eyes; if she did not interfere with me, what did it matter? She could live in my lonely house alone. Yet—by the Heaven that governs us so strangely—she was the woman whom I had once placed before the selfish calls of my own heart; she was the woman for whom I had suffered, and was still suffering, all this torment; she was the woman—and this is the deep root which gave life to my hatred—who might have saved me from all, but who had preferred to withhold her loving aid, that she might drive me the deeper into the mire of memory and remorse. . . .

---

1 See the exegesis supplied in the Editor's Introduction.

My writing was completed for the time. I pushed aside the materials, and walked across to the open window. The heat was intense, in spite of the late season, and the air almost without motion. I pulled back the curtains, then gazed forth, and laughed wildly—at what, I know not, unless it were at the shadows that had collected there in great numbers. The sky was furiously enraged; flaring clouds were rolling up from the dim horizon, twisting and writhing as though bent on the destruction of all things, while from the nearer distance came the heartbreaking lament of the sea. It was an evil night, yet I found pleasure in it, since its silent wrath accorded with my humour.

I settled myself in a chair, with a strange mood upon me. During the same minute I passed from solemnity to positive enjoyment, then back again to despair. One moment I would be biting my fingers, or clutching wildly at my hair, the next I would be shrieking with laughter at some ribald thought, or grinning foolishly, and muttering to myself in low tones. Yet I was perfectly sane. My reason was sound and unimpaired; my brain completely untouched by any flame of madness. . . .

The intense silence was disturbed only by the distant moaning of the wind as it came up with the night. . . .

As I crouched there, in a mood of ghastly cheerfulness, a palpable shudder seemed to thrill through the room, the light trembled, like the waves on a restless sea. Before I could move or stir a limb, before I could even let fall the cry of anguish which thrilled through every fibre of my being, a frightful shock flashed through my body. A touch of electric life convulsed my limbs, infested every sense, drove all humanity from me.

It had come again.

Could I fail to recognise that dire sensation which had, before that night, given my soul to the torture, and stretched my body on the rack? I tell you, as I sat there, I felt again the knife of the inquisitor's vengeance vivisecting my motionless and helpless form; I felt again the presence of that will which urged me towards self-destruction; I felt again—is there any to understand the meaning in these words?—the Presence which flowed all round me in waves of pestilential air, which circled within me from without, which beat upon me—howling—raging—burning.

My brother had come to me. He had returned, but not alone. Again he had brought that frightful monster. For the last time he had encased his soul within that living emblem of my mortal agony, and had come again to conquer, to destroy—had come invincible, armed with resolution, and power irresistible.

Fool had I been—blind, besotted, ignorant. I had taught myself to believe that I was free, that my punishment was over. Oh, implacable and most unforgiving tyranny!—the work was but commencing, the decree for my annihilation had been only recently prepared and sent forth. I had madly endeavoured to conquer the invincible and to slay the creature of eternity.

The frightful whisper rose and fell, dinning into my ears the message of death import, the text to my approaching doom,—

'You have killed your brother's body, but you cannot touch the soul. For it lies beyond your malice, and far above the destroying powers of your hand. You may strive as you will, but you shall not forget. Remorse is immortal, and the evil memory may not be destroyed. Your work has been in vain.'

And then the deep voice spoke to me again. Only a single word, yet it was to me as the 'guilty' of the jury on the criminal's ears, as the rifle missile speeding direct to the doomed man's heart.

'Look!'

I knew the meaning. I could not obey; I dared not. Then the voice laughed fearfully, and muttered again, louder and more closely to my ear,—

'Look! it is approaching you.'

I bore upon my body the agony of the entire world. With cold drops starting from every pore in my skin, with a separate anguish racking each portion of my frame, my head was turned by some occult energy. By the same power my eyes stirred, sought, and fell upon the white wall to the right—the wall where the black stain had been, the white wall where it was even then visible! No, not then, not then! It was not there; it had been blotted out; it was visible no longer. But I saw—oh, may the God against Whom I have sinned, have pity upon me in this last agony!—I saw—

It was there!

The same, perhaps, in every gruesome detail, but to me it appeared more monstrous, more irreconcilable, more loathsome.

But what of such things? Was it not sufficient to know that it was there—waiting for me? Was it not enough to know that its entire purpose was fixed upon my destruction? What mattered it, then, if the eyes were a little fiercer, the body a little larger, the entire appearance more hideous? This could bring no alteration to the manner of the end.

Quickly I perceived that I had too long trifled with the power of the unknown. The foul creature had determined to take its vengeance with speed, and to allow no second opportunity for escape.

Soon the entire ebon-like body quivered with preparation for immediate motion. As I still gazed, with fixed eyes of sheer anguish, the mass surged forward, heaved upward, each horrible leg moving slowly and deliberately, each red eye gleaming with most malignant light. The gradual and awful ascent had commenced.

My limbs were paralysed again; I was the helpless martyr at the stake. My tongue curled up inside my mouth like a dry leaf; my muscles cracked like rotten twigs; my entire mortal being lay beneath the awful rigour of death, frozen into a stern and absolute rigidity.

The second symbolic movement had taken place, when a mad revulsion of Nature shook the house. Tempestuous wind came rushing along the passage, while a malignant serpent of yellow light hissed across the open window. Then there followed other sounds beneath. A weird, wild shriek echoed within my ears.

The wind collected itself into a concrete body, and dashed against the dark door that fronted me. The wood work creaked, while the hinges shook; presently it gave way, and yawned open, falling back deliberately, while the frenzied vapour swept inwards with a hiss of menace.

And there, in the centre of that black oak frame, appeared a figure, dark and terrible. Dark, yet with white face set against the night. While every feature in that countenance formed a bitter line of inextinguishable hatred.

And again came that wild shriek from below.

CHAPTER IX

THE RETURNING OF SETH

And Cain said unto the Lord, My punishment is
greater than I can bear.—GEN. iv. 13.

8.30 p.m.

IT was my wife.

Horrible as was this fresh vision, it accomplished in part the
breaking of that terrible spell. It imparted power to my limbs, even
capability to my brain.

A resonant roll of thunder roared forth, as the door swung
back, and disclosed the hated being without. The apparition on the
wall appeared to rock backward and forward, and leap from side to
side, as though in excess of joy, or of anger at this interruption to
its work.

She advanced into the room, while a shadowy hand pulled back
the door.

'So you are here,' she said. Her eyes were like two cold stones at
the bottom of a slimy well, and her voice as the touch of the east
wind across a snow-covered moor.

It was natural that I should feel fear, for it was long since I had
seen her, still longer since I had addressed to her open speech. Now
she had sought me of her own free will, and for what purpose?
Not to offer me that meed of consolation which she had wickedly
withheld so long. She stood, and glared upon me with great, dark
eyes.

I made a mighty effort to reply. As the words rose in my throat,
hot fear burnt them up, and they shrivelled away into dry gaspings.
But as I stared at this white-faced woman, who bore a murderer's
name, stumbling feet shuffled along the passage. That fierce cry of
anger circled madly around, and there came a furious beating of
clenched fists at the door panels.

The snake-like woman, who bore my name, turned upon me.

'Do you hear that?' she cried. 'Do you know why this madman follows me about?'

I would have answered that I was not her keeper, but my tongue remained fear-bound.

'I believe you are my husband—they say that I have your name. Are you going to protect me from him? Will you—'

Shouts of anger drowned her speech. Again the door gave way. My uncle fell into the room, quivering with his madness and fury. His wrinkled face was distorted and hideous; the grey hair set along his head like wires; his eyes were distended and bloody. I saw that he had attained the final stage of his disease, that he was incontrollable, and dead to human intelligence.

The awful creature on the wall made no movement. I perceived that its red eyes were fixed steadily upon the form of my wife.

'Are you going to protect me?' she cried again. 'Or shall I call in strangers, and disgrace your house?'

'White devil!'[1] shouted the hoarse voice. His throat was rough and sore with the poisons he had imbibed. 'Ugly white devil, I have you now. Ha, ha! You cannot get away from me this time.'

I stirred, and my dry figure cracked within the chair. The sound reached his sense, and he perceived me.

'Nephew! I've been looking for you, but they told me you were buried. I said I would go and dig you up. In the early morning I was looking round for your grave. I have a fine new mixture, nephew.' We will drink it together presently, you and I. We must get rid of the tiger first. I have tracked her all day. Now I have her, nephew, I have her.'

His strange figure lurched about the room. I saw—and I under-stood the truth with a distinct sense of sorrow—that he could not possibly harm her, for he was unarmed, and weaker than a child. Also I perceived that she was aware of this, and therefore was bold.

'You miserable pair!' she cried.

I laughed inwardly, while my uncle shouted again and again.

'One of you—he is called my husband, though he has, in his cowardice, never dared to claim the husband's privileges—is mad

---

1 In John Webster's tragedy, *The White Devil* (1612), the title's oxymoron applies to Vittoria because of her ambiguous morality—"white" being her public persona of chastity, "devil" connoting the private wickedness of an evil temptress.

with the sense of his vileness. The other has ruined his soul and
wrecked his body in the drunkard's hell, which he has thought paradise. And you dare to claim brotherhood with humanity—you
two.'

'She wants to kill you, nephew. I heard her saying it. And she
wants to kill me, too.'

How was it that my wife did not blench from that horror upon
the wall? She could not fail to notice the monstrous black body
outspread on that white surface. Yet she never glanced towards it,
nor did she display any sign of fear.

'Can you not speak?' cried this malignant woman furiously.
'Why do you sit there, cringing and trembling? This creature is
your uncle, and may obey you. I am your wife, and have a right to
be protected. Tell him to go, before I have him removed by force.'

Power of speech and freedom of action had not yet come to
me. I made no motion and no sign, because I could not.

'Ha, ha! you are going to fight with me. You will show me that
you are the strongest. We shall see. We shall see. Do you see that
lizard between us?'

She drew back with a gesture of horror. The mere mention of
such objects is a terror to women. Why did not my uncle point
towards that black spider, which was so far more fearfully great
and conspicuous?

'See what I am going to do with it. I have never killed a lizard
before, but I am going to now. I will show you what I would like
to do with you.'

He sprang forward, and stamped repeatedly upon the floor,
with many hoarse cries. He slipped to and fro. He closed his eyes
at the horror of his deed. He sweated and groaned, while his feet
worked their destruction against the white carpet.

'You see it now. Look how I have mangled the lizard. It was alive
only a minute ago, but now it is all in pieces. Look at its two round
eyes rolling at your feet, and the torn shreds of its legs. That's what
I am going to do with you. My nephew will help me, for he hates
you, too. Nephew! Come here! Come here!'

I remained as powerless to stir from my position as I was unable
to respond to his fearful words.

He reeled back excitedly, with hands trembling, his fingers

gripping at the air, as though it were a thing of substance. Once his body came between me and the dark presence of the fiend; another time I thought he must surely fall upon and crush it; once he actually appeared to brush upon the bristling shape. I could even hear the dull hiss of the hairs along his coat, and I wondered at his intrepidity.

My wife took up her stand in the centre of the floor, her lips curling with passion, her eyes smouldering with hate. Even at that moment I understood that she was about to pit her forces against ours, that she was going to fight us both with her woman's cunning, and fight, moreover, to the death.

Yet it was an unequal combat, for I had but my mad uncle as an ally, whereas she had, fighting victoriously on her side, my brother, in the many subtle forms of immortality, with that livid cross-marked demon near at hand.

I marvelled at her coolness. What a fearful opponent is a desperate woman! How deliberate she is in her momentous actions! How gradually she mounts towards the apex of her retaliation, slowly, sternly, without any of those sudden impulses of fury—the mad fury that upsets calculation—of the headstrong man! What a splendid animal she is, when she has finally cast aside her wiles, her delicate allurements, her coy mask of inability, and stands out in the nakedness of self! Above all, what an infinity of power lies behind that weakness—the pride of woman, because it is her cruellest weapon of strength!

'Take care, nephew,' came in a deep voice. 'The tiger is going to spring at you. Look at her claws and her teeth. She wants to tear you in pieces, nephew.'

She moved a step towards him, and he slunk away abjectly, because he could not resist the pressure of her mind upon his impaired reason. She came between us. I lay upon the chair to the left; my uncle was upon her right; opposite, staring into her eyes with a steady gaze, was the black image of my remorse.

'You first,' she said, with a grim smile in the voice, as she turned her back upon me. 'You are a madman, I know, and for that I have pitied you in a manner, though you have brought the affliction upon yourself.'

'White devil!' he shrieked, interrupting, with glaring eyes.

She came a step nearer, and he cringed away before the power of her reason.

'So long as you kept on your way, and left me to mine, I should not have interfered—with you. Now I am forced to act, for you have threatened me. The last two days you have followed me about.'

'I want to kill you,' he shrieked forth. 'You know that I want to kill you badly. You have sucked the life out of my poor nephew. I love my nephew, and he loves me. We are going to kill you, when we get the chance. Ha, ha! I have been looking for a gun all day. When I find one, I shall come and shoot you. I will trample on you, as I did on the lizard. Then you will die, and not trouble us any more.'

She had let him go on, as though anxious to hear all he had to say.

'I thought so,' she said calmly. 'You are a weak old man, and probably harmless, for all your threats. Still you shall not stand in my way. I am going to get rid of you—and at once.'

'Do you hear, nephew?' he screamed. 'I told you what she was. Now she is going to suck away my life. Come and help me, nephew. Come and stand by me. We will fight her together.'

He slunk into the corner, his small eyes moving fearfully. Again I made an effort to move, but again in vain. I was marble, and not flesh. I was a frozen image, and not man. I could see, I could hear, I could feel the brooding horror impending. That was all.

My wife spoke again, in the tones of disdain. 'With either of you words are foolish, and yet—women have few privileges, and free speech is perhaps the greatest.'

'You tiger! You white devil! You want to murder me. I know you do. I have known it for a long time. I will stand here, and I will fight. Fight, do you hear? Ha, ha! I will fight with you. See! I have strong nails, long nails. I will tear out your two eyes, and send them rolling at your feet, like the lizard's eyes lying over there. I will—'

'Stop!' she cried with violence, and the moment she spoke the word he was silent. 'I have listened to your ravings long enough. I am going to have you removed from this house, and from association with your rational fellow-creatures. I shall see that you are taken to your proper home—the madhouse.'

I felt a shudder fall over me at that awful name. My uncle sat in his corner, and screamed in newborn fear.

'For the present I shall leave you together. I am going for the doctor, who will certify that you (pointing a scornful finger at his huddled form) are in no state to be left at liberty. You shall spend your last days in the company of those who are as yourself—hopelessly insane.'

'No, no,' he cried fearfully, the head rolling on his shoulders. 'That is not true. Nephew, tell her it is not true. I am an old man, and harmless—quite harmless. I am only the king of the insects, and have never done any harm. Tell her so, nephew. She will listen to you, for they say you are her husband.'

'He!' she cried. And then her lips closed together again. But her eyes turned upon me once, for one moment only—it was enough.

She rustled over the white carpet, like the living spirit of vengeance, clad in her black garments. That wealth of hair I had once gone mad over gleamed in the strong lamplight. Her pale lips parted once in a half smile at the thought of her coming triumph. Then she came to the door, which presently closed behind, and hid her hated figure from my view.

So she was gone, but for a time only. She would return to complete the work she had but commenced.

The demon on the wall moved his horrid legs menacingly, while, for the first time, I detected a fearful miasma, an odour of death, emanating from the awful body.

Then my uncle crept over the floor towards me on his hands and bony knees, crying like a child, and shivering with the great fear of approaching bondage—that dreadful incarceration within the living tomb of the madhouse.

## CHAPTER X

### THE SETTLING OF SHADOW

The wormwood and the gall.—LAM. JEREMIAH iii. 19.

9.45 p.m.

THE heat of the night lay around like a thick, damp mantle. The darkness was cut by thin and constant blades of lightning, while dreary thunder spoke hoarsely its messages from without.

As the yellow hands of my uncle fell upon my knees, energy flowed back in the form of speech and partial understanding. I seized his wrists, and bent down to his upturned face, which was palpitating with terror. I drew him nearer—my sole friend in the two worlds—and he came with stiff motions, until we crouched together, muttering and sweating, each shuddering with the other.

'Uncle,' I gasped in hollow accents, to test my strength. When I found that power of speech was mine, I went on, 'She is coming back again.'

'Nephew,' he panted, with lower jaw hanging dog-like. 'She has gone for the other one that tried to kill you. They are going to take me away from you, and bury me alive. I heard her say it. Nephew, will the pain be very bad? Can I stand it, nephew—I am an old man, and weak?'

'Listen, uncle. They are going to lock you up with a lot of mad creatures. You will be by yourself in a small tomb, where there is a little light, a little air, and sometimes they will bring you food to keep your body alive. If you say anything to them, they will torture you. They are devils there, and not men.'

'Nephew, I will kill them. I will pull them in pieces.'

'There are too many. There are thousands of them.'

'I will murder them all day and all night. I will drag their wicked eyes out.'

'You cannot. They are too strong for you.'

'I will bring all my subjects against them. Beetles, nephew, with great poisonous spiders—'

'That!' I shrieked, pointing with all my newfound strength. 'Take that.'

He peered round towards the monstrous horror on the white wall. 'Give it me, nephew. What shall I take?'

'That. The awful spider. That hellish demon you are looking at.'

He blinked his eyes strangely. 'Nephew, there is nothing there.'

'Nothing! It is not three yards away. You certainly must see what a frightful thing it is.'

'Where is it, nephew? Where?'

'There—huge and horrible in the centre of the wall. Its body is like ebony, except for the silver cross. Its legs are like twisted black ropes. There, you can see the stiff, bristling hair on its body, and the dull gleaming of its eyes.'

'No, nephew, no.'

'See, it moved its jaws as a sign of menace. It made a half movement. Do you know what it is about to do?'

'It is not there, nephew—not upon the white wall.'

'It will climb up that white wall, and then along the ceiling. Above my head it will stop, and hang above for a long time. Then it will drop—very suddenly, you understand. It will drop, sprawling, right across my face.'

'Nephew, there is no black spider.'

'Once before it did so, and I came near to death. My physical strength was so great that I recovered. It will drop again presently, and this time I must succumb. It will tear body and soul apart.'

My uncle partially lost his fear in witnessing mine. 'Ha, ha! nephew. This is a very good jest of yours. I cannot see any black spider there.'

'It is half the size of my body, and it swells to a greater extent each hour. Look at the great cross on its back. Why does it bear that mark? Such a sign they erect over graves. It will be placed over ours. What does it mean? What is the good of it?'

'It is another jest, nephew, a very good jest.'

'I know,' I shouted at him, as my brain dissolved. '*The Lord set a mark upon Cain.* That was the mark. It was the mark of the white cross upon the black soul. That was the mark set upon the fore-head of Cain.'

The grim thunders rolled forth in solemn corroboration of my words.

'Listen, nephew.' My uncle was pulling at my arm. 'I cannot see the black spider. Do you see that slimy snake coiling and uncoiling in the corner?'

I gazed in the direction that he indicated. There was nothing visible, only an awful blot of shadow.

'There is no snake there, uncle.'

'On that chair are a nest of horrid white creatures. They writhe and they twist, with mouths wide open. They have long pink tongues like flames of fire.'

'I see only the reflection of the lamplight.'

He pulled himself upright, and set his trembling lips against my ear. 'Listen, nephew, I have something to tell you. Listen, now. We are mad, both of us. The tiger was right. We are quite mad, but we shall be happy if she will leave us alone.'

I laughed at the hidden mockery in his words. 'I cannot see the snake and the white creatures—'

'Nephew, I cannot see the big black spider. So, you see, we are both very plainly mad.'

'But she will be coming back. She is coming back—and for you.'

His fear returned. 'She is going to take me first. She will put me in the deep tomb. Then she will come back for you. She said so, nephew.'

'Uncle,' I whispered. 'We must escape.'

His face became altered with a strange joy. 'Yes, yes, nephew. We will go away together, and never come back here. We will go quickly before the tiger comes. We have always been good friends, nephew. We will go together, and find another home to live in. Come on, nephew, come quickly. The tiger may return at any minute, and catch us in her claws.'

I gripped the sides of the chair, and struggled to force myself from its embrace. The effort was without avail. My uncle seized me with nerveless hands, and pulled at my quivering arms, yet the endeavour of each of us failed utterly. My extremities were frozen and stonelike; they had not the strength to support my body; the energies were paralysed and useless. With a fearful cry I again fell back, panting and groaning. The chair received and held me. My uncle stood in front, wringing two bony hands.

'I cannot, uncle. My strength has gone. I cannot get away.'

'Nephew, come. Come, nephew. You must, or the tiger will be here.'

'I cannot move while that is here—the black spider, uncle.'

'She will soon come. Nephew, we must escape, or she will find you in her trap. She will fasten her white claws into you, and suck away your life.'

'She is going to take you to the madhouse. Escape, uncle, while you can.'

'I want you,' he moaned. 'You have been good to me, and I love you. Try again, nephew—once again.'

I strove, until my muscles stretched and cracked, but the effort was wasted. I could not rise, nor could I even raise my body from the chair which held it. I was as powerless as the insect, that is caught and held by the sticky mesh of some spider's web.

'I am cursed, uncle,' I shouted then. 'I am damned, for the mark of Cain is on me.'

He swayed to and fro in front of me in an ecstasy of horror. Suddenly his face broke up, and he shouted at me, 'The mixture, nephew! The new mixture that I made in the blue room. It is down there now. I will go for it. There may be time, nephew—time before the tiger comes back.'

'Get it, uncle.'

'I have never made such a mixture before, nephew. It is so wonderful that I did not dare taste it by myself. We will each take half. It will give you life and strength. Then you will be able to leave that chair. We will escape, nephew—go away together. The tiger shall never find us again.' He lurched to the door, across which the lightning shuddered. 'I am going for the mixture, nephew. There will be time before the tiger comes.'

He disappeared. Once I heard him fall heavily. Then he continued his journey with many wild shouts of excitement. The door was half open, while blackness lay without, darkness where I could see awful faces of despair and pain that jeered at my impotence.

Outside, the storm increased; within, the squat demon lay stagnant on the wall, gloating over my hopelessness.

Thus I remained until the shouts and groans of my uncle came close again. He reeled into the room, clutching a bottle to his heart.

'I have it, nephew. I have the mixture,' he cried again and again, with furious chuckles.

'We must be quick, uncle,' I gasped.

'It is terrible on the stairs, nephew. I could not walk for the creatures. There are fearful creatures crawling everywhere. I kept stumbling over their slippery bodies. In the passage I trod upon a slimy snake. Didn't you hear me fall? The snake tried to bite me, but I stamped upon its head. It is dead, nephew. Ha, ha! Quite dead.'

'The mixture!'

'Ha, ha! nephew. The mixture. Yes, we will drink it together, and then we will escape.'

He put the cork to his broken teeth and pulled. It came forth, while a frightful odour crept into the room. He lurched towards a side table, and clutched at a couple of glasses. His eyes rolled, and became filled with a dull fire.

'Smell it, nephew. Ha, ha! It is a glorious mixture. It is wonderful, nephew. You shall have half. I will have half. Perhaps I shall see the black spider then.'

By a great effort he composed his body, then poured forth a half glass of the fearful compound. The liquor glittered and shone as it fell in long threads of light. Then he stopped, while the matter settled within the glass. It was like solid ebony, of a most inconceivable and dead blackness.

'Take it, nephew. Drink it. You will be young again and strong.'

I only shuddered as I looked upon it. 'Is it poison, uncle?'

'No, no. It will give you life; it will give you strength. An eternity of both. Drink, nephew.'

The odour surged up from the glass and stifled my senses. My brain revolted, while sparks of flame darted before my vision. 'I have no strength, uncle. I have not even power for this.'

'It will give you the power. Take it, nephew, and then you will move eagerly. The tiger will soon be back.'

The storm raved forth as he spoke, but surely there were other sounds, actually at the entrance of the house, or even within. A hollow clanging, then a reverberation seemed to arise from the darkness and silence beneath.

I seized the glass, raised it upward, then paused. Distinctly to my ears there came, from the distant portion of the house, a harsh opening, then a resonant closing, of a weighty door.

'She has come back,' I shrieked. Then the glass dropped from my nerveless grasp. The frightful black compound soaked itself within the white carpet, forming a gruesome, octopus-like pattern round my feet.

My uncle swayed before me, gibbering with disappointment and fear.

'Nephew!' he gasped forth. 'You have lost the mixture. There is only the half left, and the white devil has come back.'

'Uncle!' I shouted. 'She is coming up the stairs.'

'She is going to put us in the tomb—alive.'

'She is coming for you—you first.'

The monster on the wall oscillated to and fro with his joy.

'I will drink my half of the mixture. It will give me strength, nephew. Then I shall escape, and I shall be able to help you. Yes, yes. I shall help you to escape, nephew.'

He raised the glass to his lips, and it chattered upon his teeth. I could see how the deadly fumes were choking him. He gasped and gulped down a portion. Then the half-emptied glass shivered upon the floor, and he spun round towards me, his limbs jerking and writhing.

'Help me, uncle,' I whispered fearfully. 'Help me to escape now.'

A fearful thing happened. The blood rushed into his face in a torrent, and there burst through the skin. The eyes seemed to hang from his head at the end of long strings. . . . The door was forced open by a current of air along the passage, and I shrieked and shrieked again.

He staggered to the window, and held to the ledge with abnormal strength. The tongue fell from his lips, vibrating like a spring. Presently there issued a frightful voice, more hideous a sound than any that may ever have jarred upon the ear of mortality. It came to me from a distance. It impressed me—even at that moment—with a sense of the speech of the dead.

'I am very strong again. . . . I will go out by the window . . . and escape . . . then walk round to the door . . . and wait for you . . . come quick . . . nephew. . . .'

With a bound he sprang upon and through the aperture. For a second his horrid fingers showed, clutching the ledge. Then these vanished—there was an awful pause of silence.

That window was fifty feet above the level of the terrace—the stone terrace.

I realised the length of a single second of time.

There came the frightful thud of the dull flesh, as it met the cruel wet stonework of the terrace beneath.

Again there sounded the hateful rustling along the passage; again the slow, yet light, footfall. Once more the white set countenance of hate within the dark framework of the door.

Alone she came, and she entered—alone.

CHAPTER XI

IMMORTALITY AND TWO MORTALS

If you have poison for me, I will drink it.
I know you do not love me.

*King Lear*, Act IV., sc. 7.

10.30 p.m.

In a dumb marvel, like the man who falls gradually beneath the influence of a drug, I looked upon her. My senses dropped and failed, the light of the room flickered to a dull unsteady flame, while my heart lay sluggish. There was nothing to wait for, but the end, which I now perceived was at no great distance. With almost a wild curiosity I wondered what form it would take, what method would be employed by the diabolical creature for my final torturing. Yet I was indifferent almost, for the gall which flowed in my veins enervated the sense of understanding and deadened the energy of thought.

This was only the inaction prior to the struggle, the last mercy extended to the criminal before execution. The awakening was near at hand.

I presently found myself speaking. I was not conscious of the effort, yet I detected the sound of a voice, which a dull instinct suggested was mine, throbbing into my ears. I was asking a question, which took some such form as this— 'Why have you come back?'

Each syllable was a separate snake bite to her, for she turned upon me the head of a Medusa, and the face of a Fury. Her voice, when she spoke, suggested the horrid, stagnant pool of unknown depths, which the traveller may sometimes find frowning sullenly before him, in some black and lonely forest.

'You ask me that—you. Where is *he?*' She looked round and cast her eyes into each corner.

I grinned with the agony of that question. I was fearfully alone, for my last companion had been snatched from me. There was none for me to look to now.

'Where has he gone? I have been for the doctor, but he is away. Perhaps he will come presently, and then we shall end all this. Your uncle shall go to his own fitting place, while you will be left—here.'

'You want him,' I whispered hoarsely. 'You are looking for my uncle. Shall I tell you where to find him?'

'Where is he?' she only asked again sternly.

'He heard you coming, so he went out by the window to escape. He is out on the terrace now—the stone terrace. I do not know what he is doing there.'

The lights of the night struck upon her face. It was very white and set in fear.

'Then—he has killed himself.'

'No—no,' I said, with the cunning in my nature arising. 'It is not so. There is murder here. He heard you coming; he knew you wished to destroy him. He would not have gone from the window, had it not been for you. You have killed him.'

She went back a little at that word. But the next moment she remembered, and again came forward.

'You have murdered,' I chuckled, pointing. 'There is the red mark upon your forehead also. I shall tell all the world that you have murdered my uncle.

'Is that all the tale you will have to tell?' she said, with a fierce smile.

I would have answered her, but a dull sound near caused me to start round with full remembrance of my fate. The sound increased into a sharp rustling of wire-like hair.

The monster on the wall had altered his gaze from my face to hers. Suddenly he turned, dropped to the carpet, and placed his body between myself and the door. The dreadful crawling of that hideous shape filled my being with a shuddering sense of sickness. This change was quickly marked by my wife. She noted my distracted gaze, so turned, and there, standing not more than a yard distant, was the foulest object ever born into this world.

With a savage triumph I looked for her to scream, to fall down in a death-like fit, or at the least to shrink away in horror as far as possible from that enormity. But she did none of these things. Not

even did she stir, nor make any sign of fear, when the loathsome
mass raised two red-hot eyes to hers, when he dug his pointed
claws into the carpet, and dragged himself nearer, when even he
raised himself on quivering legs to caress her hand, and to press his
poisonous jaws upon her skin. Intrepid and fearless woman! She
had no fear for that which had driven me to the brink of madness.

There was a voice within the room. It was surely my own,
for her lips did not move, but my ears gave no recognition to the
sound.

'You see it now—the devil that tortures me?'

She set her cold eyes towards me. 'Of what are you speaking?'

The voice came again. 'That—the great spider. The monster
that shows love for you, that is caressing you now.'

A fearful smile grew round her mouth. 'Madman!' she muttered. 'You are being punished indeed.'

'I am. Why have you come back? Why do you add to my
agony?'

Then she came a step towards me, and spoke furiously,—

'Why? You know that better than myself even. You understand
what I have suffered through your wickedness, and you know what
has brought me here to-night.'

I shivered as the cold hailstones of speech beat around me.

'All this time I have watched you, silently and secretly. Long
ago I wrung the dark secret from your mind. I have looked upon
you from the shadows of the garden. I have seen you holding your
hands to the Heaven that hates you. I have heard you crying forth
in your anguish. I have gazed upon you in the dark corridors, while
you have paced to and fro, with the groans falling from your lips.
I have seen you start aside, when the shadow of some harmless
object has fallen across your path. And I noticed your horror of
the night.'

I shouted aloud, and cursed her with a dying effort. When
strength fell from me, she went on with the same cold fury,—

'I have kept by you, when you were unaware of my presence. I
have listened to your every utterance. I have marked the dim mutterings of your tongue. I have overheard the confession of your
heart, when it has been wrung forth by the strong hand of terror.
Often, at many times in the day, beneath the sunlight, at night

from the darkness, or to the white glimmer of the moon, I have heard the words of meaning. Shall I repeat them now?'

To that I could make no answer. She continued pitilessly. '"Oh! my brother—you are surely avenged. Rest now; for the love I bore you, rest, and leave me." Can you remember those words?'

I laughed aloud in my delirium. 'Then you have suffered, too. I am glad of it.'

'I have suffered. You, with your guilty heart and fear-stricken mind, can you form any idea of that burden which I was compelled to sustain by day and by night? The slow forming of the suspicion, the gradual acquiring of knowledge, the sudden shock of the certainty, finally the crushing weight of the truth. This I have borne, while you have walked alone, with your malice, and the low cunning of the animal that strives to escape the nets which have been spread for its entanglement.'

'Woman!' I shouted at her. 'Reflect on my punishment. Think on what I have undergone, then strive to compare the least of my sufferings with the greatest of yours. What torture has burnt away your heart? What canker of remorse has eaten into your soul? You are free, and can look the world in the face. You may sleep by night unmoved. You can walk forth without a tremor where the shadows lie. What more can you desire?'

Then she smiled at me, and I learnt that the smile of a vengeful woman is more terrible than her frown. She smiled, and came nearer to my crushed figure. She paused, and spoke again,—

'You have suffered only from remorse, and the memory of evil accomplished. What do you know of the heart of sorrow? You have only feared the daylight, but I have never seen it. You have shrunk from the night, because of its blackness, its horror, but to me it has been the same as the invisible day. What do you know of the keen edge of grief?—you, who have madness to assist you in bearing the sorrow of your own creation—'

I broke in upon her words, howling and raving in my fury. 'Madness! I am not mad. I am more sane now than you have ever been.'

'Enough,' she cried fiercely. 'I am not here to discuss such questions.'

I fell into a calmer mood, and even laughed at her pale

countenance. 'Remember that you bear my name. The husband should hold no secret from the wife, so it is right that you should know all. But the world will not listen to your testimony. After you have done your best to ruin the man whose name you bear, they will only jeer at you. They will call you the murderer's wife. They will say that you are the partner of the man who killed his brother. It will be a good jest.'

She writhed, like a wounded snake, and I thought I had beaten her. But the woman is at her strongest when trampled upon. She will not turn to inflict the fatal blow, until such time as her defeat seems assured.

'You asked me why I am here. As yet I have not told you. Listen now, for I wish you to hear the truth. Tell me this—why did I marry you?'

I grew cunning again, because I saw her falling into my snare. 'You are a woman, and I am rich,' I gave her answer. 'By nature you envied my wealth, nor may I blame you for your covetousness, since you are a woman. Wealth is all that you can love, and wealth you have acquired. May you rest miserable in its possession.'

She came even nearer, until she cried into my face, 'Man, have you no heart?'

'Woman,' I called back, 'I have none. You have stifled and corrupted it.'

She gave a groan, and I thought it was of pain, but I was mistaken. 'Then I have obtained my wish.'

I stared fearfully, while the black monster made a vile movement towards her, and the storm rattled the window sashes. With scarcely a break she resumed,—

'I married you, not for yourself, not for your wealth—but for the sake of revenge.'

The apparition was at her side, beaming upon her with awful eyes.

'You—even you cannot think that I married you for affection's sake. Search the world for the most depraved and deformed being that bears the name of man. Him would I promise to love in preference to you. I would say that I hated you, but the word is ineffectual. When I consented to be your wife, I could have bitten out your heart.'

Her words hissed round me like whip thongs. They stung my body with the bite of scorpions.

'What do I care for wealth? Money may perhaps purchase puppets, painted and perfumed toys, that move and breathe. But nothing will buy womanhood, except the wealth of a pure heart of love. When you stood at my side on the cliff, with the lying vow on your lips, and the brother's blood on your hands, had you that to offer me? Can the man who has murdered his brother swear to dedicate a loyal life of service to her—to her whom the brother loved?'

My voice was broken, and hollow as the rifted organ pipe. 'You knew nothing—then,' I muttered.

The remark reached no ears. With restored calmness she continued. 'For there was one man whom I loved. To him I had sworn to consecrate my life, while his heart for me was faithful and true. His was the pure heart that weighs heavier than earthly possessions. The name of that man you know.'

I shivered anew, yet more with passion than with fear. I had been completely and miserably duped.

'That man was your brother.'

I knew it, but to hear the truth from her false lips stabbed another thrill of anguish through my body. 'He was a vile traitor,' I muttered. 'See what I had done for him. Judge him by the return he made. He robbed me. He betrayed me.'

'And you killed him,' she finished, with her woman's bitterness.

'He deserved it. He should have been made to suffer more. No punishment is too heavy for such a man.'

'Except for that one who has done murder,' she added again. 'But now I will finish. You say that I never knew what your madness had accomplished. Was there none, then, who could have warned me?'

'Who?' I ejaculated, as I fell drunkenly from side to side in the chair.

'Yet you declare you are not mad,' she cried in the voice of scorn. 'Can you not guess, fool, that it was he who warned me?'

'But he was dead then. The dead are silent.' I refrained, for I had cause to know that the voice of the dead can never be hushed.

'Before that. The very night of his disappearance. Ah! you

alone know the true history of that. He had spoken to me; he had warned me of you and your strange moods. Even then he was afraid of you, and shrank from you. His one fault was his love for an unworthy brother. He dared not speak the truth, for he feared lest he should give you pain.'

I gnashed my teeth, and twisted my fingers together until the muscles cracked.

'When I heard the tale that broke my heart I guessed the truth. After that I could only hate—hate and avenge. I resolved to marry you, that I might increase your desolation and despair, that I might drag you towards the fate which was yours by justice. In your house I might watch your every movement. I might be sure that you could not escape my plan. I had fully determined to drive you to the end of your earthly existence. I had resolved to hang over you, like the vampire, the fury, until you should set the seal upon your wicked actions, and sink to your damnation by the frenzied act of the suicide.'

She spoke deliberately. Each ice-cold word fell upon my red-hot brain, and there hissed.

'I had not fully determined upon my course of action,' she added wearily, with again that ghastly smile; 'but after a few days I perceived that I had but to leave you alone, and allow you only an occasional glimpse of my person in the house or garden. I under-stood that remorse was doing its own work—and doing it with its usual thoroughness.'

No ingenuity could forge reply to this. I remained speechless and fear stricken.

'Day after day I watched you, as you struggled wildly to escape from the invisible presence which hung always to your footsteps. I perceived the growing ascendency of its influence, and I rejoiced at the sight. Then one day I came to the library, where I discov-ered the work of the Norse philosopher that lay open upon the table. I had often seen you with this roll of manuscript. There were passages marked, most evidently by you. These I copied, and had translated. So I began to understand the state of your agony, could comprehend those ghastly suspicions that were gradually arising in your mind, the fear lest that remorse, the natural con-sequence of your vile actions, should slowly form into material being, should cover itself with flesh and skin, and finally appear before you, visible to your eyes.'

I gnawed my hands in the fury of complete impotence. This woman had read me like a book, had played with me as a child would toss a ball.

'Who has won? You, or I, or the being who stands between us—your brother and my husband?'

'It is a lie,' I muttered forth at length. 'You were never his. You are the wife—blench from the truth though you may—of the fratricide. The stain of blood rests upon you.'

'The ramblings of a madman are of small account,' she returned, with bitter scorn. 'Even though it be yours, I bear your brother's name. I gave him my heart—to you the meaningless promise of involuntary lips. My soul was his, and is linked to him beyond death. I lived that I might see him avenged. I became your wife in name that I might accomplish this work. Now we have reached the last stage of that duty.'

'We,' I shouted, until the voice cracked in my throat. 'You are here alone. This is all your work, and there is none to help you.'

'Fool!' she cried back at me. 'You have the two of us to contend with in the two worlds—your brother in eternity, and myself here.'

Once more I laughed, though it was the grin of the martyr upon the rack. 'I will tell you where he is,' I said in a wonderfully cunning tone. 'Go out through the garden, and by the gate in the hedge along the cliff path. Then you will find yourself upon a grass ledge, beneath which—hundreds of feet below—the black sea dashes and roars. I led you to this spot on a certain evening. It was here that you consented to become my bride. But you had not my eyes, sane as you call yourself. You could not see all that was lying upon the grass. There was blood, I tell you. We were wading in it, while beneath—how many fathoms deep I cannot tell you—there was a body; a body which could not hear, nor see, nor speak. But for all that it was moving. It stirred up and down with the restless motion of the undercurrents. It rose and fell upon the soft sand bed. At times it rested lightly upon the fragile shells; at other times it bounded with force against sharp rocks. Once you loved that body. But what of it now? How will it serve you? Those arms cannot hold you in the embrace of love. Those sunken eyes cannot gaze into yours with the light of adoration. Those cold ears are covered now with clinging shell fish and briny weed, so they cannot listen to your soft speech. Those blue rotting lips can never again press—'

'Fiend!' she screamed, interrupting me in my last pleasure. Then she crouched before me, like some gaunt tiger. More she would have said, but the words cloyed in her throat, and utterance was choked. I experienced a strange, hot joy in seeing her writhing beneath the torment of my words.

'Perhaps your ears have become deadened to sounds from without. Perhaps you have not listened with my attention. I have often sat up in my fearful bed, when the night was very black. I have then plainly heard a dull scraping of bones against the wet rocks. When the sea was calm, that sound would be scarcely audible, but when the wind rose and shrieked I was quite unable, by even any mechanical effort, to shut forth the ghastly rattling of bone with rock. For the waves were heavy, and there was no rest for the dead on such a night. Could you not hear those muffled movements beneath the sea? Yet you say you loved him.'

She stood by me, panting, with hands to her breast.

'By day the tumult of the world usually drowned these sounds. Yet you might have gone forth to the cliff, and from there have gazed down upon the heaving waters. After a short time, if your eyes were steady, you would have noted a strange glow arising, as it were, from the bottom. This tinged the white foam with the red of the western sky. The colours would deepen, until presently you would have seen nothing beneath but a turgid, sullen, boiling torrent, that was like blood. And then—but only if your senses had been particularly acute—you could not have failed to notice a mysterious odour that crawled up the face of the cliff. Was all this lost upon you? Yet you say you loved him. I hated him—and yet I missed none of it.'

She was calm again: calm as the Arctic day, where Nature is frozen to silence.

'That body you may call yours. The soul, which you have tried in vain to touch, is mine. All that lies at the bottom of the sea is nothing but a reminiscence, a faded flower of the past, a broken thought, which I may now dismiss, and exchange for hope. The life of your brother is not there, but here with us in this room.'

The black enormity, that she would not notice, dragged himself forward, as though to corroborate her statement. Together they stood there, side by side, a gruesome and most malignant couple.

'Yes—here. He is prepared to drive you to the self-destruction that your deeds have merited. Your two enemies stand before you, and where—where are your friends? You have refused mercy, and cast aside opportunity for amendment. Your fate has come, and it is time.'

There was a rattling of thunder through the stifling air. My brain rocked to and fro, while the heart burnt through my stone-like flesh.

'Your brother is here.'

She looked around her with the air of victory, yet not down upon the dark horror which raised himself upon horrible legs to greet her outstretched hand. Then again he settled himself upon the carpet, squat and silent. Yet it never withdrew from my crushed and helpless figure the awful gleaming of those hot, cruel eyes.

The pallor on her face increased as she drew back a pace. Perhaps she had noticed the death tints breaking out on my forehead.

'I have finished now.'

But when I perceived that she was about to leave me to an eternity of desolation, the agony of my whole horror rushed forth in a mighty torrent. True indeed that I hated her, yet when she was present the monster was inactive. Now she was deserting me, for her portion of the work had been accomplished. She was leaving me to the furious will of the unutterable demon, that squatted crab-like upon the floor. She was abandoning me to the vengeance of that awful partner. I should be alone—alone again with That. The very thought made me look upon death with a smile.

I prayed, I wept, I raved. I gave many a blind promise. I made many an incoherent vow. I swore that I would perform things that were impossible, if she would only release me from that foe. Free once more, I would alter the very morals of the world. I would change the evil fashions of its inhabitants. Nay, more, in that maniacal fury, I declared that I had discovered a process by which the dead could be raised again to life. I would restore to her my brother in the form she had loved.

In that agony I taught the very devils how to blaspheme.

She smiled, that same fearful smile, then came towards the table at my side. Something flashed from her dress. That something she set down within reach of my hand, and then she turned away again. The door fell back before her, while the web of blackness spread sable wings beyond. She paused there, and looked back.

'We shall meet no more. Though we are both immortal, I shall never look upon your face again, nor you upon mine. This is the farewell of eternity, my husband—my husband.' And she laughed aloud. 'Here we separate, and I leave you with that which may help you to the end.'

The object she pointed at, and which I now saw clearly for the first time, was a long, sharp-pointed knife. The handle was towards me. The keen edge glittered in that light.

I was as lead that melted in the furnace. I could not speak. I could not even cry forth for mercy. All that I might do—and that most horribly—was to behold, and to listen.

The door went away from me, and closed. The white face of desperation, with its weird smile of triumph, became hidden. The light sprang up into a cloud of sharp rays, to die away in a fearful mist, where shadows writhed and grinned in agony. Small echoes of the dying storm ran muttering round my head. All last traces of manliness within shrivelled away in a dry corruption. The black horror of the spider, the child of the Shadow, prepared himself for immediate action.

But she had gone—she had gone, while the door was closed and locked.

## CHAPTER XII

## TENEBRAE

Staggering, blind with folly, on the brink of Hell,
Above the everlasting fire-flood's frightful roar.
ORIENTAL.

Midnight.

I WRITE these closing words, with brain and mind alike collapsing. I shall continue to write, so long as I have strength to control the pen, or until the guardian demon in front tires of his vigil.

He has taken up his position between my chair and the door. Effectually he closes the way, most hideous of gaolers. There is to be no attempt on my part at bursting that locked door; there is to be no further trifling with the unknown; there is to be no second escape from the icy clutch of death. He crouches there, gaunt, virulent and irresistible. Never for a second does he withdraw his fearful gaze; never does he change his position. Never even does he move one of those eight black legs of horrible shape.

The storm outside seems to have arisen into fresh fury. Lightning pours into the window, while the artillery of the thunder rolls across the sky. What will have happened to my body by the time these clouds of tempest break? To what dark, hopeless land will the immortal essence of my being have journeyed by the time the early sun appears, when the world rejoices, and those who sleep between the hours of honest labour awake to the freshness of the new day? . . .

It is surely many years since the woman, whom I have known as my wife, departed. Since that event I have lived a thousand lives. I have passed through all the stages of human passion. I have stepped from one gradation of madness to another. I have experienced a scorching heat, and a searing cold. The sword hovers over my head, supported, so it would appear, by nothing, and yet it does not, it will not, fall. What a refinement of torture is here! I long for the end. I reach out my hands towards it. I pant to grasp it to my heart. I strive to draw it into my body. But no—not yet. The pain is to be prolonged, until all reason departs; the body is to be stretched above the flames, until the anguish is forgotten, until it comes to laugh at the torment, and to regard it as a thing to be even desired.

I am seated in the chair by the table, in the same spot where I have sat for ages. Here I can watch the monster, and note his every movement. Here, also, he can, with better advantage, proceed against me. When he advances I cannot go back—I cannot, unless in my agony I may force this tortured body through the wall of solid masonry. To go forward a few paces would mean falling into his awful clutches. . . .

My legs are frozen stiffly, and would not bear my weight. . . .

The most torturing of all reflections is that fact—which at first I banished from my mind as a thing too horrible for contemplation—that the light, supplied by the single lamp, is dying down slowly. Whether this be the work of some infernal hand, or whether it be owing simply to a natural failure of the oil supply, it is impossible for me to say. In another hour, at the most, I shall be plunged into the depth of a profound, a sepulchral, a most tangible, darkness. No longer shall I be able to see the grim shape of my destroyer. He will advance upon me, will seize me suddenly; the octopus-like legs will wind round my body in the dense gloom. Perchance I shall receive warning—awful indeed, yet better than complete ignorance. It may be that I shall still be allowed to behold the dull, hot gleam of his vindictive eyes, stabbing towards me through the sombre dividing curtain of night. . . .

Hard by me lies the long knife, gleaming menacingly into my face. Of what use is this pointed implement? I may not use terrestrial weapons against the foe. Can I make use of it for other purposes? No—Heaven's mercy and pity, no. I cannot, I will not, fall into the clutches of the grave by the miserable death of the suicide. . . .

Give me again one hour of that sacred time, when the world was one garden of flowers, when the bright butterflies of pleasure flitted unceasingly from side to side, when fear was unknown, when care was a fable, when, above all, the criminal conscience was a creation unmade. Give me one breath of that untainted air, again one glance into that paradise, again one reflection of that glorious and most perfect rapture. Lift me, raise me, if only for the moment, from this ecstasy of horror, this delirium of condemnation. Set me on the most slender pinnacle of the temple of hope. I have wealth; there is still much in the name of a dying man. Take this, take everything, and leave me naked. But give me, one minute, if I ask too much, one second, of the past happiness, give me again one throb of the heart that knew not sorrow. Refreshed by such strength, I could face the end, even though it be enveloped within most unimagined horrors. I could set my face against the monster opposite with a stern courage; I could meet his poisonous embrace without blenching. But none of this is possible. The worlds are against me. Heaven curses me. The face of earth-nature shudders at my presence. My only friends are the devils, and even these torture me. What is there in the future which may fortify me with hope for any end to my misery? There can be no hand to ease my body, there will be no balm to be applied to the comfort of my bruised soul. There is no pity here. There will be no mercy hereafter. . . .

My heart will continue to beat, the pulses will throb forth a knell of departing life, until I exchange a world of anguish for an eternity of remorse. . . .

Have I ever repented of putting an end to my brother's life? Yes, surely yes. Daily I have sweated with fear. I have shuddered through long nights of direst woe. I have shed tears whenever the beauty of the world has passed before my vision, when I have realised that none of it was for me, when I understood that I might not partake of the pleasure of life. I have torn the air with my cries. I have made Heaven weary of the sound of my lamentations. No ingenuity may conceive what torments I have undergone; no pen, not even my own, may narrate them; least of all could any mind grasp them, were they set forth faithfully. Are such mental and physical sufferings any contrition for evil accomplished? Again, I may not tell, for my brain is past all reasoning. . . .

Some men there are, who suddenly come to the end of life with an unrepented sin of great magnitude weighing upon their souls.

Who wrote these words? Surely not I; yet they stand and stare at me in my writing. This was no thought of mine. Is there some devil standing beside me, that guides my trembling hand? . . .

The room is falling into an awful gloom. The storm, also, is dying away, so even that must have an end. It is raw and cold. There will be a fog at the sun-rising. At the sun-rising! By that time I may be a thing of the forgotten. The shadows pass and cross above me. The black monster lies still and malignant. His eyes already begin to glisten horribly through the collecting darkness. The time is short, very short now. Ruin in every form gathers around more closely. Death rattles a few dry bones and casts to the winds the last sands of my wasted life. . . .

I can do little more. Terror consumes me outwardly and the fire inwardly. There is a mirror on the wall directly opposite. I look into it, and I can see myself through the mist. Is this hallucination again, or do I look upon reality? As I gaze into that glimmering delineator I behold a frightful scene. I am falling to pieces before my own eyes. The limbs drop off and shrivel on the floor. The head falls and rolls aside, with the two eyes trailing behind.

And yet I see—by some mystery, I see. I am crumbling into dust. I rejoice at the sight fiendishly. There will soon be nothing left for the demon yonder to glut his lust upon. . . .

The light drops down, and begins to shudder ere expiring. My pen moves over the paper, but I do not know if words are being traced. . . .

I am mad at last. I confess it now. Perhaps I have been mad before without knowing it. The shadows are thicker than ever. They fall around me like the dried dead leaves of autumn. My head is a furnace . . . my body a molten mass of consuming fire . . . yet some occult power still continues to guide my hand. . . . Why does not the lightning strike me into insensibility? . . .

Pity, O God. Mercy, O God. Pity, O God. . . .

There is scarcely any light . . . the monster is preparing himself for action. . . . He moves from side to side slowly . . . he raises each black leg, waves it solemnly in the air, digs it into the carpet, and pulls at the body. . . . His head sways hideously . . . the jaws stir with horrid meaning . . . the flame in his cruel eyes grows redder and hotter each second. . . .

The dying light darts up, and bursts against my eyesight . . . in a minute of time it must disappear for ever. . . . I shall cringe in that fearful blackness with the wall behind . . . with the invisible and avenging horror advancing silently. . . . Uncle—uncle, where are you? . . . Where is my brother? I am not your keeper. . . . What have I done to merit this? . . . You are avenged, surely you are avenged, so rest in your grave, and leave me to mine. . . .

It has gone out . . . no, the flame springs up again into a feeble glimmer. . . . I see for another moment of torture. . . . I can see. Ah! I can see the light. . . . But the monster is stirring . . . he is moving . . . he is coming towards me. . . .

The ebon body is dragging along over the white carpet. . . . He has moved a foot forward . . . another . . . now a third. . . . Personification of agony, he has reached the middle of the floor . . . he is still advancing. . . .

Why is this knife here so close to my hand? He is not two yards away. The black hairs bristle along his unspeakable body. He comes on irrevocably. . . . This knife is sharp, and the point glitters keenly. With such a weapon did I insult my brother's unconscious body. . . .

But nearer, closer. The awful appearance. Those glaring eyes. That pestilential breath. . . .

Not a yard separates us. He is crouching, and prepares to spring at me. Where is my brother? Not in that shape, not with that vile covering. . . .

He crouches still more, while the legs quiver like wires. The room swims in blood. That knife again. It is the left side, the left side. He is going to spring upon me. The light has gone. . . .

CONCLUSION

CONCLUSION

WRITTEN BY THE DOCTOR

AFTER reading the pile of manuscript, which I discovered within the writing-desk, I have bestowed a great deal of thought upon the strangest history that is ever likely to come within my knowledge. Before I comment upon it I will give an ending to this sad story.

Hardly had I sat down to breakfast, on that memorable morning after the storm, when I was interrupted by the news that a man was waiting, who must see me at once. I went out into the hall, with my professional, 'Well! what is it?' But there I stopped, for I recognised the man. He was in a nervous state of fright, and his eyes were staring.

'Doctor!' he gasped, 'there's been awful work up at the house.'

'What?' I exclaimed.

'I came along to fetch you as soon as I could, sir. I've got the cart waiting at the door,' he continued.

'I was coming. Your mistress was here for me last night. Is your master ill again?'

'We don't know what to make of it, sir,' said the man fearfully. 'His bedroom wasn't used last night, and he can't be found. The door of the room which he generally uses of an evening is tight locked. There's no sound inside. We don't like to break it open without orders, sir.'

'But your mistress,' I began.

'There's another strange business, sir. She's gone, too. She must have walked it, wherever she went. Through the storm, sir.'

'Didn't anyone see her leave the house?'

'No, sir. They hadn't seen each other for I can't tell you how many days, but they were together last night. In the room that's locked now, sir. Once I came to the end of the passage, and I could hear her shouting and crying at him. I couldn't hear what she said, but it was a terrible quarrel they were having, sir.'

'This is a remarkable story, my man, a most remarkable story,'
I muttered.

'It's not the worst, doctor,' he went on in a strained voice. 'We
found the old mad gentleman lying out on the terrace not half
an hour ago. He'd been there a long time, sir, for he was stiff and
cold.'

'What! Dead?' I exclaimed.

'He must have fallen from the window of that same room, sir.
His neck was clean broken.'

'I will come with you at once,' I said, turning away quickly for
my hat and overcoat.

'It's a fearful thing. It looks like murder, sir—though I know it's
not my place to say so.'

We drove along in silence through a heavy mist. Presently we
entered the carriage road, and rattled towards the gloomy house
between dripping and melancholy plantations. In the dark hall
stood a knot of frightened servants, anxious to do something, yet
not knowing how to act without a master. On a table lay the dead
body of the old man. A passing glance at that was sufficient, then I
went upstairs with the gardener, and the butler, who had come
for me.

It was dreadfully oppressive in that solemn house. I never wish
to repeat the sensation. The creaking stairs, the mournful pictures, the dark wainscoting, the weird ticking or striking of distant
clocks through the loneliness, the empty rows of chairs, the silent
and familiar furniture, the gradual settling of the dust, with a host
of other things, impressed my mind strongly with a sense of the
mysterious and the certain presence of death. We came along the
silent passage, where a few sickly gleams of raw morning sunshine began to fall, and reached the door. I knocked slowly and
deliberately. There was no reply, but a singularly hollow echo, so I
knocked louder. After another pause, I turned to the gardener, and
said shortly, 'Use your feet.'

The fellow looked at me, and understood. He lifted a great
boot, and battered at the door vigorously. The lock gave, the door
swung back, and I entered.

At first I thought that the room was untenanted, but, when my
eyes grew accustomed to the gloom, they distinguished a strange

shape in the distant corner, beside a great writing-desk. I crossed over, looked, bent down, and looked again. Then I believe I cried out, though I am a man of fairly strong nerves. There were two white faces staring behind me.

Huddled up in a corner lay the dead man, with half the blade of a long knife buried in his breast. It was the expression of agony upon the frigid features that caused my momentary weakness. Upon the forehead were drops of blood, which had not proceeded from any abrasion of the skin. These drops, which resembled small red beads, had sweated through the pores before death.

. . . . . . . . . . . . . . . . . .

And now for a few words of explanation, by way of conclusion. This dead man had beyond doubt been mad from the time he murdered his brother. Probably the germ of insanity had always been present in his body. For proof of this, I may mention the episode upon the moor, when he encountered me that wild wet evening. At that time I thought he had been drinking, and as I knew him to be a man with strange opinions and an excitable temperament, I did not feel called upon to interfere. Latterly I knew very well that his reason was affected, but he seemed harmless, and no complaint ever reached my ears.

After jealousy had been aroused by his brother's conduct, the madness developed rapidly, assisted by two things—the Bible story of Cain and Abel, and his natural horror of the spider. Both are explicable. Personally, I am physically unable to touch a spider, and there are many who are similarly afflicted. The terror upon a mind partially demented would certainly be far greater. The incident of the world's first criminal sin implanted in his mind the perfectly coherent doctrine of the Shadow, the haunting fear and remorse which follows as a natural consequence of crime. From his manuscript I find that the idea dawned upon him in the following light:—

In the earliest days there was no such thing as shadow; neither the sun nor the moon had the power to reproduce the image of a man, or indeed of any solid body. Cain's crime called shadow into birth. *And now art thou cursed from the earth, which hath opened her mouth to receive thy brother's blood from thy hand.'* This curse of the earth was the imprint of shadow, which continually followed, haunted, and gradually maddened the first criminal. As shadow was the consequence of crime, so it was the avenger. Seth, the son born to Eve, 'instead of Abel, whom Cain slew,' was, in fact, nothing but this shadow. He it was, who, though the Bible is silent on the subject, haunted Cain to his miserable death—which was probably that of the suicide. This was why he gave to the imaginary spider, which became visible during the course of his mental *delirium tremens*, the name of Seth.

And what sane man has not, at some period of his life, been frightened by shadow, let it be his own, or that of some other object? Is it not true that after any act of wrong-doing this shadow is specially an object of fear? Shadow, as he somewhat truly remarks, in one of the many analytical pages I have omitted, is simply remorse made visible.

I suppose every man has suffered from this remorse at some time or another.

Undoubtedly the fear brings with it the suggestion of a presence. As you walk along, you start in sudden terror, and look over your shoulder. You do not really expect to find anyone or anything there—yet you are relieved to find that there *is* no one. As remorse increases, the shadow may be truly said to blacken and develop.

Here are some of his own ideas in his own words:—

'For the first time came a foretaste of my approaching fate. What further proof of the soul's eternity can be needed than the fact of the indestructible nature of those compounds, which make up the despised weed we crush beneath our foot? Nothing can be annihilated, no body may be obliterated from space.

'Cain slew Abel's body, but Seth rose as a conqueror. Seth sprang from the ashes of the dead brother, a re-incarnation of that life, endowed perhaps with the same immortal soul, his flesh perchance built up of those very constituents which had passed in the form of invisible gases from the decaying body of the murderer. Seth was the result of a crime. Above all, he was the avenger.

'And what was this being, this symbolic Seth, but a vague shadow, to which we have since given the name of memory or remorse?

'The vapour of memory, like the invisible gases of the atmosphere, might solidify beneath enormous mental pressure, and take finally that form which should be most suited to it. Memory was a thing present with me night and day, not as a dim spectral figure of a dream-like uncertainty, but rather as an omnipotent force which could not tire. It was my constant companion; it spoke to me in a fierce whisper; it gazed at me with wild eyes; it kept step with me as I walked; it cast a second shadow by the side of mine. Call this demon what you will—memory, remorse or madness—the name of the disease is nothing to a dying man—it had become a part of myself, but it refused to stop there. It had been ordered to claim me altogether, and wreck me irremediably.

'What was this creation of the Shadow? What, but a frightful blending of fear, agony, remorse and memory, to constitute a being of shape and powers unknown? The living, moving, breathing consequences of a great crime, such as, shall we say, the wilful destruction of life; a commingling of all the fearful essences in Nature, for the formation of a hideous creation.'

Comment upon this seems to me to be unnecessary. What his agony must have been, on seeing the creature advancing towards him, when the light was flickering out, and the madness was consuming him, no man can imagine. It is sufficient to reflect that, at the awful moment, he did that which he had all along shrank from—killed himself. This is what he says in another place upon suicide:—

'Why did I not put an end to this torment of the body? I hated my life, but I dared not lose it. Willingly would I have surrendered breath and sunk into the clammy grave, were it nothing beyond the general human idea—silence and complete rest. These were the two blessings I hungered and thirsted after; but what might be the unknown accompaniments?

'The final compulsory recession from life was so dim, so hazy, in its distant uncertainty, as scarcely to be a terror. I was young, and still very strong. But the actual breaking off abruptly from that existence, the establishing of a fixed hour for the fatal secession, the cold calculation of the act, with the deliberate setting of time and place between metes and bounds—all this is an impossibility for a mortal, yet an immortal, who is forced to face the racking problem of eternity.'

Any pang was preferable to falling into the clutches of the monster, and the weapon had been vindictively left within reach of his hand. I think he acted then as most men would have done under similar circumstances.

The crumpled and ink-stained pages of manuscript, which mutely proclaim a pitiful tale, I shall always keep. The first chapters are beautifully and carefully written, though occasional passages are much slurred, the spelling being curiously deranged. On proceeding, the composition grows worse, until at the end it is almost, in some places quite, illegible. The closing pages are most awful. The very paper seems to scream with torture, and the ink turns to blood as I ponder over the strange markings. I have been compelled to construct a good deal, as in many places long tortured lines, like writhing serpents, take the place of words, and this frequently continues for pages. These I have endeavoured to fill up, as I think he might have written them, but of course I am unable to compose beneath the pressure of his agony of mind. I am thankful that I cannot. There is one noticeable point—the chapter that describes the brother's murder is written with red ink.

I think the vanished wife is more to be pitied than blamed. She was not mercenary, but too loving, and she was not allowed to enjoy her love. From my studies and the lessons of my profession, I feel safe in laying it down as an axiom that—there is no fury like a woman who has been wilfully and violently robbed of her love.

Still, it will go hard with her if captured in her flight. Coroners are, for the most part, narrow-minded men, and juries are composed of dull-witted fellows, to whom a spade can never be anything but the veriest spade. I must produce this manuscript, but of course they will laugh at it, because people always revile things they cannot understand. I fancy she is well away by this time. I hope she is, for I cannot help pitying her.

I feel it my duty to make this confession of a murderer public, not because I wish to advance any new theory, but because I feel that it may be of a certain interest to some. We have it on excellent authority that there is nothing new under the sun, and these words were written over a thousand years ago.

And this is surely true. Things appear new on account of man's forgetfulness. Even our present-day ideas, so fresh and vivid in themselves, are but the shadows of decayed dreams of thinkers in the past. The great inventions, of which we are so proud, are but re-discoveries; our wonderful and novel scientific theories have been discussed on the Euphrates, in the Agora, in the Forum, *ad unguem et ad nauseam,*[1] by forgotten masters of the world. And while we fight for preference in art, the highest place in letters, vast treasure-cities moan in oblivion beneath the sea, the mysterious deserts conceal marvels to stagger our enlightenment, and gaunt Egypt stands in eternal ruins.

*To that end must we all come.*

THE END

---

1 With great precision (literally, to the fingernail) and to the point of sickness.

CPSIA information can be obtained at www.ICGtesting.com
Printed in the USA
LVOW120819081012

301928LV00002B/37/P